Praise for *Once Upon a Summertime*

"A hardworking girl finds her happily-ever-after ending in Melody Carlson's heartwarming tale. Readers will cheer Anna's journey as a summer of new beginnings becomes a summer of unexpected love."

—**Lisa Wingate**, bestselling author of *The Prayer Box* and *The Story Keeper*

"Carlson (*The Christmas Joy Ride*) kicks off her new series with this heartwarming and uplifting novel about taking a chance on fulfilling your dreams. Carlson's fairy-tale romance is not without its ups and downs, but readers will root for her likable protagonists to find their happy ending. A pleasant summer escape for readers of new adult fiction and contemporary romance."

—**Library Journal**

"Sweet, romantic, and endlessly entertaining, this romp through the storied streets of New York City will enchant readers. Melody Carlson has created characters so charming that readers will long to meet them in the lobby of the stunning Rothsberg Hotel."

—*Christian Manifesto*

"In this the first in the Follow Your Heart series, Carlson takes readers to New York City and the exciting world of starting and running a hotel. Anna is an enchanting character, and the romance develops naturally. Overall, this is a fun new series."

—**RT Book Reviews**

"This perfect summer read for a day at the beach is sure to fill many readers' summers."

—*CBA Retailers + Resources*

All Summer Long

Other Books by Melody Carlson

FOLLOW YOUR HEART SERIES

Once Upon a Summertime

All Summer Long

HOLIDAY NOVELLAS

Christmas at Harrington's

The Christmas Bus

The Christmas Shoppe

The Joy of Christmas

The Treasure of Christmas

The Christmas Pony

A Simple Christmas Wish

The Christmas Cat

The Christmas Joy Ride

All Summer Long

A San Francisco Romance

MELODY CARLSON

Revell

a division of Baker Publishing Group
Grand Rapids, Michigan

© 2016 by Carlson Management, Inc.

Published by Revell
a division of Baker Publishing Group
P.O. Box 6287, Grand Rapids, MI 49516-6287
www.revellbooks.com

Printed in the United States of America

Library of Congress Cataloging-in-Publication Data
Names: Carlson, Melody, author.
Title: All summer long : a San Francisco romance / Melody Carlson.
Description: Grand Rapids, MI : Revell, a division of Baker Publishing Group,
    [2016] | Series: Follow your heart ; 2
Identifiers: LCCN 2016000790 | ISBN 9780800723583 (softcover)
Subjects: LCSH: First loves—Fiction. | GSAFD: Love stories. | Christian fiction.
Classification: LCC PS3553.A73257 A795 2016 | DDC 813/.54—dc23
LC record available at http://lccn.loc.gov/2016000790

16 17 18 19 20 21 22   7 6 5 4 3 2 1

1

Tia D'Amico was sick of pasta. Not sick of consuming it—no self-respecting member of an Italian family would admit to as much. She was tired of making it. Whether it was fettuccine, tortellini, rigatoni, cannelloni, or even today's special—ravioli filled with spinach, ricotta, and morel mushrooms—she'd grown weary of the process. That was embarrassing to admit. Especially when she used to love the sweet simplicity of mixing semolina and eggs and watching the shiny machine do its magic until the dough was just right, followed by the process of rolling, pressing, molding, cutting, drying, and finally serving up the pasta to the restaurant's appreciative guests. Pasta used to make her happy.

"This is not why I went to culinary arts school," she told her uncle as he carried a crate of seafood into the kitchen. Uncle Tony was her father's brother as well as her boss and favorite uncle. With his dark grisly beard and faded denim shirt, he looked more like a crusty fisherman than a prosperous restaurateur, but there was no one better to teach her the ropes of the restaurant business than her uncle.

Her short-term plan, after graduating, had been to return to her hometown in Norton, Washington, and to work at D'Amico's for a season or two. Long enough to build up her résumé, and then she'd move on to something bigger and better. Unfortunately, nothing bigger or better had surfaced in the two years she'd been here. But, to be fair, with all the hours she was putting in at the popular Italian restaurant, she had little time to job hunt—or have a life.

"Why *did* you go to cooking school?" Uncle Tony dropped the crate onto the maple butcher block with a loud thud. "You were on your way to becoming a perfectly good chef before you went off to that fancy-dancy school in Seattle. And what you didn't know, I was happy to teach you. If you ask me, *cara mia*, you just wasted a bunch of your papa's hard-earned money on a silly pedigree."

"It's not a pedigree." She wrinkled her nose at him as she rolled the cutter across the pasta dough. "I'm not a poodle."

"Getting generous with your filling there." He poked a puffy ravioli square. "Trying to make me go broke? Put me out of business?"

"Yeah, right." She laughed. "Like that's going to happen." It was no secret that D'Amico's was the most popular restaurant in the small town in northern Washington. Tia's great-grandparents had started it with only eight small tables shortly before World War II. Since that time it had more than quadrupled in size, and when Uncle Tony retired next year and his son Marcus took his place, it would become a fourth-generation business.

"Phone for Tia," Marcus called from the dining room. "It's Aunt Julie on line two."

"Aunt Julie?" Uncle Tony frowned as Tia reached for the

kitchen phone. "My baby sister is calling to talk to *you*, not her big brother?"

Tia made a face at her uncle as she greeted her aunt. "Uncle Tony is about to throw a knife at me if you don't at least say hello."

"Tell big bro hey for me. Give him my love, then tell him I called to talk to *you*."

Tia relayed this information, then asked Julie, "What's up?"

"Well, Roland's father passed on a couple months ago."

"Oh, I'm sorry," Tia told her. "I hadn't heard. Give Roland my love."

"Thank you. But it's not like we were surprised. Roland's dad was pretty old. He'd enjoyed a good full life. Really, that's not why I'm calling you, Tia. Here's the deal . . . Roland's dad left us a boat."

"A boat?" Tia used her free hand to run the cutter between the ravioli squares. Julie had called to talk about a boat?

"Not just any boat. It's this beautiful luxury yacht. Well, actually it's a luxury yacht in need of some TLC, but that's another thing. The real reason I'm calling you is because Roland has given the yacht to me, and I would like to turn it into a restaurant."

"A restaurant?" Tia stopped cutting ravioli.

"A really upscale restaurant with sunset dinner cruises and birthday parties and anniversaries and weddings and all sorts of fun events."

Tia felt her interest rise. "You'd run this floating restaurant on the San Francisco Bay?"

"That's my plan."

"Wow, that sounds really fun."

"I know! And I got to thinking I'd need a top-notch chef,

and I remembered how you graduated from that culinary school last year. I got to thinking you might be just the ticket."

"Seriously? You'd consider me for a position like that?"

Uncle Tony stopped sorting the shrimp, pausing to scowl at Tia.

"Absolutely. The thing is, I need more than just a chef, Tia. At least to start with. I need someone with youth and ideas and lots of energy. Someone to help me get things going, to assist me in getting the boat set up as a lovely restaurant. Do you think you'd be interested?"

"Of course!"

"When can you come down here?"

"I don't know." Tia covered the mouthpiece on the phone. "Julie is offering me a job. She's starting a restaurant. She wants to know when I can start."

Uncle Tony just shook his head in a defeated way. "When does she need you?"

"When do you need me?" Tia asked.

"Is *now* too soon?" Julie giggled. "Tony will kill me."

Tia looked at Uncle Tony. "She says 'now.'"

Uncle Tony rolled his eyes. "My baby sister knows I could never say no to her. Better go home and pack your bags, *cara mia*."

"Uncle Tony is telling me to go home and pack!" Tia exclaimed.

"Fabulous! Call me back when you get home, and we'll go over the details. I'll start looking for flights. Do you really think you can leave right away?"

"No reason I can't."

"Great! My goal is to get the restaurant running by mid-summer. Roland thinks I'm crazy, but I think it could happen.

Anyway, you better let me talk to my big brother before you hang up. I have a feeling I owe him big-time."

Tia handed the phone to Uncle Tony. And as she continued to happily cut the ravioli, she listened to her uncle making a huge pretense of grumbling and complaining, acting like Julie was stealing the best cook he'd ever had and going on about how it would ruin his business. It was all baloney, but he seemed to be enjoying it. Besides, maybe it took leaving a job to get the appreciation you deserved. Tia wasn't even sure she cared right now. The good news was that she was getting out of this little Podunk town! Life was suddenly good!

She'd only been to San Francisco once before, but she had fallen in love with the unique city on the bay. She'd been sixteen when Aunt Julie had invited her down there for the summer. Tia had known her parents' marriage was on the brink just then. But she'd pretended to be oblivious during her visit at Julie's. It was easier. And she'd suspected her aunt's generous hospitality was an attempt to give Tia's parents a chance to work things out without an observer around. But by the time Tia got home, it was over. Mom moved on to a new life in Florida. It had been just Tia and Dad since then, although her dad had started dating someone last year. Maybe their romance would progress better if Tia was out of the picture.

"You're still here?" Uncle Tony feigned surprise as he hung up the phone. "I thought you'd be on your way to the airport by now."

"You don't really want me to quit today, do you?" She peered curiously at his gruff, unshaven face. Her uncle was like a lobster—hard and crusty on the outside but soft and sweet underneath.

He shrugged. "Maybe finish the raviolis first."

"Seriously? This is really my last day?"

"Sure. It sounds like Julie needs you. Roland is having some health issues, going into early retirement. She thinks this restaurant boat idea is just what they need." He shook his head. "But I'm guessing it'll sink them." He chuckled. "No pun intended."

"Sink them?" She spread out another sheet of waxed paper and laid the freshly cut ravioli on it.

"You remember when I had my boat. Thirty-two-foot beauty, inboard-outboard, cabin that slept six. My big plan was to take it on the Sound during my free time." He sighed. "Free time—ha!"

"I do remember that boat. It was really nice, but I never got to go out in it."

"No, it was *not* really nice. It was a hole in the water that I threw money into. I only took that stinking boat out once. The rest of the time it was in the boat shop getting fixed."

"Oh."

"They say the two happiest days in a boat owner's life are one"—he held up a finger—"the day you buy the boat, and two"—he held up a second finger—"the day you sell it."

"Really?"

"Trust me. I don't make this stuff up."

"Well, Julie didn't *buy* her boat—it was a gift. So maybe that's different."

"She may not have bought the boat, Tia, but she will end up paying for it. Take it from me. I know what I'm talking about. And even though you're determined to go down there to help her with this crazy plan, I'm warning you, it could turn into a big fat mess."

Tia considered this as she continued cutting ravioli. "Are you saying I shouldn't go?"

He closed the freezer door with a loud bang. "No. I think you should go." He came over to the pasta station with a somewhat sly smile. "It will be a learning experience for you."

She held the pasta cutter up in the air. "You mean like the school of hard knocks?"

"Maybe a little, but I can tell Julie really needs you."

"And *you* don't need me?" She frowned at him.

"Of course I need you, *cara mia*. You are irreplaceable. But it's June and kids are home from college. I've already turned several job hunters away. I can find someone to cover for you." He winked. "Until you learn your lesson and come back to me."

She laughed. "You seem awfully sure of yourself."

"Time will tell." Uncle Tony grabbed her head, planting a kiss on her forehead. "I hope you have a great adventure, *cara mia*. You deserve it."

"Thanks."

"Just don't do anything I wouldn't do." He winked again as he headed for the door.

"For sure!" She laughed as he left, then returned to putting generous dollops of filling on the ravioli dough. She knew D'Amico's would continue on just fine without her, but to her surprise she felt a tiny wave of sadness to think she was leaving. Since she was a little girl she'd always loved this place—the smells, the sounds, the sights—but most of all she had loved the feeling of family and heritage, of being a part of something bigger.

Even so, it would be exciting to be part of her aunt's new venture—and to be part of San Francisco too! The change would definitely do her good. As she pressed the top layers of thin dough around the mounds of filling, her favorite memory of San Francisco flashed through her mind. She sighed happily as she let it play out like a movie.

It had been late August and the last day of the sailing camp that despite Tia's adolescent reluctance, Aunt Julie had insisted she attend. At sixteen, Tia had felt too old for any sort of camp. Fortunately, she'd been wrong. It was no ordinary camp. The two dozen campers got to be the working crew of a forty-foot sailboat. The captain and first mate, a twentysomething married couple, taught the teens sailing terminology and how to handle all the elements of the boat. The youthful crew basically kept the boat sailing smoothly for a whole week.

Although the bulk of Tia's working time had been spent in the sailboat's galley (after it was discovered she was the best cook of the bunch), she was forced out on deck for that final day. It had been purely magical. No trace of fog and just a gentle breeze. The bay was topaz blue and smooth as glass, and the sky was azure and cloudless. But best of all was the boy she got partnered with for the day. *Leo Parker*. Tall and muscular, Leo had sandy blond hair and ocean blue eyes—and all the girls had been drooling over him for the whole week.

But as the day progressed and Leo helped her with the ropes and sails, patiently explaining some of the training she'd missed while cooking down below, Tia had felt a real connection with him. When the day was over and the boat was docked with their duffle bags all piled on deck, the two of them had crowded together in the narrow bowsprit, looking out over the water and the other boats. Totally out of the blue, Leo had leaned over and kissed her on the lips. She still got slightly dizzy just thinking of that amazing moment—her first kiss. But as quickly as it had come, it was over. Suddenly everyone was grabbing their baggage, saying good-byes, and disembarking to go home with their families.

"Tia!" Marcus exclaimed as he burst into the kitchen. "Is it true? You're really leaving us?"

She smiled at her favorite cousin. "Afraid so. Think you can get by without me?"

He frowned. "I doubt it."

"Sorry, but Aunt Julie needs me just now." She put the last ravioli on the tray. "But if your dad's right, her project will sink even before it starts, and I'll be back here older and wiser." She untied her apron and hung it on the rack by the door.

"Well, have fun anyway. And give Julie my love." He hugged her and wished her luck, then returned to the dining area. Tia removed the red bandana she'd tied around her hair that morning, got her bag from her locker, and finally gave the large, well-equipped kitchen one long last look before she quietly let herself out the back door. She felt a strange twist of melancholy as she left, but as soon as she stepped out into the summer sunshine, she broke into a happy dance. Life was waiting for her!

2

What do you pack when life is waiting? Tia wondered as she unlocked the front door to her dad's townhouse. He'd gotten this place while she was in culinary arts school, downsizing from her childhood home in order to help her with tuition. After graduation, she'd taken over his guest room with plans to find a place of her own later. But somehow, although she'd been saving up, she'd never quite gotten around to it.

She went to the cluttered bedroom, trying to decide where to begin. On one hand, she wouldn't mind leaving everything here, just in case. That seemed unfair to her dad, though. She knew this space had been his prized home office while she was in school. Oh, he'd never complained, but she felt pretty sure he'd like to use it again.

For that reason she spent most of the day going through her piles of stuff, boxing up some of it for storage and some to be sent to her later (if all went well), and bagging the rest of it to be donated to St. Vinnie's. She carefully folded her culinary clothes, a mishmash of checkered, striped, and black pants along with her white chef's coats and kitchen clogs. On top of this pile, she added her ukulele and her art case. So far she had plenty of room in her oversized suitcase.

And as she sorted through her nonwork clothes, it was obvious she would be traveling light. She picked up a well-worn Seattle Seahawks T-shirt that she was reluctant to part with. Not exactly the sort of thing she wanted to sport on the chic streets of San Francisco. She frowned at her garments. Clearly this was the wardrobe of a woman who spent most of her time in the kitchen—a woman with little or no social life. She was just tossing the T-shirt on her giveaway mound when her cell phone jangled.

"I've got your flight booked," Julie told her. "Considering the short notice, not such a bad deal either. You ready to head out tomorrow?"

"I'm packing my bags right now." Tia threw her favorite pair of jeans onto the "take" pile. "In fact, I was just wondering what sort of clothes I should bring. To be honest, my wardrobe is pretty pathetic."

"Well, bring your chef's clothes for sure," Julie told her. "And some old work clothes too. Stuff you can just use and lose."

"Right." Tia reached into the giveaway stuff, extracting the Seahawks shirt and a couple of other raggedy things to put on her "take" pile. "I can't wait to see you, Julie. And your boat."

"I can't wait to have you here to help me. It's overwhelming. I'm so glad Uncle Tony agreed to let you come so quickly."

As Julie gave her the details for tomorrow's flight, Tia felt her stomach tighten. She'd only flown once before, and that had been a nerve-racking trip. Why hadn't she suggested going down there by train or bus, or even hitchhiking?

"Your flight's scheduled to land at 6:38. Roland and I will meet you at passenger pickup around 7:00. Unless there's a flight delay. Just call my cell if there's a problem. We'll be driving my Subaru. It's just your basic white SUV. I'm hoping you'll be hungry because I made us a dinner reservation at this really cool restaurant, Le Bernard. I think you'll appreciate it."

"Sounds good." Tia tried to block the nervous feeling building up inside her.

"It's actually sort of like dining espionage, because I'd love to copy their menu for our dinner boat."

"Well, imitation is supposed to be the highest form of flattery. Hey, maybe I can sneak a photo of the menu with my phone."

Julie chuckled. "That might be pushing it. But at least you'll get to sample the food and get a feel for the place."

After Tia said good-bye, she took a deep breath. *Flying is not a big deal*, she told herself as she looked around at the messy room. She picked through her piles of clothes, trying to find something that would be swanky enough for a nice dinner in a stylish San Francisco restaurant. Nothing seemed remotely appropriate. Especially considering how chic her aunt could look when she dressed up for a night out. Tia would look like a frumpy old frau next to Julie. Like a boring piece of flatbread next to a fluffy golden croissant.

Just like that, Tia decided to do something she hadn't done in ages: go shopping. After a couple hours of walking around their small town, which had a definite shortage of clothing shops, Tia had somehow managed to put together a fairly decent traveling outfit that would work for a night out as well. While she was shopping, she also picked up a few other items that would definitely improve her sparse wardrobe. She was just carrying an armload of bags to the townhouse when her dad pulled in. He hurried out of his car to help her.

"What's going on here?" he asked with amusement as he relieved her of some of her packages. "My earth muffin girl turning into a shopaholic? What is the world coming to?"

She started to tell him about the job in San Francisco, but he stopped her. "I already know," he said as he opened the front door. "Tony called me this afternoon."

"That tattletale." She dumped the bags by the door, shaking her hands to get the blood flowing in her fingers again.

"He called because he was worried." Tia's dad peered curiously at her. "He's concerned that he encouraged you to do something you'll regret. And if that happens, he'll feel responsible."

"Well, you can tell him that I'm doing this because I *want to*. He bears no responsibility whatsoever."

Dad pointed at the mess of bags on the floor. "What is all this?"

She explained about the fancy restaurant and her lack of wardrobe, and her dad just laughed. "What's so funny?" she demanded.

"Nothing. It's just such a relief to see my little girl is growing up."

She frowned at him.

"I'm sorry, Tia. It's just that you're such an attractive girl." He tweaked her long brown ponytail. "But you never seem to do anything about it." His smile faded. "Sometimes I think that's my fault."

"Why on earth would you say that?" She bent down to gather up the packages from the floor.

"Well . . . after your mom left . . . I probably didn't encourage you much. At least not as far as fashion and girly things go."

She dropped the bags and threw her arms around him. "You did just fine, Dad. I'm the way I am because that's just who I am." She stepped back and shrugged. "Glamour girls don't really fit into commercial kitchens. And that's fine with me."

He patted her cheek. "But don't kid yourself, Tia. You are a beautiful girl. I guess I should've told you that more while you were growing up."

She laughed as she picked up the bags again. "That's sweet, but I wouldn't expect a dad to say anything less to his only daughter." She headed for her room with him tailing her with more shopping bags.

"Deanna was coming over for dinner tonight," he said as he set the packages inside her door. "But I didn't realize you were leaving so soon. Tony said you might be gone by tomorrow."

"That's right. But you don't need to cancel your plans with Deanna." She tossed the packages on the bed.

"But I want to spend time with you," he protested. "We all know how you usually hide out in here when Deanna's around."

"I just do that to give you your space," she confessed. "I'd like to see her before I go."

"Really? You'd join us for dinner?"

"Sure, if you want me to. FYI, I actually like Deanna. I think you guys make a good couple."

"You do?" He looked genuinely surprised.

"I do. And maybe you'll make more progress with her after I go."

His brow creased. "But that's not why you're—"

"No, of course not. I'm going because I *want* to. It sounds exciting."

He looked relieved. "Well, I'm sure Julie is thrilled to get you. Tony said that Roland's had some health problems and plans to take early retirement. It's time for them to change their lifestyle."

"Yeah, I know." As she unloaded a shopping bag, she told him about tomorrow night's dinner plans with Julie and Roland.

"Sounds like fun."

"By the way," she asked, "who's cooking dinner tonight?"

"Not you," he assured her. "Deanna offered."

"Good." Tia chuckled as her dad left. The truth was, Deanna was a pretty pathetic cook. But one night of a Deanna dinner wouldn't kill her.

As it turned out, the Deanna dinner wasn't half bad. The green salad was edible, and although the halibut was dry, the sauce she'd bought at the fish market helped. Tia wasn't sure if it was just her imagination or simply the fact that she was distracted about her upcoming trip, but Deanna actually seemed a lot sweeter than usual too.

"Tia got some new clothes for San Francisco," Dad told Deanna as the three of them cleared the table.

"Good for you," Deanna told her.

"Yeah, you're probably thinking it's about time." Tia rinsed food scraps into the disposal.

"I didn't say that." Deanna put a hand on Tia's shoulder. "But I've often thought you could do more with your looks. You really are a gorgeous girl." She looked closely at Tia. "In fact, I've often felt you resemble Penélope Cruz."

"Uh, thanks." Tia turned on the disposal, hoping the loud roar would discourage more conversation about her looks. This was definitely not her comfort zone.

"But running around with your hair pulled back so tightly, not a speck of makeup, and your unisex cook's clothes . . . well, who could tell?" Deanna chuckled.

Normally a comment like this—coming from anyone but Dad—would put Tia off, but tonight she felt curious. "Well, you'll be relieved to hear that I actually bought some *girl* clothes." She peered at her dad's girlfriend. Although Deanna was seventeen years older than Tia, she could easily pass as her sister. Deanna's appearance was always impeccable, which was probably one of the reasons Tia could never relate to her. "But I'm interested in your opinion. What else would you suggest?"

"Seriously?" Deanna broke into a big smile. "You're asking *me* for help?"

"Well, you're the expert." Tia made a stiff smile. She knew that Deanna's side job was selling Terry Fay cosmetics. Tia had even heard Deanna mention that she'd made more money selling Terry Fay than selling real estate. Of course, that was when the housing market had been pretty depressed.

"Oh, Tia, I would just love to give you a makeover. And I just happen to have my Terry Fay sample case in my car. Would you really consider it?"

Tia felt like she was biting a bullet as she nodded. "Sure. Why not?"

"Well, I'm going to run out there and get it right this minute." Deanna thrust her kitchen towel at Dad. "You know what they say—strike while the iron's hot."

After Deanna left, Dad peered curiously at Tia. "I think

it's really sweet of you to let Deanna do this. She looked like you'd given her the moon. But are you sure you don't mind being worked over?"

Tia just laughed. "Hey, it might be fun." Also, she thought, it might distract her from fretting over tomorrow's flight. For whatever reason, she was feeling haunted by it.

As it turned out, Deanna was much better at makeovers than she was at cooking. She started by giving Tia a facial that smelled like cucumbers and oranges. "Your skin is really good," she said as she wiped on the goop. "But working in the kitchen will take its toll, if you're over a hot stove so much and not cleansing and hydrating properly."

By the time Deanna removed the goop, Tia could tell the difference. Her cheek was soft and smooth with a fresh, tingly feeling. Deanna went through a bunch of other steps, most of which were lost on Tia, although she didn't really mind. The whole process was surprisingly relaxing. Even if she wound up looking like Dolly Parton, it wouldn't matter because she'd simply wash it off before bed anyway.

"I realize that you're more of a natural girl." Deanna removed the band that had been containing Tia's ponytail, taking a few seconds to fluff out her long hair and letting it tumble down around her shoulders.

"Don't you mean 'earth muffin,' like Dad's always saying?"

"I don't know about that. But I did feel you needed a softer touch in the makeup department. And I respect that." Deanna closed her sample case. "So I've tried to keep it casual."

"Thanks." Tia smiled.

"Aren't you going to go look in the mirror?"

"Oh, yeah." Tia went into the living room where a mirror hung over the gas fireplace. "Wow." She peered at herself in wonder. Her skin seemed to be glowing, and her eyes looked darker and bigger. Even the lip gloss color, a soft shade of coral, was very becoming. With her hair loosely framing her face, she thought perhaps she really did resemble Penélope Cruz. "That's actually not half bad, Deanna."

"Not half bad?" Deanna came over to stand by her. "It's really quite good. What do you think, Vince?"

Tia's dad looked up from his ball game, then let out a low whistle. "I told you she was a beauty," he said to Deanna. "Nice work."

"All I did was draw attention to her fabulous natural features." Deanna pointed at Tia's face. "See these high cheekbones? Girls would kill for that. And those big eyes with the thick, dark lashes. And her lips are so nice and full, and—"

"Oh, you guys." Tia laughed as she waved her hand at them. "I don't think I can take too much more of this. I'm going to bed."

"But it's early. You should take that gorgeous face out on the town," Deanna told her.

"No thanks." Tia shook her head. "I still have a lot to get done before my flight tomorrow."

"By the way, how are you getting to the airport?" Dad asked.

"I hadn't really figured that out yet." Tia grimaced at the realization. "I'm guessing they need you at work. I should get to Sea-Tac around 3:00, which means I'd need to leave here around noon. I thought about taking a taxi. Or maybe I'll ask—"

"I'll take you," Deanna said suddenly.

"Really?" Tia blinked.

"Absolutely. I'd love to. I don't have anything important going on tomorrow."

"Are you sure? It'll take a good chunk of your day, you know."

Deanna nodded. "And I plan to drop off a going-away present for you tomorrow morning. I'll stop by before I check in at the real estate office."

"A present?"

"I'm going to print out instructions for everything I did here tonight. And I'll give you the same products I used on you. That way you can do it yourself before we head for Seattle."

Tia wasn't sure what to think but simply nodded. "That's really generous, Deanna. Thanks. For everything." Thinking Deanna and her dad might like to be alone now, she told them good night and returned to her room to finish organizing and packing. But when she noticed her image in the mirror above her dresser, she had to do a double take. She really did look pretty good—and not overdone either. She felt almost as if Deanna had worked some sort of magic on her.

Tia felt like someone else as Deanna drove her to Sea-Tac airport the next day. First of all, it was unbelievable that she was getting out of Norton and going to San Francisco—to work on a floating restaurant that she was going to help set up. That was totally amazing. But almost equally amazing was that for the first time she could remember, Tia actually felt pretty. It was partly due to the new outfit, which was a relatively simple ensemble but made her feel good. Her little black dress, which fit perfectly, was made of a silky knit fabric that was not supposed to wrinkle during the flight. Over that, she had a lacy, pale gray cardigan that reminded her of a spider web, but in a good way. Instead of her clunky Dansko clogs, she had on a pretty pair of black Nine West sandals. Topping it all off was the makeover that Deanna had helped her with again this morning. All together it seemed to elevate her confidence to a whole new level. Now if only it could increase her courage for this upcoming flight.

"You better keep in touch," Deanna said as she pulled into the passenger drop-off area. "Send us lots of photos. And not just of the boat and scenery. Send pictures of yourself too."

"I will," Tia promised as they got out of the car to get her bags. "Thanks so much for everything." She hugged Deanna tightly. "Tell Dad I'll call him when I get there." Just like that, Tia was on her own, feeling like a million bucks as she walked into the terminal. Oh, she knew she was earlier than necessary. But she hoped that having time to walk around and acclimate herself would help with her flight phobia. Plus, it would help her to avoid the stress of running late. Just like in the kitchen, preparation and organization were her keys to success. Or so she hoped.

Tia waited in line for an e-ticket machine, but she immediately felt flustered and frustrated when it didn't seem to work like it was supposed to. "Come over here." A woman behind the ticket counter waved her over.

"Thank you," Tia said gratefully. "I honestly don't know what I'm doing. Or I'm just too nervous to do it right. This is only the second time I've flown. And I'm not sure how I'm supposed to check my bag."

"Only your second flight ever?" The agent looked skeptical as she took the e-ticket.

Tia assured her it was, and then, as the woman typed something into her computer, Tia explained about San Francisco and the restaurant boat and Julie.

"Interesting," the agent said. "Well, it's not a very full flight today, and since you got here early and you look so nice, I've upgraded you to an empty seat in first class."

"Seriously?"

The agent smiled as she tagged the bag to be checked. "You don't have to mention this to anyone. Don't want to create passenger envy."

"I won't say a word." Tia pointed to her large suitcase. "Do you think my ukulele will be okay in there?"

The agent blinked as she handed Tia her ticket packet. "A ukulele?"

"It's in a hard case," Tia said quickly. "With clothes packed all around it."

The agent laughed. "Well, your suitcase looks pretty sturdy too. I'm betting your ukulele will be just fine." She stuck an orange sticker on the bag. "But this will remind the baggage guys to take it easy. Now have a good trip."

Tia thanked her, and feeling much lighter both physically and mentally with only her small carry-on bag, she made her way through security and then to the gate. So far so good. Her flight fears seemed to be shrinking. With plenty of time to spare, she picked up a couple of magazines, some water, and a bag of mixed nuts, then found a seat near her gate.

She almost felt relaxed as she flipped through the first magazine. But just as she was reaching for the second magazine, she noticed the other people in the waiting area anxiously pointing to the TV screens and talking amongst themselves with worried expressions. She looked up at one of the screens, only to see what looked like airplane wreckage over a body of water. She read the words beneath the picture—a French jetliner had gone down somewhere over the Atlantic. She took in a deep breath, willing her pounding heart to slow down as she stared up at the frightening scene.

Really, she asked herself, *what are the odds of two passenger jets crashing on the same day?* But before she could answer that question, the gate agent called for first-class passengers to board. Praying a silent prayer, she headed for the short line already forming. A man in a dark suit stepped aside to let her go ahead of him, nodding with what felt like approval. As she thanked him, she glanced down at her traveling outfit, so unlike her usual kitchen garb, and smiled to herself. Well, at least if she was going down, she was going down in style.

3

Tia's fear of an air disaster turned out to be completely unfounded. In fact, she actually sort of enjoyed the uneventful flight. Well, up until that brief frightening moment when she honestly thought the plane was going straight down into the gleaming blue San Francisco Bay. Thankfully, they landed perfectly on the strip. The flight attendant explained that the airport was almost surrounded by water and added, "It often catches first-time flyers by surprise."

By the time Tia was strolling toward baggage claim, she was feeling rather happy and festive. She'd made it here! No problem. She turned on her phone as she waited at the carousel. Not surprisingly, she had a text from her aunt, sent while she'd been in flight. But as soon as she started to read it, she knew something was wrong. Very wrong.

Headed to hospital. Roland. Very bad. Pray.
Call me.

Tia said a silent prayer for her uncle as she hit the speed dial for Julie's phone. *Please, let him be okay—please, don't let him die.* She knew that her desperate prayer was partly selfish. If Roland had died from a heart attack, she knew that Julie would be shattered. Her boat restaurant venture would come to a screeching halt. And who could blame her?

"Tia," Julie said eagerly. "You're here!"

"How's Roland? What happened?"

"He's okay. Well, *okay* is an overstatement. Poor guy! He'd been feeling a little off all day. But we were out at the marina and neither of us paid much attention to his symptoms. A couple hours ago, he started having severe chest pains and we knew it was serious. Fortunately, the paramedics got there fast."

"So he's okay?"

"Well, aside from needing a quadruple bypass."

"Oh, wow." Julie watched baggage sliding onto the carousel. "I guess he's lucky to be alive."

"That's for sure. His surgery isn't scheduled until Monday, but the doctor wants to keep him here over the weekend. Just to be safe."

"Yes, that sounds wise." Tia went to snatch her bag from the carousel. "You must be relieved. I mean, that he's in good hands now. Not that he had a heart attack."

"Well, we knew there was a problem. He was scheduled to see the cardiologist next week." She let out a loud sigh. "But you're right, I am relieved. And feeling pretty thankful too. I don't know what I'd have done if he'd died. It was really touch-and-go there for a while. But enough about that. Where are you? Did your ride find you yet?"

"My ride?"

"Yes. When I realized I couldn't make it to the airport, I asked an employee to pick you up. He's my boat captain.

Leonard. You should see him holding up a sign with your name on it somewhere."

"Oh . . ." Tia glanced around the crowded baggage claim area, imagining a rough-looking, gray-haired fellow in a captain's hat.

"I better go," Julie said quickly. "Roland needs me."

"Okay."

"Just look for the sign, Tia. You'll be in good hands."

"Tell Roland I'm praying for him." As she slipped her phone into her bag, she noticed a white placard with her name printed clearly across the front. But it was the tall, sandy-haired man holding the card that got her attention as she waved at him.

"Tia D'Amico?" he asked politely as he joined her. "Julie Sheffield sent me to pick you up." He paused to study her more closely, a look of realization washing over his face. "Are you the *same* Tia, the one from sailing camp—about ten years ago?"

She felt speechless as she nodded silently.

"The girl who liked to cook." His ocean blue eyes grew wide with wonder. "Seriously?"

She smiled. "Yeah. And you're Leo."

"Wow." He reached over to pick up her big bag. "This is amazing. You're Julie's niece? The cook for her big restaurant project?"

"And you're the captain?" Tia felt like she was walking on air as they made their way toward the doors.

"I am for this summer. I told her I'd see how it went. And after hearing about Roland, I'm already having my doubts." They paused outside, waiting for a break in the traffic before crossing the street.

"It's a pretty big venture to take on," she said, trying to sound calmer than she felt about being there with him. It was all so amazing—like a wonderful dream. "My uncle—he runs a restaurant too—he has some serious doubts. But I'm ready to give it my best shot. I just feel badly for Roland."

"Yeah." He linked his arm in hers, ushering her across the busy street with him. "They were lucky to get to the hospital when they did." To her disappointment, he released her arm on the other side of the street. Pointing to his left, he explained that his car was over there.

"I'm still sort of shocked to meet up with you again," she said nervously. "I mean, it's kind of crazy, don't you think?"

Leo nodded. "Threw me for a loop. But now that I think about it, I'm putting the puzzle pieces together."

"How so?" she asked.

"Well, Julie and Roland go to the same church as my parents. My mom told Julie how I'd been working as a ferry boat captain, but my boat got retired. That's when Julie called me. What I didn't know was that the new cook—Julie and Roland's niece—was that girl from sailing camp." He laughed. "Small world, huh?"

"I'll say."

He stopped by a Jeep Wrangler with the top down. "I hope your bag will fit in my trunk." He reached to open the small space, then managed to cram her suitcase into it. "Your carry-on too?" He held out his hand.

"Why don't we just throw it in the back?" she suggested.

"Oh, yeah, I forgot to tell you. Julie insisted I keep her reservation at Le Bernard tonight. And we don't want to leave anything valuable in an open vehicle."

"Okay." She eagerly handed him her bag. "See if it fits."

"There." He gave it a firm shove, then slammed the trunk closed. "Hopefully you don't have anything fragile in there."

She smiled. "No worries."

He paused to carefully look at her. "You look really nice, Tia. I hope you don't mind riding in the Jeep."

She laughed. "Not at all!"

"I know some girls don't like getting all windblown. I probably should've put the top on, but it was so nice today."

"Really," she assured him. "I like it."

"Cool." He grinned as they got in and he started the engine. "I still can't believe it. You and me meeting up again after all these years."

"I know." She shook her head. "Crazy."

As he navigated his way out of the parking lot, she called her dad, telling him she had arrived safely and also about Roland and his scheduled surgery. "Julie is still with him in the hospital."

"So what are you doing? Getting a taxi to Julie's place?"

"Julie sent her boat captain to pick me up," she explained. "And ironically, he was someone I already knew." She glanced over at Leo, feeling a thrill rush through her as she watched his sandy hair blowing in the breeze. "A guy I met at sailing camp. You know, that summer I spent at Julie's. Anyway, his parents are friends of Roland and Julie. Funny, huh?"

They talked a bit longer, then Tia wrapped up their conversation, probably faster than she normally would. She was anxious to learn more about Leo. She turned to study him more carefully as she put her phone away. "You haven't changed much," she told him. "I mean, you look a little older. But I would've recognized you anywhere."

He grinned. "You sound like my mom. It's what she calls

my boyish good looks." Stopping for a red light, he turned to look at her. "You've changed some. Not in a bad way. But you've definitely grown up."

She suppressed the urge to laugh. Good thing he hadn't seen her yesterday—dressed in her shabby chef's outfit and before Deanna's makeover. "So you were a captain on a ferry boat? That sounds interesting."

"It was more interesting at first. I have to admit it got a little boring doing the same route day after day. When the ferry got retired, I started to wonder if I should head back to school and finish my law degree."

"Is that what you want to do?"

"Not exactly." He frowned. "I quit college short of my master's. My folks weren't too pleased, but pursuing a degree I didn't plan to use felt wrong to me. I love being on the water—it's where I feel most alive. During high school and my four years of college, I spent every summer working on boats. Got my captain's license when I was twenty-one. Went to work on the ferry right after I graduated."

"That's impressive that you got your captain's license. When Julie told me I was being picked up by her yacht captain, I imagined this old dude with a skipper's hat, a grisly beard, and a corncob pipe." She laughed.

"My little sister actually got me a corncob pipe for Christmas one year." He laughed too. "Haven't tried it out, though."

"I think it's great you're pursuing your dreams," she said. "I get that. I only did two years of college. My dad wanted me to be a CPA, just like him. All because I won a mental math contest in fifth grade." She laughed. "Can you imagine?"

"Actually, I can. My dad's an attorney. He assumed I would follow in his footsteps."

"What's up with that? Parents thinking they should direct our futures? What happens if we end up in careers we hate?"

"Exactly."

"I'll admit I wanted to please my dad. But after a couple years, I realized it was a total waste of time and money. I'd rather cook beans than count them."

He chuckled. "And I'd rather eat beans—well, as long as I could be outside on the water—than be stuck in a law firm."

She laughed. "The upside for me was that taking those accounting classes convinced me that I really wanted to be a chef. My dad was concerned at first, but he grew up in the family restaurant. So he sort of got it. He knew I loved to cook."

"A family restaurant? That sounds interesting."

She told him about D'Amico's and a bit of its history. "As a little girl, all I wanted was to grow up to work there. Everyone thought it was just a phase. But I think it was in my genes."

He chuckled. "Maybe that's my trouble too. My grandfather captained a cutter in the Navy—during Korea. Must've got his DNA, but it skipped a generation because my dad doesn't even like boats."

"Same thing with my dad. He has absolutely no interest in the restaurant—well, aside from balancing the books. And it's probably good he doesn't want to be in the kitchen. A family restaurant can only support so many people."

Leo got quiet, but she was so nervous and happy that she just kept on chattering. "It was actually harder to leave the restaurant than I expected it would be. I mean, I really thought I was over our little town and ready for a change. But when it came right down to it, I was sad to go. But at the same time I wanted something new." She glanced at Leo, still absorbing the fact that this was the boy who kissed her in the bowsprit. Did he even remember that day? "Now that I'm here, I don't regret it a bit."

"Even if it all falls apart?" He exited the freeway, heading into the city.

"Falls apart?"

"You know . . . with Roland and everything."

"Oh, yeah." The seriousness of her uncle's health situation came crashing down on her. "I guess that would change things."

"I was talking to my mom before I left to pick you up. She has serious doubts that Julie will continue with the boat project if Roland's not well . . . or if by some chance he doesn't make it."

"Yeah, I had the same thought. Quadruple bypass surgery sounds very serious."

"He's got a bunch of folks praying for him." Leo turned down Market Street. "Including me."

"Me too," she declared.

"Sorry, I didn't mean to get you down." He stopped for a traffic light and turned to look at her. "I'm sure he's going to be fine. Julie said that he was out of pain now. And she insisted we shouldn't worry about him tonight. She made me promise to be sure you have a good time. So let's just send our prayers and good thoughts to Roland, then concentrate on making your first night in San Francisco as welcoming as possible."

"Sounds good to me." She took a deep breath, admiring the architecture of the tall old buildings illuminated by the golden light in the western sky. "San Francisco is such a beautiful city. For some reason it makes me feel right at home."

"Maybe because for a big city, it's not really that big."

"Oh, it's big to me," she admitted. "My hometown is tiny. Population less than fifteen thousand."

"Wow, that is small. Where is it?"

"Norton, Washington," she told him. "You probably never heard of it. About three hours northeast of Seattle."

He drove a couple of blocks before entering what looked like a private parking garage for some kind of law firm, slipping a card into the machine and waiting for the gate to open. "My dad's an attorney here. He lets me use his spare ID card when I come down here during off hours. Easier than trying to find a closer place on a Friday night. And you can never fully trust valet parking."

"Is the restaurant nearby?" she asked as they got out.

"Not exactly." He reached into the backseat to pull out a tan sport coat, hooking it over his arm. "Ready?"

"I am."

He looked down at her delicate-looking shoes. "Mind walking a few blocks?"

"Not at all," she assured him.

"I think San Francisco is putting on her best face for you tonight," he said as they emerged from the garage. "Pretty balmy for us."

Tia took in a deep breath as they walked down the street, looking all around and trying to soak in all the elements of the cityscape. The sun was low in the sky and the clouds on the horizon seemed to be promising a pretty sunset. Perfect . . . everything was just perfect. Like a fairy tale.

"Mind riding the cable car?" he asked as they reached Powell Street.

"Really?" she said with as much excitement as she'd felt ten years ago.

"It'll be quicker."

"And more fun," she added as they went over to wait by the turnaround. About a dozen other people were already gathered there. Most looked like tourists. Even though Tia knew she was a tourist of sorts, it was fun to pretend she was a resident like Leo, out on the town. Really, wasn't she?

Before long the *clang-clang-clang* of the bell announced that the cable car was coming and suddenly people were pouring out of it. With Leo's help, Tia climbed on board. "Want an outside seat?" he asked.

"You bet," she said.

He paid their fares, then joined her on the old wooden bench that faced out from the car. "I like the wind in my face," he said as he sat next to her.

"This is just perfect."

"There's Union Square." He pointed to the park as they passed by.

"As I recall, there's some good shopping around here," she said as they clattered along.

"Yeah. Your aunt's probably the expert in that department." He pointed again. "See the Transamerica Pyramid?"

"Oh, yeah." She nodded eagerly.

"And if you look really quick down California Street, you might catch a glimpse of Chinatown Gate." He put his face close to hers, pointing down the intersection. She nodded, although she couldn't really see it. But she enjoyed feeling his face so close to hers. Everything about this evening felt magical and amazing, like she was starring in some fabulously romantic movie that she hoped would never end.

"We get off at the next stop," he announced as the car slowed down. It had barely stopped when he leaped off, reaching out to help her down. But as her feet hit the pavement, her heel caught on something and she felt herself tumbling—straight into his arms.

"Wow," he said as he helped her to stand. "That was close."

"Thanks." She put her hand on his chest, getting her bearings. "I'm glad I didn't do a face-plant on my first night in San Francisco. Very unbecoming."

"Not to mention painful." He reached for her arm, hooking his into it as he guided her across the street and down about a block, finally stopping in front of what resembled a lovely Parisian café, complete with black-and-white striped awnings and lots of curly black ironwork. "Well, here we are. Le Bernard."

To her disappointment, he unhooked his arm when they came to the door. Standing next to the outside dining area, she checked out the small round marble-topped tables lined up alongside the restaurant. There was only room for six tables, and all of them were filled, mostly with couples, sipping wine and enjoying the sunset-painted sky. She realized Leo had released her arm in order to tuck in his pale blue oxford shirt and pull on the tan sport coat he'd been carrying. He grinned as he retrieved a navy striped tie from the pocket. "It's required here." Struggling to get it under his collar, he grimaced as he fumbled with the twisted tie. "Stupid things. I avoid them as much as possible."

"Can I help?" she offered.

"Seriously?" His eyes lit up. "You know how to tie a tie?"

"Yep. Been doing it for my dad since I was a kid."

He held his hands to his sides and leaned forward. "Go for it."

She took her time straightening the tie inside his collar. She enjoyed feeling this closeness with him, relishing every step of the process until she got the knot just perfect. "There," she proclaimed, stepping back to admire her work. "Stunning." And she wasn't exaggerating. Leo could make the cover of *GQ*.

"Thank you." He smiled at her. "So are you."

"Oh, I'm probably all windblown." She started to smooth her own hair into place, but he reached up to stop her.

"No, it looks great like that, Tia. Really."

"Oh . . . okay." She honestly felt like she was floating as they went inside. As Leo checked on their reservation, she considered pinching herself. Was this really her life? Or was she simply caught up in one of her favorite romantic comedies . . . or just dreaming?

"I forgot to mention, we're meeting someone," he said when he came back. "She's already here, saving our table."

She? Tia felt like a soufflé that had just gone flat. "Who are we meeting?" she asked, trying to keep her voice light and carefree.

"My fiancée." He made a funny half-smile. "Guess I should've mentioned that sooner, huh?"

"Oh, no," she said quickly, fighting the urge to turn around and flee this place. "I'd love to meet your fiancée." As he led her through the crowded dining room, she pasted on a forced smile. Really, she should've known better than to get her hopes up. A guy like Leo couldn't have possibly been single. Really, what was she thinking? She should've guessed that someone like him would at the very least have a girlfriend. Of course he had a fiancée. Good grief, he was probably nearly twenty-eight by now. He might've easily been married. And even if he was unattached, what could he have possibly seen in her?

4

Tia spotted her from across the room. She didn't want it
to be the gorgeous blonde sitting by herself at a corner table,
but somehow she knew that it was. Wearing a strapless knit
dress of turquoise blue, she looked impeccable.

"Tia D'Amico," Leo said politely, "I'd like you to meet
Natalie Morgan."

Natalie extended a perfectly manicured hand, grasping
Tia's warmly. "I'm so happy to meet you," she said with
what seemed genuine sincerity. "Welcome to San Francisco."

As Tia thanked her, Leo pulled out a chair. But after she
was seated, Tia couldn't think of a thing to say. She was
literally speechless.

"I already ordered hors d'oeuvres," Natalie announced.
"I hope you don't mind," she told Tia. "I know you're the
foodie, right? But I thought you guys might be hungry." She
pointed to her nearly empty wine glass. "Plus I needed some
food to go with that moscato. But I hope I didn't overstep—"

"Not at all. That's fine." The truth was, Tia would've

liked to have made her own choice, but what could she say? "What did you order?"

"The chicken liver pâté, which is awesome. And the onion tart."

"That sounds good." Tia scanned the hors d'oeuvres section of the menu, thinking she would've preferred the coquilles Saint Jacques and the baked Camembert. But really, despite having had no lunch, she had no appetite.

"Did you have a good flight?" Natalie asked.

Still perusing the menu, Tia explained how she'd been upgraded to first class.

"Oh, good for you," Natalie said. "It's the only way to travel. Flying coach is like being in a cattle car."

The waiter arrived to take their drink orders. Dressed in traditional black and white, he was strikingly attractive in a dark, mysterious way. His attention was focused on Tia, but before she could say a word, Natalie spoke up. "We must have champagne—to celebrate." She reached for Leo's hand, caressing it. "Or haven't you heard the news?" she asked Tia.

"News?" Tia shrugged.

"That Leo proposed to me today."

"*Today?*" Tia looked curiously at Leo. "You told me you were engaged, but I had no idea it was so recent. Congratulations—to both of you. How exciting." For some reason this aggravated Tia even more. Not only had it felt like Leo had kept this information from her, but to hear he'd only gotten engaged today, well, she felt slightly blindsided.

He nodded. "So far only our parents know about it."

"So, to celebrate, we want champagne," Natalie told the waiter. "Your Cuvée Brut, please. The Vilmart, 2000."

"Very good," he told her. "Anything else?"

"I'm fine with water," Leo said without much enthusiasm.

"Yes, water's fine," Tia echoed. She suspected the champagne that Natalie had just picked was well over a hundred dollars. She hoped Leo could afford it. But even if he couldn't, it wasn't her problem. She focused her attention on the handsome waiter as he recited the specials, feigning interest despite knowing that most restaurant "specials" were simply the product of surplus food items about to go bad.

The waiter left to get their champagne, and she returned to studying the menu. She couldn't help but notice that the prices were exorbitant—probably as much to do with the location as the quality of the food. She also knew that since her aunt and uncle weren't here, she should be prepared to pay for her own dinner tonight. It wasn't like she was Leo's date.

"I feel a bit intrusive," she admitted as she laid her menu aside.

"Intrusive?" Natalie said. "It was your aunt who set up this reservation for you. If anyone is intruding, it's probably me."

"Except that you guys got engaged today. You should be celebrating with a nice romantic dinner, and, well, here I am." She made a meek smile. "Kind of like a third wheel."

"That'd be a tricycle," Natalie teased. "I loved my trike as a child. And I'm very happy to share this evening with you, Tia." She turned to Leo. "Aren't you?"

He nodded with an uncertain look. "Of course."

The waiter returned and set up the ice bucket next to Leo. "This is a very good year," he said as he worked the cork out, releasing it with a festive pop. "The lady knows her champagne."

"Well, I had time to study the menu," Natalie admitted

as the waiter poured the first glass, handing it to her with a flourish. "I would love to have something this good at our wedding, but I'm afraid Daddy would put his foot down over the price."

Leo's brow creased as if curious as to what this bubbly was going to cost him, but he said nothing as the waiter handed a glass to Tia. She really didn't want any, but the least she could do was sip to a toast. Unfortunately the rest of her drink, probably around $25 worth, would remain in her glass. Not to be rude, but simply because she didn't care for champagne.

After the waiter left, Natalie and Leo lifted their glasses and Tia, feeling very much like a bulky third wheel on a sleek racing cycle, raised hers. But no one said anything until Natalie looked at Tia with raised brows. "Will you do the honors?" she said politely.

Tia swallowed hard, then nodded. "Here's to the most glamorous-looking couple I've ever had dinner with." She made a nervous smile, knowing that was a pretty shallow toast. "May your lives together be truly blessed, filled with love and happiness." As everyone clinked their glasses together, Tia longed to disappear. She would rather be anywhere just now. She wished she was back in D'Amico's, even if she'd been demoted to peeling potatoes. She could not remember the last time she'd felt as miserable as she felt tonight.

When the waiter took her order, Tia made her requests in French, ordering *soupe a l'oignon* and *sole meuniére*. "I know the onion soup is a little repetitive with the tart," she told him, "but I'd really like to try it."

"Very good." He smiled pleasantly.

Natalie's order was more complicated, but it was plain to see she was comfortable with the menu. She asked the kinds of questions that servers liked to hear. This was a woman who knew her way around good cuisine. Judging by her hair, clothes, and jewelry as well, Natalie was well-off.

Leo's order was simpler and to Tia's surprise, he ordered the *sole meuniére* as well. Was it because it was the cheapest entrée on the menu or simply because he liked fish? Why should she care? The sooner this evening ended, the happier she would be. Somehow she made it through the hors d'oeuvres, making idle conversation as she pretended to pick at the onion tart and liver pâté. It wasn't that the food was bad. It was really quite good. But her stomach felt as if she'd ingested a bag of cement for lunch.

Suddenly she realized the table was quiet, and she suspected it was due to her presence. She was obviously putting a damper on what was meant to be a festive evening. "I must apologize," she told them. "I think I've been worrying about Roland again." Okay, it was a flat-out lie. She hadn't actually thought of him since meeting Natalie. But she didn't know what else to say.

"How about if I text Julie?" Leo offered. "See how the old guy is doing?" He looked at Natalie. "Do you mind?"

"Normally, I would. But under the circumstances."

"I'd appreciate it," Tia told him.

"How upsetting for you," Natalie told her. "To come all this way to help your aunt, and on the same day, your uncle nearly dies."

"On the same day . . ." Tia shook her head. But again, instead of fully focusing on her ailing uncle, she was thinking it was *on the same day* as Leo went and got himself engaged—to another girl. "Tell me, Natalie," Tia said when she saw that Leo was still focused on his phone, "how did you guys get engaged? Did Leo do some amazing stunt, like all those ones you see on YouTube?"

"Julie says that Roland is feeling much better. He even ate dinner and he's resting comfortably now."

"Oh, good." Tia thanked him as he put his phone away. "That's a relief." She turned back to Natalie. "And now for your engagement story. I'm dying to hear it." That wasn't completely disingenuous. She did feel like she was dying in some ways.

"Well, it's not very exciting," Natalie admitted. "Nothing anyone would want to watch on YouTube." She poked Leo in the shoulder. "Mr. Parker here is not exactly a romantic."

Leo made a guilty-looking shrug. "Sorry about that."

"It's okay, baby. I'm sure it's partly my fault." She refreshed her glass of champagne then turned to Tia in a confidential way. "You see, we've known each other for, well, *forever*. Our parents have been friends since long before we were babies. In fact, our mothers made a secret pact, back when we were both in diapers, that we would marry one day." She laughed. "But then Leo went his way and I went mine."

"Uh-huh." Somehow Tia could imagine this. The two beautiful blond babies playing together, their mothers speculating about what a lovely couple they would make someday. They *did* make a lovely couple. Already Tia had noticed other guests in the restaurant peering at them with curiosity, almost as if they suspected the handsome pair were celebrities. They just had that sort of look.

"Anyway, I graduated from Stanford Law School in March." Natalie took a sip of champagne. "And went straight to work at the firm." She turned to Leo. "That's where both our dads work, and where James—that's Leo's dad—had hoped that his only son would come join him someday." She smiled as she poked Leo again. "Anyway, Leo and I started spending time together a couple of months ago and, well, one thing led to another. Today we met for lunch downtown, and I took the bull by the horns." She grinned at Tia. "I made my demands."

Tia was confused. "Huh?"

"Natalie?" Leo put a hand on her shoulder.

"Oh, it's okay." She waved a hand. "We can trust Tia, *can't we*?" She turned back to Tia with a furrowed brow. "You just have that sort of face. *Trustworthy*." She patted Tia's cheek. "And very pretty too. Did anyone ever tell you that you resemble Penélope Cruz?"

"Actually, my dad's girlfriend said the same thing." Tia looked curiously at Leo. Was Natalie getting tipsy?

"I told Leo that it was time to fish or cut bait." She frowned. "However that saying goes. Anyway, I told him that I was not going to hang around forever. Good grief, I'm almost twenty-nine." She finished off her champagne. "And I've heard that most women who wait until thirty to marry, don't."

"Don't?" Tia was confused.

"Marry." Natalie pointed at Tia. "How old are you?"

"Twenty-five."

Natalie nodded. "Oh, well, that's okay. You have plenty of time."

"Oh."

Natalie held her glass out to Leo again, but this time he shook his head. "You need to get more food into you." He put a piece of the onion tart on her plate. "Eat up."

"But I'm telling Tia our story."

"You eat a few bites first."

Natalie took a big bite, then turned back to Tia. "I made him propose to me," she declared. "Can you believe it?"

"You didn't *make* me," Leo gently told her.

"No, I didn't, did I?" She gave him a sweet smile.

"As my dad can attest to, no one can make me do anything." Leo put the cloth napkin over the champagne bottle as if to hide it from Natalie.

"Oh, yeah." She nodded as she chewed on a piece of baguette with pâté. "You *are* a stubborn man. You proposed to me because you wanted to, didn't you?"

"That's right."

After the waiter brought their entrées, Leo asked him to bring Natalie a cup of espresso too. Then he looked at Tia with what seemed an apologetic expression. The table got very quiet as they started to eat. Uncomfortably quiet. Tia attempted to make small talk, focusing on their food and the restaurant.

"The reason Julie wanted me to come here tonight was to be a culinary spy," she confided. "I offered to take photos of the menu, but Julie said no." She laughed. "I wouldn't really do that. But I did study the menu pretty carefully. It's definitely a good one. I'm not sure if Julie wants only French cuisine on the boat, but I wouldn't mind."

She told them about how she'd been cooking Italian for the past couple of years. Leo asked her more about her family's restaurant, and she was relieved to fill him in on everything she could think of to fill the space. Meanwhile, Natalie concentrated on her food. By the time they were finished and Natalie had consumed most of her meal and her espresso, she seemed to be returning to normal.

"We have to do dessert," she told them with renewed enthusiasm. "No one should leave Le Bernard without dessert." She pointed at Tia. "Besides, you're doing research, remember? You can't ignore their dessert."

Tia had no appetite, but to pacify Natalie, she ordered crème brûlée with an espresso. As she poked her spoon through the crispy burnt sugar, she wondered if she'd ever had such a deliciously despicable dinner. Hopefully this nightmare would end soon.

When the bill came, she reached for her purse, but Leo told her to stop. "Your aunt insisted that tonight's meal was on her."

"But I—"

"No arguments, Tia. Julie will cover your meal. I'll cover the rest."

"Okay." Feeling more awkward than ever, she excused herself to the "little girls' room." As she pushed open the door, she realized that Natalie had followed.

"I'm sorry I acted like such a moron," Natalie said as they went in together. "I should've known better than to have a second glass of champagne."

"Well, I'm glad you're feeling better," Tia said uncomfortably.

"I just hope I didn't ruin your meal." Natalie peered into Tia's eyes with real concern. "Please, tell me I didn't."

"Of course you didn't," Tia said lightly. "It was a delicious meal. I know why Julie speaks so highly of this place."

"Oh, good." Natalie hugged her, holding her tightly. "And what I said about twisting Leo's arm to marry me . . . I hope you'll chalk that one up to too much champagne." She released her and giggled. "I mean, of course, it's partially true. But it's not something I want repeated, if you know what I mean."

Tia put a forefinger over her lips. "It stays here."

"Thank you." Natalie pointed to the available stall for Tia to go in. "I knew I could trust you, Tia. That wasn't the wine talking. I can tell you're a loyal friend. And believe me, I'm good at reading people."

"Oh." As Tia went into the stall, she suppressed the urge to stomp her feet and scream in frustration. Why did Natalie have to be so nice? Especially when all Tia wanted was a good excuse to hate her. Oh, that's right, she had an excuse. Natalie had taken the only guy that Tia had ever felt seriously interested in.

By the time Tia emerged from the restroom, the table they had occupied was empty. "Your friends said they'd meet you outside," the server said with what seemed a flirtatious smile. "But if you want to lose them, I'll be off work in an hour. Buy you a drink at the bar while you wait."

As uninterested as she was in his offer, she felt a strange sense of comfort that he found her attractive. "Thank you." She smiled. "I have to decline, but I do appreciate being asked."

"Another time." He winked, then headed for the kitchen.

Bracing herself, she went outside to find Leo and Natalie embracing. She turned her back, extracting her phone from her purse and pretending to be engrossed in the messages there. All two of them. One from Julie, telling her how to get into the house. And the other from Uncle Tony, telling her he missed her.

"I miss you too" she texted Uncle Tony back. *More than you'll ever know*, she thought as she hit send, still waiting for Leo and Natalie to remember she was with them. A taxi slowed down in front of the restaurant, and she was tempted to raise her hand and jump in, but before she could pull off this childish move, Leo and Natalie came over.

"Sorry," Natalie said. "I had to apologize to Leo too." She sniffed, almost as if she'd been crying. "So embarrassing."

"You're sure you don't want me to give you a ride?" Leo asked her.

"No thanks, the valet already went for my car." She smiled brightly. "Really, I'm fine, baby. The food and coffee did the trick. Plus there's no way I'm leaving my car here overnight. I'll be home in ten minutes." She pointed to the street where a small silver Porsche was pulling up to the curb, then leaned over to give Leo one last peck. "See you tomorrow, baby," she called over her shoulder as she hurried to her car. She tipped the valet and, looking sleek and glamorous, climbed in and took off.

"You really think she's okay to drive?" Tia asked with concern.

"Yeah." He nodded glumly.

"How about you?" Tia asked as they walked toward Powell Street.

"Huh?" He frowned. "You think one glass of champagne would impair my driving?"

She shrugged. "That wasn't what I meant."

"What then?" he asked as they crossed the street.

"You just seem a little sad. Like something's bothering you."

"I'm fine," he said in a clipped tone. Neither of them spoke as they walked to the cable car stop. Tia felt like she'd stepped over some invisible line. Almost like she should apologize. Except that she wasn't sure what she was sorry for. Well, other than the fact that Leo was engaged to someone else. She was definitely sorry for that. Not that she planned to admit as much—to anyone.

5

The cable car ride back up the hill was nothing like the earlier one. Besides the awkward wall of silence between Tia and Leo, the fog had rolled into the city, making it decidedly chilly. Damp and cold and dark. Kind of like her mood.

"You're shivering," Leo said as he removed his sport coat, draping it over her shoulders. She murmured a quiet thank-you but wished he hadn't been so chivalrous. It would be easier to hate him. Not that there was any real chance of that.

To make things worse, she'd stupidly taken the seat "up-hill" from Leo, and every time the cable car made a choppy lunge forward—and there were many times—she couldn't help but slide backward on the worn wooden bench, straight into Leo. It would've been pleasurable a few hours ago, before she knew about Natalie. Now it was pure torture.

They finally reached the turnaround on Market Street, and once again he helped her down from the cable car. "Don't know where this fog came from," he muttered as they walked

back to the parking garage. "The weatherman never mentioned anything."

"It's San Francisco," she said dryly. "It's supposed to be
foggy."

"I just hope you won't get too cold on the way to Julie's,
with the top down."

"It's okay." She wanted to tell him there were worse things
than hypothermia . . . like broken hearts.

"Do you want to get anything out of your luggage?" he
asked as they walked through the garage. "Some layers to
keep you warm?"

"Do you want your jacket back?" she asked a bit sharply.

"No, no, that's okay. I'm pretty warm-blooded. I don't
need it."

"Then I'll be fine." She felt horrible for being so snippy,
but she couldn't seem to help it. Besides that, it seemed her
best defense against breaking down in tears. No way did
she want him to know how she really felt. She knew it was
childish and selfish and totally ridiculous. Just because an
eighteen-year-old boy had kissed a sixteen-year-old girl, ten
years ago, was no reason to go to pieces. Really!

Of course, he would open the door to his Jeep for her. She
forced a grateful smile as she slipped inside, telling herself
that somehow she was going to become Miss Congeniality
during the ride home.

"I'll turn the heater on full blast," he said as he started
the engine. "That should help take the chill off."

"Thanks." She faked a cheery tone.

He let the engine run as he pulled out his phone. She
wondered if he was checking on Natalie, making sure she'd
made it home okay. "Julie texted to ask how our dinner went.

Actually she copied you on the same text." He turned to Tia. "What should we tell her?"

"That dinner was delicious and we had a wonderful time." Tia waited for him to type his response.

"She says she plans to spend the night at the hospital with Roland tonight. And told us where their house key is hidden." He slipped his phone back into his pocket. "And that she expects me to get you safely home." He made a lopsided smile as he backed out.

"Thanks." She attempted to return his smile. Even if she was faking it, she was determined to appear grateful. "And thank you for taking me to Le Bernard tonight. It was really good to see the place. It'll be helpful for Julie's restaurant. I mean, if a picture's worth a thousand words, sampling food must be worth about ten thousand. Or more."

"I feel like I owe you an apology," he said as he pulled out onto the street.

"An apology?" She tried to sound oblivious. "Whatever for?"

"Maybe I imagined something, but it seemed like things changed between us when you found out about Natalie."

"Oh . . ." Tia didn't know what to say.

"I realized that I should've said something about our engagement a lot sooner. I feel kind of like I was stringing you along somehow. Really, I didn't mean to do that. To be honest, I almost told you as we were leaving the airport, but you seemed so happy to see me. And hey, I was pretty thrilled to see you again too. It was fun catching up. The more we talked, the harder it seemed to be to tell you. How do you just blurt out, 'I got engaged today,' you know?"

His sincerity caught her off guard. "Yeah, that makes sense."

"And then, when we got to the restaurant and I realized that not only had I neglected to tell you about Natalie but that Natalie was already there . . . man, I felt like the biggest jerk."

She turned to look at him. Why did he have to tell her all this? Why did he have to be so nice and understanding? Didn't he know it would be a lot easier if he really was a great big jerk?

"So, anyway, I just want to apologize. I hope you don't hate me."

"Of course I don't hate you. The truth is, I did feel a little awkward. I mean, it's not like I thought we were on a date or anything. That would be ridiculous. But the last time I saw you . . . a lifetime ago . . . well, the last thing I remembered was . . . oh, you probably don't remember the . . ." Somehow she couldn't bring herself to say the word *kiss*. For all she knew, Leo had kissed every girl on the boat. She was certain they all would've enjoyed it.

"The good-bye kiss," he said quietly.

She felt a tinge of bittersweet relief. "Yeah. I was only sixteen and probably pretty impressionable, and you seemed so grown-up to me. So today there you are, Julie's boat captain picking me up at the airport, and, well, I nearly fell over from the shock."

"Hey, I was shocked too. You may not realize it, but I thought about you a lot over the years."

"Really?" She felt her hopes start to rise . . . then drop. "I don't believe you."

"It's the truth. I could tell you were special, Tia. Even if you were only sixteen. You had this air of confidence about you. Like you knew where you were going and couldn't wait to get there. I admired that. I mean, here I was about to start college and I had no idea where I was going or what I wanted out of life."

"I never would've guessed that," she admitted. "To me you were confident and capable. Of all the kids on the boat, you really knew what you were doing."

"That's because we were on a boat. I loved boats. It was my comfort zone."

"Oh."

"As soon as I got home, I wished I'd thought to get your address or email or something, to keep in touch. All I knew was that you were Tia D'Amico, the girl from Washington State. I didn't even know that you were related to Julie and Roland. Not until I picked you up from the airport today."

Stunned and dismayed, she replayed his words. He had wanted her address? He'd wanted to keep in touch? Unbelievable. But what was the point of sharing this now? Once again, she was speechless. They rode through the city without speaking, until finally she could stand it no more. Somehow they had to move on. She couldn't bear to remain stuck like this.

"You and Natalie got engaged today," she stated. "You must be pretty excited about that."

"Yeah, sure. Natalie is great."

"She seems super sweet," Tia admitted. "I'm not just saying that. She seems like a genuinely nice person. I really like her." She didn't add that it would be much easier to despise the beautiful woman.

"She's one in a million. No doubt about it. I think Nat mentioned that she's an attorney, but she probably didn't admit that she graduated at the top of her class. Could've had her pick of jobs, anywhere in the country. But she wanted to work with her father. And my father too, of course."

"You must feel very lucky." She wanted to ask, *But do you love her?*

"I know I'm lucky. Nat could have her pick of guys. I'll bet she's had at least a dozen proposals by now. But she's turned them all down."

"Sounds like she was waiting for you."

"That's what she says."

"It's nice that your families are good friends."

"Pretty convenient, that's for sure. Our parents were ecstatic. I'm sure our moms have already started making wedding plans."

"That should be fun for them." Tia took a deep breath, inhaling the cool, damp air and then slowly exhaling as she looked around, trying to think of something else to talk about. "Is that the Presidio?" she asked as the pristine buildings and parklike landscape came into view.

"Yeah. Have you been there before?"

"Julie and Roland took me once. During the day, of course. But it looks different at night. Really pretty lit up like that." She pointed ahead. "And there's the Golden Gate Bridge. Now it really feels like I'm in San Francisco."

For a minute or two, neither of them spoke. To break the awkwardness, Tia went into chatterbox mode, trying to fill the silence with a myriad of words as they drove over the bridge. As Leo navigated the winding road to Julie and Roland's house in Sausalito, she attempted to recall every detail about her visit there ten years ago—talking nonstop about everything she could think of—touring Chinatown, having lunch on Fisherman's Wharf, seeing the wax museum, having tea at the Japanese gardens, shopping with Julie in Union Square, going to a Giants game with Roland.

She babbled on and on about everything that had happened that summer. Everything except that week on the sailboat . . . that kiss in the bowsprit. Finally, just as she was running out of steam and words, he pulled into the driveway of her aunt and uncle's beautiful bayside home. She eagerly jumped from the Jeep, peeling off his jacket and shoving it at him as she hurried to the little trunk to extract her baggage. But Leo seemed determined to play the gentleman to the end, stepping in front of her and getting the bags himself.

"I'll show you where they hide their key." He set her bags on the oversized front porch, then went over to where a bunch of flowerpots were clustered in a corner. "Julie said it's under the big cast-iron flowerpot with the sunflowers." He lifted the heavy black pot, pushed aside some dirt on the porch, and produced a key. "Voila." Still being the gentleman, he went to the tall double doors. Unlocking one, he pushed it open, then set her bags on the foyer's slate floor. "Do you want me to go through the house to be sure the bogeyman isn't here?" He placed the key in her hand, allowing his fingers to linger just long enough to send a shiver down her spine.

"No thanks." She clasped the key, jerking her hand away. "I'm not worried."

He just nodded as he stepped out the door. "I figured as much." Still, he didn't go. His brow was creased, and she suspected he still felt remorseful for not telling her about Natalie sooner.

"Let's make a deal," she said slowly.

"Huh?"

"If you promise not to feel bad about tonight, I promise not to feel bad. Okay?"

He nodded with an uncertain expression. "Okay . . ."

"While we're at it, let's just forget about what happened ten years ago." She gave another forced smile. "It's all water under the bridge. Bygones being bygones. Clean slate. Pick your metaphor. It's over. Okay?"

He nodded with what looked like true relief. "Okay. Thanks!"

"Really, you should be celebrating your new engagement, Leo. It's very exciting. I hope you and Natalie will do something really special tomorrow—just the two of you."

He chuckled. "Don't worry. I'm sure we will."

"Thanks for everything." She kept her smile pasted on as she started to close the door.

"Wait a second." He stuck his foot on the threshold. "I forgot to say that Julie asked me to take you out to the boat tomorrow. She doesn't expect to be able to go and she really wants you to see it. Maybe even start to work, if you want. Do you?"

"Yeah, sure. Why not?"

"I plan to head out around 8:00. Can you be ready by then?"

"Of course."

"Wear your grubby clothes," he called out as he went down the stairs. "Lots of work to do."

Tia had barely closed the door when her eyes began to sting with unshed tears. She told herself she was simply weary and homesick. She was missing Dad and everyone at D'Amico's. Plus, she was anxious about Roland's condition . . . and worried that Julie's restaurant venture was sunk and that Uncle Tony had been right all along—she had come here on a fool's errand.

But as tears trickled down her cheeks, she knew the truth. Her heart was breaking. She felt like her life had finally been beginning and was now crushed. She felt like a child who'd been awarded a big beautiful prize, holding it in her hands, and suddenly it was plucked away and given to someone else. All she could do was cry.

6

Blowing her nose, Tia scolded herself for being such a big baby. Normally she wasn't an overly emotional or dramatic sort of person. She considered herself a realist, pragmatic and practical. If something broke, she would try to fix it. If it couldn't be fixed, she would move on. In this case, she needed to move on. If not physically, at least emotionally. Lecturing herself on these things, she wandered aimlessly around her aunt and uncle's beautiful home.

To distract herself from her heartache, she tried to see what had changed in this house since her last visit ten years ago. She had been impressed with the sprawling ranch home back then, but somehow she felt even more impressed now. Perhaps it was because she had a better understanding of money and how hard it was to come by. Things she'd taken for granted as a teen suddenly captured her attention. The original art, old Persian carpets, interesting antiques. The house was a showplace. She knew this water-view home had to be worth more than a million dollars. Probably more like two or three. Kind of mind-blowing when you came from a middle-class family in a small Podunk town. Dad and Uncle Tony sometimes made fun of how Julie had "married up."

It was no secret that Roland came from an extremely wealthy family. And he'd worked quite successfully as an investment broker. He'd been so successful, in fact, that according to Tia's dad, Julie had embarked on numerous small business ventures simply to "lose" money. "A tax write-off," Dad explained to her after she returned from San Francisco wanting to know how Julie could afford to run a fancy clothes boutique without being very concerned over her lack of clientele.

According to Dad, the recent economy had changed some of that for Julie and Roland. Walking through their home, though, it seemed obvious that they were still very well off. Their kitchen, which had been a little dated when Tia had visited before, was completely remodeled. Subzero fridge, commercial-grade gas stove with an oversized hood, two built-in convection ovens, wine fridge, double drawer dish-washers—not to mention fabulous cherry cabinets, granite countertops, and all the trimmings. Judging by appearances, the Sheffields were definitely not hurting. Well, except that Roland was in the hospital, facing life or death surgery in a few days. Money wouldn't be able to fix that.

Tia stood before the tall stone fireplace, studying a recent photo of Julie and Roland. She knew it was recent because although Julie looked pretty much the same, Roland looked so much older. He still had his beard, but it was completely white now. Tia knew that Roland was fourteen years older than her dad, which meant he was about sixty-five. Meanwhile Julie was barely forty.

Suddenly Tia felt a deep pang of compassion for her aunt and uncle and grabbed up her phone to send a quick text, asking how Roland was doing and if there was anything she could do to help tomorrow. As she hit send, she hoped Julie would ask her to come to the hospital to keep her company or perhaps to do something around the house. Any excuse for not going to the boat with Leo tomorrow. Within minutes, Tia's phone was ringing with a call from Julie. First she gave the update on Roland. "He's stabilized, and of course, he thinks because he feels fine, he should come home. What he doesn't fully appreciate is that without all these machines and blood thinners and whatnot, he would not be alive. But it's going to be a long weekend. I plan to be here most of the time."

"Tell him I'm still praying for him," Tia said. "Send him my love."

"I'll do that. And thanks for offering to help," Julie said. "But the most helpful thing you can do right now is to keep the renovations on the boat moving along. I've lined up various workers, but there's a lot to do before they get there. Maybe it was naïve, but I'd imagined you and I doing it together. Our way to get ourselves familiar with the boat, you know?"

"I'm willing to do whatever you need," Tia told her.

"Great! I left my boat bag on board." She explained that her "boat bag" was actually a big blue canvas case where she kept a notebook, samples, and catalogs all pertaining to the boat renovation. "The notebook has a long to-do list right in the front. You'll see that I've made some progress, but if you could start attacking it again, I'd be so grateful, Tia."

"You got it."

"The bag is in the stateroom."

They talked a bit longer, but as they said good-bye, Tia realized that she had no good excuse not to go with Leo tomorrow. Julie needed her help on the boat, and Tia was determined not to let her down. Since it was getting late and tomorrow would be an early day, Tia turned off the house lights and went to the guest room—the same one she'd occupied during her last visit. Judging by the fresh flowers on the dresser next to the neat stack of towels and basket of toiletries, she was in the right room.

As Tia got ready for bed, she blocked all thoughts of Leo from her mind. Or nearly all. But as soon as she turned out the lights and got into bed, it all came flooding back at her. She could feel the lump in her throat as the tears gathered again. Instead of surrendering to it, she pulled out an old trick that Grandma D'Amico had taught her to use after her parents' divorce—a way to trick your mind into thinking about something else until you fell asleep. She started to count her blessings in alphabetical order.

After tossing and turning all night, Tia didn't wake up until 7:45. Scrambling to get dressed and a bite to eat, she was just putting her hair into a ponytail when she heard the doorbell ringing. It was barely 8:00, but feeling no need to primp today, she was ready. Since Leo appeared to believe in promptness, she grabbed her sweatshirt and backpack, then hurried out to join him. As she went, she told herself that today was just about work. That was all. She would not let her emotions or her imagination run away with her. If they did, she would do something drastic—like jump into the bay—to make it stop.

"Good morning," Leo said brightly as she emerged.

"Morning!" She forced a cheery smile as she locked the front door. She figured she'd be doing a lot of fake smiles today. Might as well get used to it.

"Ready to rock and roll?" he asked.

"You bet." She slipped the spare key into her backpack and looked all around. "Looks like the fog's gone."

"Yeah, it's supposed to be another sunny day."

"Cool. I can't wait to see the boat." She hurried down to the Jeep, opening the passenger door before Leo could do it first. Hopefully she was sending him a clear message—she did not need him to be a gentleman.

"Well, the *Pacific Pearl* is a real beauty," he said as he slid into the driver's seat. "Okay, I guess she's a beauty in disguise. But she's a classic. Circa 1958, but completely restored a few decades ago. Roland's mom wanted to give the *Pearl* a 'modern' update back in the 1980s." He shook his head in dismay as he backed out of the driveway. "Lots of pink and plum and lavender colors, and this horrible flowery wallpaper. Fortunately, they only covered the surfaces. Most of the original stuff, all that mahogany and brass and teak, is still underneath."

"Sounds interesting."

"The one good thing about their restoration is that they completely overhauled the engine room—and they did it right. The *Pacific Pearl* has guts. She can go."

"How big is she?"

"Not too big. At least by today's standards for yachts. Just sixty-two feet. Julie estimates that after it's opened up inside—she's taking out all but the one stateroom that's clear in the back—there should be enough space for tables to accommodate fifty diners. And up to seventy-five if it's not seated dining."

"That sounds like a nice number." Tia nodded. "Not too overwhelming."

"Yeah, we figure the smallness will be part of the attraction," he explained. "There are a lot of big dinner yachts already running the bay. But most of them are huge and corporate owned. You feel like you're on a mini-cruise. The *Pearl* should feel more intimate, more luxurious. Plus you've got that old world classic feeling."

"With fewer diners, I'm guessing it's more about quality than quantity, so Julie can probably charge more than those big lines."

"That's the plan."

They continued chatting about the boat as he wound his way down to the marina, and for a few minutes Tia nearly forgot all about her broken heart. It wasn't until he had parked and they were walking down to the wharf that she noticed how handsome he looked. He was casually dressed in worn khaki shorts and a faded gray T-shirt, and his sandy hair was blowing in the wind. But it was the earnest expression in his ocean blue eyes that got her. As he gazed out over the bay, eagerly taking it all in, she was reminded of the boy who had kissed her ten years ago. Her steely resolve to keep her mind under control was crumbling.

However, she was not about to jump into the bay. Instead, she mentally slapped herself and followed up with a silent scolding. *Get over it!*

"You okay?" he asked as he led her down one of the docks.

"Yeah, sure." She shrugged. "Why?"

"You just looked so serious, like something was wrong."

He switched the small duffle bag he was carrying to the other hand as he paused to study her. "Did you hear from Julie lately? Is Roland okay?"

She filled him in on what Julie had told her last night. "Mostly I think Roland is getting antsy. Can't be fun being stuck in the hospital over the weekend."

"Maybe we should run over and visit him after work today."

"I would like to see him," she admitted.

"It's a date."

She bristled at that word. Did he have to call it a *date*?

"Well, there she blows." He pointed to a long white boat occupying half the length of the dock. "The *Pacific Pearl*."

She studied the sleek body of the craft. The upper portion, made of gleaming wood, was somewhat boxy—giving it a retro look. But all in all it was absolutely delightful. She wished she had her sketch pad with her because she'd love to sketch it. "I love it!" she exclaimed. "It's a gorgeous boat."

"Well, be warned, she looks better on the outside than the inside."

"She's such a classic." Tia sighed. "All those windows— that will probably be great for the diners."

"Yeah. Julie wants both indoor and outdoor dining, but knowing San Francisco, the indoor dining will probably be the most useful." He pulled a long plank from behind a Dumpster, leaning it onto the side of the boat like a gangway. He grinned as he reached for her hand. "Come aboard."

She reluctantly took his hand. Okay, she was partly reluctant and partly rejoicing. But it was the rejoicing part that needed to go jump in the bay. "Thanks," she said as she made her way up the slightly wobbly gangplank. Once she was on board, she looked around the decks. "It looks like it's been beautifully maintained," she said in wonder. "I thought Julie said it needed work."

"The exterior's in excellent shape," he agreed.

"What kind of wood is this?" She ran her hand over the glossy exterior wall of the cabin. "It's so rich looking."

"Most of the exterior wood is teak," he said as he unlocked the cabin door.

"It's beautiful."

"Brace yourself." He grinned as he opened the door. "Welcome to the eighties."

She stepped into the main cabin, grimacing at the pastel upholstery, floral print wallpaper, whitewashed wood cabinets, and plum shag carpeting that was sun-bleached in places. "Ugh, this is really bad."

He pointed to a section of wood that had been stripped of the whitewashing and restored to its original rich red-brown tone. "Fortunately, the mahogany can be brought back."

"That's good."

"But most of these interior walls are going to be removed." He opened a door on the back wall, leading her down a dark, narrow hallway. "The berths and stateroom are back here. But most of this will all be opened up to accommodate seating. That's why Julie decided to wait on the wood refinishing. Wait until the footprint is done."

"Makes sense." Tia peeked into one of the berths, surprised to see that it was almost as big as the bedroom she'd had at her dad's house. But it could have slept four passengers with two sets of bunk beds. The next berth was a bit larger with two twin-sized beds and some nice built-ins.

"This must be the stateroom," she said when she came to a door at the end of the hall.

"Yep. It's the only space that Julie plans to pretty much leave as is."

She opened the door to reveal a fairly large room with a queen-sized bed and lots of handsome built-ins. Unlike the main cabin, this room had its original wood, and other than the flowery bedspread, it was fairly nautical looking. "This is actually quite nice."

"Yeah. Not sure how it missed the eighties makeover, but lucky that it did."

"For sure." She spotted the canvas bag on a dresser. "That must be Julie's boat bag. I'm supposed to start working on her to-do list."

"Great. So you're all set then?"

"I guess so."

"I'll either be working on some things outside on deck, or in the engine room, or in the cockpit. If you need me, just go outside and holler—or ring the bell by the door and I'll hear you."

She thanked him and, relieved to be alone, opened one of the portholes to let some fresh air into the musty stateroom. The bedspread reminded her of an old woman's overgrown flower garden. Roland's mother obviously had a penchant for these colors and prints, but seeing the original woodwork and untouched built-in cabinets gave her hope.

"You're such a beautiful boat," she said as she retrieved Julie's canvas boat bag. "I'm glad you're going to get some help." She emptied the bag onto the queen-sized bed. She admired the various samples for fabric and paint and wood stain and all sorts of things. There were also catalogs of hardware and fixtures and furnishings and kitchenware. Many of the pages were flagged with Post-its. Julie had clearly been doing her homework.

The more Tia studied the contents of the boat bag, the more she understood where Julie was headed. Her vision for the boat's interior was classic. The color scheme was simple. A crisp, clean off-white and nautical blue, offset with the rich mahogany and golden brown cork floors. There were even some hand-drawn blueprints for the boat's decks. The main cabin area was all opened up with spaces for tables, pretty much like Leo had described, but she was actually starting to envision it now.

The to-do list started with lots of hands-on tasks like removing wallpaper, carpeting, and furnishings. Tia had seen a fair number of home remodeling shows and suspected this would be considered a gut job. She wondered what the kitchen (aka the galley) was like. That was the area that really interested her. Since she hadn't seen any sign of it on this portion of the boat, she suspected it was on the other side of the cabin, or even on a lower deck.

She left her backpack and sweatshirt in the stateroom and set out to do some more exploring, taking the notebook with her. It was fun having the place to herself—or nearly so, because she could hear some thumping and bumping going on somewhere on the boat. She assumed it was Leo, but it was possible that other workers were there too.

She eventually found a steep ladder that led to a small galley beneath the main cabin. After a quick inventory, it was obvious that the galley would be a gut job too. No way could the four-burner propane stove produce quality cuisine for fifty to seventy-five diners. She poked around some more, discovering some storage areas as well as what must've been berths for crew members. If it was all taken out, the kitchen easily could be expanded. She would recommend that a dumbwaiter be installed too.

Since she hadn't seen any drawings of this in the blueprints, she decided to make a rough sketch of her own, trying to design what she felt would be an efficient commercial galley within a relatively small space. It was a challenge, but after several failed attempts, she thought she was getting closer. It was at least a jumping-off place. She would show it to Julie when they went to visit this afternoon.

Another thing Julie would need to address was the restrooms—or "heads," as they were called on a boat. Julie had probably already considered this, but just the same, Tia made notes and suggestions.

Finally, after she felt fully familiar with the interior spaces, she was curious to see what the outside decks were like. How many diners could be accommodated out there? Stepping out, she was impressed again with how handsome the exterior part of this boat was. It would look classy and elegant cutting through the bay. Not to mention romantic. It had that kind of old Hollywood appeal. And with a few strings of white lights in the right places, perhaps some festive lanterns, it would be a fabulous place for an anniversary party or even a small wedding.

As she stood there in the bowsprit, her mind sprinted ahead, and she was suddenly imagining her own wedding. It came rushing at her so quickly that she couldn't stop it. Or perhaps she didn't want to. She saw herself in a lovely but simple white dress, and she was barefoot, with her long hair flowing freely on her shoulders and a sea breeze gently blowing over her sun-warmed skin. Beside her stood her handsome groom, and together they faced the minister, who was leaning against the bowsprit railing. Meanwhile, the sky on the horizon was painted with the most beautiful sunset colors. And standing behind them were only their closest family and friends. After the ceremony, they would dine on a fabulous catered seafood dinner.

"What's up?"

Tia spun around in the bowsprit to see Leo curiously watching her. "Nothing," she said quickly, stepping down from the bowsprit. "I was just getting a feel for the boat. Imagining how we might run strings of white lights around this banister. When the weather is fair enough, the diners could eat outside." She pointed to the wide deck area. "I think we could probably get four or five small tables out here. That would seat about twenty diners. Not bad."

He nodded with a thoughtful expression. "Sounds like you've really been giving this some consideration."

"I have," she said as she pushed past him. "And now I'm going to go strip some wallpaper."

"Need any help?"

She wanted to yell, "No, I don't need any of your help!" Instead she just turned and glared. "Don't you have work to do in the engine room or something?"

"I already told Julie I'd help with the wallpaper stripping."

"Oh."

"Do you even know how to strip wallpaper?" he challenged.

She shrugged. "How hard can it be?"

He chuckled. "That just shows that you don't know what you don't know. As it so happens, I've stripped lots of it from my grandmother's house. So I'm experienced."

"Then I guess I should be grateful for your help." She made a stiff smile.

"Cool. I'll grab some tools and be there in a minute."

As she went inside, she knew it was hopeless. Trying to control her feelings toward Leo was like trying to control the tide. She stared out the window into the shimmering blue bay. Maybe it really was time to jump overboard.

7

As it turned out, removing wallpaper wasn't as easy as she had expected. Fortunately, Leo had all the right tools. Together they steamed and scraped, and by 1:00, one exterior wall of the main cabin was free from the flowery paper.

Leo paused from scrubbing the leftover paste from the wood. "I think it's coming back," he said as he rinsed his sponge in water.

"Very nice." She ran her hand over the rich, warm brown mahogany.

"I don't think it needs to be refinished." He used a rag to dry the wood panel, rubbing it until it shone. "I'm guessing they used spar varnish."

"What's that?"

"Spar varnish is a boat's best friend. Well, if the boat has a lot of wood. Spar varnish is impervious to water. That's why the exterior wood looks so good. Roland's dad must've had someone give it a fresh coat not too many years ago." He peered more closely at the wall. "This might need another coat too. To really brighten it up and protect it."

"You seem to know a lot about restoring boats," she said as she compacted the shreds of wallpaper into the trash bag.

"I've worked on a few."

"You really do love boats, don't you?" She picked up the trash bag, hoisting it over her shoulder to take out to the Dumpster.

"Pretty much." He made a lopsided grin. "My parents think it's something I'll outgrow in time, but I really don't think so."

"I don't see why you should outgrow it," she said as she opened the cabin door. "My uncle is always saying that if you love what you do for a living, it's not really work."

"Is that how you feel about cooking?"

"Absolutely." She nodded as she went outside, stepping around some of the smaller furnishings that they'd moved out to the deck. As she carefully made her way down the wobbly gangplank, she had to admit that Leo was fun to work with. Not only was he knowledgeable and a hard worker, he was good at conversation too. Still, as she tossed the bag into the Dumpster, she felt aggravated. It would be a whole lot easier on her heart if he was a bossy grump.

"You hungry?" Leo asked as he came out onto the deck.

"Now that you mention it."

"There's a little place within walking distance. It's called the Fish Shack, and that pretty much describes it. But their fish and chips are killer."

"Sounds good to me." She pointed at the furnishings on the deck. "What do we do with all this stuff?"

"We can set it on the dock with a 'free' sign to see if anyone wants to do some salvaging. But we need to have it out of here by the end of the day."

"Maybe we should move it to the dock before we leave," she suggested.

He looked skeptical. "It'll take both of us to get some of those bulky pieces off the boat. You think you're up for that?"

"Sure." She picked up a small pink ottoman, carrying it to the gangplank. "I'm stronger than I look." Of course, as she walked down the wobbly board, she didn't feel as confident as she sounded. Fortunately, she did not fall in.

Together they worked to get all the pieces onto the dock. "It looks like a yard sale," she said as she taped the "free" sign onto a coffee table.

"An eighties yard sale." He put on his sunglasses and rubbed his stomach. "I don't know about you, but I'm starving."

"I hear those fish and chips calling my name."

"I hope I didn't get your hopes too high," he said as they strolled down the dock in the afternoon sunshine. "I'm not really a connoisseur of fine cuisine."

"I'm so hungry, I'm not sure I care."

As they walked, they talked about the boat, discussing what they'd accomplished and what they hoped to get done after lunch. "I'm impressed with what a hard worker you are," he said when they reached the tiny restaurant.

"Thanks. I was thinking the same about you." Tia looked up at the limited menu painted on the side of the small shack. "I'm going to stick with the fish and chips," she said as they stepped up to the window to place their orders.

Before long, they were seated at an outside picnic table that was splattered with seagull droppings and sticky from the previous diners' meals, but as Tia bit into her crusty piece of halibut, she really didn't mind. "This is fabulous," she said as she sprinkled some malt vinegar onto her fries. "I know it has about a million calories, and I don't even care."

"That's my kind of girl," Leo said.

Tia tried to hide her irritation as she bit into a fry. She knew he was simply trying to be nice. He probably couldn't help it. His mama had brought him up right. But she wished he could be a little bit rude, self-centered, or arrogant.

"I always thought sea captains were supposed to be kind of curmudgeons, you know? Crusty old cusses. Growling at their crew to swab the decks."

"Make 'em walk the plank if they don't toe the line?" he teased. "Sounds more like pirates to me."

She took a sip of her lemonade. "Maybe so."

"Besides, I'm still young. I'll probably turn into a crusty curmudgeon later on." He held up his hand. "Maybe I'll have a hook by then."

She frowned. "Hopefully not."

"Hello there," called a voice from behind Tia.

"Natalie." Leo stood with a surprised expression.

Tia turned to see Natalie striding toward them. Dressed in white capri pants, cork-soled sandals, a blue-and-white striped shirt, and a chic straw hat, she looked like an ad for the Ralph Lauren nautical line. Like she should be posing on the deck of a fabulous yacht.

"What are you doing here?" Leo asked as he went to meet her.

"Looking for you." She smiled at Tia. "Nice to see you again."

"You too." Tia suppressed the urge to smooth her messy ponytail—especially since she knew it was pointless.

"Do you want some lunch?" Leo asked her. "I can go place an—"

"No, no," she told him. "I don't want to interrupt your meal. I'll just go grab a Diet Coke."

While she was ordering her drink, Leo used his napkin to wipe the seat next to him, and when Natalie returned he warned her that the table was a little sticky.

"No problem," she said lightly as she gingerly sat down on the bench. She pointed at Tia's half-eaten meal. "You're a brave woman."

"It's actually really good."

"Oh, I'm sure it is. But if I ate that it would probably go straight to my hips." She laughed.

Tia wanted to point out that Natalie was thin enough that it probably wouldn't matter, but instead she just looked down at her food.

"Well, Tia's working so hard that she'll probably burn that off in a couple of hours," Leo said.

"I saw all the junk on the dock." Natalie wrinkled her nose. "What a mess, huh?"

"We're making good progress," Leo told her.

"I'm starting to get a vision for it," Tia added. "It's going to be really lovely when it's finished."

"I guess I'll have to see it to believe it." Natalie took a sip of her drink. "Leo, I came over here to talk to you about the wedding."

"The wedding?" Leo's brow creased as he chewed.

"Yes." Natalie nodded firmly. "I've decided that we should have a short engagement."

Leo stopped chewing with a slightly perplexed expression. "Really?"

"I know, baby." She reached over to rub his back. "It probably sounds a little crazy, huh?"

"I don't know . . . What do you consider a *short* engagement?"

"I—uh—maybe I should go," Tia said uncomfortably. "I mean, this seems like a conversation you should have in private."

"Oh, no," Natalie assured her. "It's okay." She turned to Leo. "That is, if it's okay with you."

"Yeah, I don't care. But a short engagement? What do you mean?"

"I think we should get married before the end of the summer."

"Wow, that is short." He frowned. "But I thought you wanted some big huge wedding."

"I do. But I've always imagined getting married in the summer, ever since I was a little girl." She glanced at Tia. "I'll bet you understand that. A girl has certain dreams for her wedding. Guys just don't get it."

Tia just nodded, taking a small bite of her fish, which now tasted more like deep-fried cardboard than halibut.

"Anyway, I don't want to wait another whole year," she continued. "So I think we should tie the knot this summer." She beamed at Leo. "What do you think, baby?"

"I, uh, I don't know."

"Well, I already told my mom and she's told your mom and they both think it's an excellent idea."

"They do?" He took a long, slow sip of his lemonade.

"The biggest challenge will be securing the venue."

"Uh-huh . . . ?" Leo picked up a fry with what seemed disinterest.

"I really want an outdoor wedding, but most of the best spots are already booked for this summer."

Leo's eyes lit up as he turned to look at Natalie. "What about the boat?"

"What boat?" Natalie cocked her head to one side.

"The *Pacific Pearl*," he said with genuine enthusiasm.

"You mean the *Minnow*?" Natalie snickered.

"The what?" Tia looked lost.

"Ever seen *Gilligan's Island*?" Leo asked her.

"Of course."

"Well, Nat thinks the *Pacific Pearl* looks like a large version of the boat on that show. It was called the *Minnow*."

"Oh." Tia suspected that was not a compliment.

"The *Pearl* will be completely renovated and operable by mid-July. If we set a date for, say, mid-August, we could have a really fun wedding on the water."

"On the water . . ." Her brow creased. "Really?"

"Yeah," he continued eagerly. "I'm a captain. Getting married aboard a boat? Can you imagine how cool that would be?"

"I, uh, I don't know."

Tia felt her spirit shriveling. It was bad enough they were discussing their wedding plans in front of her, but hearing Leo suggest a boat wedding and Natalie obviously hating the idea . . . well, it was just more than she could stomach.

"I think I'm done here." Tia picked up her lunch things and stood. "I'll be at the boat." Before they could dissuade her, she dumped her trash and took off. As she hurried down the dock, she fought back the lump forming in her throat. *Put on your big girl pants*, she told herself. *Don't be such a big baby!*

She took in a bunch of deep breaths, gazing out over the

bay as she walked, and by the time she got to the boat, she felt better. She was pleasantly surprised to see that several of the pieces of furniture had disappeared. That was progress. Relieved that Leo and Natalie hadn't followed her, she went aboard and opened the windows in the stuffy cabin, then started up the steamer and went to work stripping paper.

It felt good to have a task to focus on. Carefully using the broad knife just like Leo had shown her, she gently worked the damp paper from the wall without gouging the handsome mahogany. All in all, it was a rewarding process. Maybe it was because she felt a satisfying sense of control. Something that seemed missing from her personal life right now.

"Ahoy there, mate," Leo called as he boarded the boat.

"Ahoy, Captain," she called back as she moved the steamer over a strip of the hideous wallpaper.

"Wow, you've already made some good headway," he told her.

"What a mess," Natalie said as she stepped over a trash bag.

"Yeah," Tia said lightly. "Sometimes you gotta get messy in order to clean up."

Leo chuckled. "That's true."

"Well, as much as I'd love to stick around and help." Natalie laughed. "*Not!* I have some wedding errands to run in town." She kissed Leo good-bye. "See you later, baby." She waved to Tia and took off.

The cabin grew quiet as they worked together, taking turns with the steamer and broad knife. While one steamed, the other peeled paper. For quite some time, neither of them spoke. Finally, tired of the silence and slightly curious, Tia spoke up. "Sounds like you guys worked things out."

"I guess you could say that."

"Did you decide on a venue for the wedding?" Tia used the broad knife to carefully remove a nice long piece of flowery paper, tossing it onto the growing pile.

"Not exactly."

"I love your boat idea," she said with enthusiasm, then regretted it. When would she learn to keep her mouth shut and her thoughts to herself?

"You do?" He sounded surprised.

"Sure. The *Pacific Pearl* is going to be a great wedding venue. It would be truly memorable."

"That's what I thought too. But Nat is definitely not on board." He chuckled. "Pun not intended."

"Why not?" Tia picked up the steamer. "Is she worried it won't look nice enough? Because I can just imagine it all finished. You could have strings of lights and garlands of flowers along the railings, maybe a string quartet on the upper deck, drinks and appetizers . . . It would be delightful."

"She says the *Pearl* is too small. She wants a really big wedding. Like four or five hundred guests. I told her she should just rent Oakland Coliseum."

"Oh." Tia nodded. "I hadn't thought about that."

"I asked her why we need to have such a humungous wedding. I mean, this boat could probably handle a hundred guests. Not for a sit-down dinner, but that's not necessary, is it?"

"I, uh, I really don't know." She wished she could think of a gracious way to change the subject that she'd so stupidly brought up.

"Why do we need more than a hundred guests anyway? I'd prefer to have just the people I really know. Close friends and family, you know?"

"Uh-huh." She set the steamer down, reaching for the broad knife.

"I just don't get it."

"Get what?" She said absently as she peeled the paper from the wall.

"Why the guy doesn't have an equal say. I mean, it's my wedding too, isn't it?"

"Yeah, sure. Of course."

"So why is the guy always pushed out of the wedding plans?"

"I don't know. Maybe it's because most guys don't care. They just let the girl handle everything."

"And this whole idea of a short engagement." He reached for the steamer. "Where did that come from?"

"She told you. She wants a summer wedding," Tia said in a flat tone. Really, did they have to keep talking about this? He obviously didn't know he was torturing her. Just then she realized something: perhaps this was like taking medicine or getting vaccinated—it felt lousy at first but made you feel better afterward. Maybe talking about Leo and Natalie's big fat wedding would inoculate her against feeling so miserable later on. Maybe it was time to take the bitter pill. "If you don't have your wedding this summer, you'll have to wait a whole year or more. Natalie said she doesn't want to wait that long. What's not clear about that?" She snatched the steamer from him.

"Some of my friends were engaged for a couple of years. One friend has been engaged for three or four years and they still haven't set a date. What's the big deal?"

"I don't know," she said. "But to be honest, I think I agree with Natalie on this."

"Seriously?" He threw a strip of paper on the pile, then came over to stare curiously at her. "Why?"

She set down the steamer, then reached for the broad knife, focusing her eyes on the paper as she talked. "Well, I think if you truly love someone, if you know you want to marry them, you know you want to spend the rest of your life with them, why would you want to wait? Wouldn't you be eager to begin your life together?" She turned to look at him as she dropped the strip of soggy paper onto the pile. "Well, wouldn't you?"

Leo's face was blank, and instead of responding, he picked up the steamer and went back to work. She knew she'd probably stepped over some line as they continued stripping paper together, neither of them speaking. The only sounds that broke the silence were their tools, occasional noises from people on the dock, the *slap-slap-slap* of the water against the side of the boat, and the random cries of seagulls flying overhead.

It was actually quite peaceful, except that Tia's mind was waging a huge war over the cause of Leo's silence. On one hand, she might've struck a chord with him. Perhaps he really was unsure about his feelings toward Natalie. Maybe he needed more time to think this whole thing over. But more than likely, he'd recognized the sensibility in Tia's suggestion. He may have realized she was right—if you really love someone, why delay a wedding? Thanks to Tia's big mouth, he was probably getting ready to give Natalie the green light for her dream wedding. Well, fine—the sooner the better. At least Tia would be able to move on with her life.

8

They were just taking out the last load of ugly plum carpeting when Tia paused to survey the mishmash of furnishings still piled around the Dumpster. "Didn't you say these things had to be gone by the end of the day?" she asked as she brushed grit off her jeans.

"My friend Jake's coming by to get them. Promised to be here by 5:00." He glanced at his watch. "Guess he's running late." He reached over to pluck a piece of carpet scrap from her hair.

"We made good progress." She knelt down to examine a round coffee table that was partially buried in chair cushions. "This actually looks like it might be a nice piece," she said absently. "I mean, if someone removed this ugly whitewash paint." She attempted to scratch it with her fingernail.

Leo removed the chair cushions, then tipped the table up to see beneath it. "Hey, you're right. This looks like solid teak."

"I'll bet it would be pretty if it was stripped and refinished."

She frowned. "If I had a real place to live, I'd salvage it myself."

"Do you think Julie would want it?"

Tia considered this. "Probably not. I mean, you've seen her house. And I doubt there'll be room for a coffee table this size in the restaurant. Dining space will be at a premium."

"But you're right," he said. "It does seem like a quality piece. Maybe I'll keep it."

Tia started poking around some more. "I wonder if there's anything else in here worth saving."

Leo chuckled. "Sounds like you're a good scavenger."

She held up a table lamp. "I do believe in reusing and recycling. Even if I don't like this stuff, it seems wrong to let it become landfill. Someone would like it."

"I know. Jake is taking it all to a nonprofit thrift store that helps support a local homeless shelter."

"Oh, that's great." She set the lamp down, then pointed up the dock. "Here comes your fiancée." She waved as she watched Natalie strolling toward them. She'd exchanged her nautical clothes for a chic sleeveless white dress paired with tan pumps and matching bag. She looked classic and stylish—and totally out of place on the rustic dock.

"Hey, kids," Natalie said with a slightly creased brow. "Still working?"

"Just finishing up," Leo told her. "You look nice."

"Yeah . . ." She tapped him on the chest. "I thought we had a date tonight."

"Oh?" Leo looked slightly blindsided.

"Remember last night, before I left the restaurant, when I asked if we could have a proper celebration? You know, for our engagement?"

He nodded.

"I thought you understood I meant *tonight*. Didn't you get my text this afternoon? I got us reservations at Plouf."

"I must've missed that." Leo pulled out his phone. "I wonder if Jake texted me—"

"The only reservation I could get was kind of early. It's for 6:30, Leo, so if you head home right now, you should have time to clean up and make it on time. If you hurry"—she stroked his cheek—"you could even shave."

He pointed to the junk on the dock. "But I need to stick around until Jake gets here to pick up—"

"You're going to blow off our celebration dinner in order to see this garbage gets picked up?" She made a pout. "Seriously?"

"I need to help Jake load it in his pickup," Leo told her. "Julie could get fined if we don't get it out of here tonight."

"I can help your friend load it," Tia offered.

"I don't want you to—"

"Really," she assured him. "I don't mind. Go ahead and take off. I can probably walk back to Julie's. I can use my phone's GPS. I'm guessing it's only a couple miles."

"Three and a half," he told her. "Besides that, I promised to take you to the hospital to see Roland tonight." He turned back to Natalie. "Could we celebrate our engagement tomorrow?"

Her faced hardened.

"I can take a taxi to the hospital," Tia told him. "Really, *just go*. I helped you get this stuff out of the boat. I'm sure I can help your friend get it onto his truck."

Leo looked unsure. "I realize you're pretty strong for your size, but I hate just ditching you like this."

"Really, it's okay," she told him.

"Hey, there's Jake's pickup now," Natalie exclaimed. "Problem solved!"

Tia looked down the dock to see a dark green pickup slowly backing toward them. "I hope Jake's good at backing up," she said nervously. She didn't want to admit it, but she'd probably be in the bay by now if it was her. Of course, driving was not her strong suit. She'd never owned a car and avoided being behind the wheel as much as possible. Fortunately, Leo's friend was fine with it, and before long a tall, lanky guy with shaggy dark hair hopped out of the pickup. "Sorry I'm late, man," he told Leo as they shook hands. "I was giving someone a landscape estimate and got stuck longer than I expected." Jake pointed to the pile of junk. "Looks like the nineties are calling and they want their furniture back."

"Try the eighties," Leo told him.

"Hey, Natalie." Jake grinned. "You look a little overdressed for this."

"Funny." She smirked. "Leo is taking me out tonight. To celebrate."

"Celebrate?" Jake frowned.

"Didn't Leo tell you that we're engaged?"

"Leo?" Jake looked at him with shock. "Seriously?"

"Yeah." Leo nodded.

"Well, congratulations, man." Jake suddenly seemed to notice Tia. "And who are you?"

"Sorry." Leo quickly introduced her. "Tia is Julie's niece and she'll be the chef on the boat."

"You're a cook?" Jake's eyes lit up. "Cool."

"Well, today I'm more like the cleanup crew," she admitted.

"Anyway, we wondered if you could give her a ride home," Natalie said to Jake. "Because Leo is taking me to Plouf tonight. Our reservation is for 6:30."

"Plouf?" Jake pointed to Leo. "You'll need to dress a little nicer than that, buddy."

"Yes," Natalie agreed. "Slacks and jacket required."

"How about we get this stuff loaded," Leo told Jake, picking up a couple cushions and tossing them into the back of the pickup. "I want to load this table last so we can drop it at my place before you head back to town."

"Why do you want this at your house?" Natalie stared down at the table.

"Because I'm keeping it," Leo said as the guys hoisted up a chair.

"Keeping it?"

"Yeah, it's a cool old piece. I'll restore it and—"

"But it's so bulky and clunky and ugly."

"It's solid teak, Natalie. And it's nautical. Probably as old as the boat," Leo explained.

"I'm going to get my stuff and lock up the cabin," Tia said quickly. "You need anything inside, Leo?"

As he called out a "no," Tia went on board, but she could hear the discussion continuing. Clearly Natalie didn't intend to have any "old junky pieces" of furniture in her home. Apparently that meant Leo couldn't either.

By the time Tia returned, they seemed to have smoothed things over. Jake was pointing out that they could pay a lot for a piece like that from Restoration Hardware, so Natalie announced she would reserve her final opinion until after she saw it refinished.

"See you back at my apartment." Natalie kissed Leo and

hurried off down the dock. Then Tia helped with the last of the items to be loaded, and the three of them climbed into Jake's pickup.

"So you're really going through with it, man?" Jake spoke over Tia's head as he slowly drove up the dock. "Getting ready to put on the old ball and chain?"

"Funny." Leo looked out the side window.

"I mean, Nat's a nice girl. And I know you guys have been friends forever. But I really expected you to be the last one to fall, man. I'm not sure what to think."

"Well, don't strain your brain over it," Leo teased. "I wouldn't want to be the cause of reducing your already limited brain cells."

"Nice way to talk to your best friend. Hey, does this mean I gotta rent a tux and be best man at your wedding?"

"That's right," Leo told him. "Misery loves company."

"Ooh, better not let Nat hear you talking like that."

"Here's my Jeep." Leo opened the door before the pickup was completely stopped. "Maybe I should just take Tia home so you can—"

"I don't mind taking Tia home."

"Yeah, but you have to drop off my table and make it to the thrift store before they close."

"Oh, sure," Jake said with a sarcastic tone. "You get to be engaged and take the cute little cook home and everything. *Real fair.*"

Tia laughed as she got out. "Pleasure meeting you, Jake."

"Pleasure's all mine. And maybe Mr. Selfish will let me take you home next time," Jake called as she closed the door.

"Your friend's a card," Tia said as she got into the Jeep.

"He's a funny dude, all right." He started the engine. "I feel bad that I'm not taking you to the hospital. Especially after I told Julie I'd pop in and see Roland tonight."

"How about if I send your love?" she offered.

"Thanks. Tell them I'll come by tomorrow." He drove without talking, and for a change, Tia felt no need to fill up the empty space with words. She decided as he pulled into the driveway that she was glad he wasn't taking her to the hospital. It would be a relief of sorts to get away from him. "Have a good dinner," she said brightly as she hopped out. "And thanks for the ride." Before he could say anything, she shut the door and hurried up to the house.

After a quick shower to clean up, she called Julie to see if there was anything she wanted from the house. Julie gave her a short list, then asked if Tia could bring her ukulele. "Seriously?" Tia asked as she removed the towel from her damp hair. "No one in the hospital will mind?"

"I don't see why. And Roland asked."

"Then I'll definitely bring it. I took a bunch of photos to show you what we got done today," Tia said cheerfully.

"I can't wait to see them. And you too."

"Well, I just need to dry my hair and get a bite."

"Take your time. They're just bringing in dinner now anyway. No hurry."

Tia felt clean and refreshed as she carried her ukulele up to the hospital entrance. She wasn't too thrilled about how much it had cost to take a taxi up there, but it would be worth it to spend time with Julie and Roland. Maybe she could talk Julie into going home with her. She felt certain her aunt would be in need of a good night's sleep by now. Roland ought to be able to get along without her for one night.

"There she is," Julie announced as Tia poked her head into the private room.

Tia held up her ukulele case. "I hear there's a need for some island music in here."

"Tia!" Roland's face broke into a smile. "Welcome to my world."

Julie was already across the room, tightly embracing Tia and exclaiming how glad she was to see her.

"Come over here," Roland commanded. "Let me get a better look at you."

Tia complied, going to stand by his bedside, trying not to stare at all the tubes and wires connected to him. "How are you doing?"

"Depends on who you ask," he said wryly. "According to the nurses, I'm doing great. But the doctors won't let me go home. And if you ask Julie, I'm just downright cantankerous."

"I never said that," Julie protested.

"You don't have to." He winked at her, then grasped Tia's hand. "You are even more beautiful than the last time I saw you. You and Julie must've got all the pretty Italian genes in the family." He chuckled. "We know they skipped Tony completely."

"Thanks." She smiled shyly.

For a while they just chatted congenially together, catching up on the latest news back in Norton and the restaurant, and how Tia had been upgraded to a first class flight, and what she'd ordered at Le Bernard last night.

"Where's Leo?" Julie asked. "Parking the car?"

Tia explained about Natalie's restaurant reservation. "It

kind of caught Leo off guard. But it was to celebrate, you know."

"Celebrate what?" Julie asked.

"Their engagement," Tia told her.

"What?" Julie and Roland said simultaneously.

"Oh, yeah, it's pretty recent news." She told them about how the couple decided to become engaged over lunch yesterday, including the part about how Natalie gave him an ultimatum. Suddenly she remembered and said, "Oh, I wasn't supposed to tell that part. Sorry. Just pretend like you never heard it."

Roland chuckled. "It figures that Natalie would have to twist Leo's arm."

Julie didn't say anything, but her brow was creased.

"Anyway, Leo sends his love, and he wants to stop by tomorrow."

To change the subject, Tia produced her camera and started to show them the pictures of the wallpaper being stripped and finally of the completely emptied main cabin.

"Wow," Julie exclaimed. "It looks bigger."

"And it looks like a boat again." Roland described how he remembered the boat as a small child, before his mother gave it the "English flower garden makeover," as he called it.

"I know your notes said that you wanted it all gutted," Tia said to Julie. "All the furniture, carpeting, and wallpaper removed. But there was one piece that seemed worth saving."

"I can't imagine what."

Tia explained about the big round coffee table. "Underneath the whitewash, it looks like solid teak. I hated seeing it go to the thrift store and Leo decided to keep it. Is that okay?" She looked from Julie to Roland.

"It's fine with me," Roland said.

"Me too." Julie peered at the last photo. "The only room I plan to keep is the stateroom. Although I want it freshened up." She put her hand on Roland's shoulder. "I want you to like it too. Because no matter what you said a few weeks ago, I think you're going to want to go out on the boat sometimes."

He looked into her eyes. "As long as you're there, I will be glad to go out."

"You might even enjoy it."

"I expect I will."

Julie leaned down to kiss him.

"Say, Tia, do me a favor, will you?" Roland said.

"Of course."

"Take your aunt to get a real dinner."

"But I already ate—"

"I saw you picking at the sad excuse for a Swiss steak," he told her. "Go with Tia and get something good to eat. Please, I think I could use a break."

"But I—"

"Take her, Tia," he commanded. "Even if you have to drag her kicking and screaming."

"Come on, Aunt Julie." Tia took her by the arm. "Let's give Roland some breathing room."

"We won't be gone long," Julie called over her shoulder.

"No, I didn't think so." He waved. "Tia still has to come back and play some island music for me. I want to daydream that I'm sunbathing in Maui." Tia returned his wave, feeling a twinge inside of her as she imagined what a grim place the world would be for her aunt if Roland didn't make it. How sweet—and yet precarious—it must be to love someone so dearly.

9

As they went into the elevator, Julie let out a long, weary sigh.

"You must be exhausted," Tia said as she pushed the button for the correct floor.

"It's only been about thirty hours, but I feel like I've been in this dreary place for at least a week."

"How about if you come home with me tonight?" Tia urged her. "I'm sure Roland can get by without you for one night."

"I can't leave him, Tia. Not for more than just a few minutes. And not overnight."

"But you look so tired." Tia studied her aunt's pale face. "No offense, but you look like death warmed over."

"Thanks." Julie pointed up. "I'll blame the fluorescent lighting."

"You really won't consider going home to sleep in your own bed?"

"That recliner in his room isn't too bad, actually. I'm fine, really."

"You're sure I can't persuade you?"

"I promised myself that I wouldn't leave until Roland's had his surgery and is completely out of the woods."

"Oh."

As they exited the elevator, Julie grabbed Tia's hand, looking intently into her eyes. "If I went home and Roland died . . . well, I would never forgive myself."

"So it's still that close—touch and go?"

Julie nodded grimly. "Those tubes and wires are literally keeping him alive. If a machine quit working, or an alarm didn't sound, or the nurses didn't come in time . . . well, that could be the end." She started to cry, and Tia wrapped her arms around her, hugging her tightly.

"I get it. I know how much you love him, Julie. I can understand why you wouldn't want to leave." She sighed. "You guys are really lucky, you know?"

"I know. And I'm just not ready to lose him."

"Of course not."

Julie stepped back, retrieving a tissue from her pocket to wipe her face. "I only leave his side when he's fully awake. I figure if something went wrong, he would be able to press the help button or even call out. But if he were asleep, well, I just don't know."

"Okay, I get that." They continued walking.

"You see, I'm a very light sleeper."

"That's good."

"Even though the staff here keeps telling me it's okay and that I should go home, I'm digging in my heels." They went into the cafeteria.

Tia nodded. "I won't nag you about it anymore. I promise."

"Thank you." Since neither of them felt particularly hungry, they got chicken noodle soup and found a vacant table in a quiet corner. But after only one bite, Tia knew she wouldn't be finishing it.

"How do you mess up chicken noodle soup?" Julie asked quietly.

"Pour it from a can?"

"You really think?"

Tia shrugged. "Kinda tastes like it."

"People always joke about hospital food, but I never really took it seriously. I'm not complaining since I haven't had a real appetite lately. But I do feel badly for Roland. It's like adding insult to injury. Here he is bedridden, but they have to torture him with bad food as well?"

"I wish I could cook you and Roland something good to eat."

"Wouldn't that be wonderful?"

"Do you think it's allowed?"

"As far as I know, he doesn't have any food restrictions until the night before his surgery. That's tomorrow night. And, of course, no alcohol."

"Maybe I could prepare a healthy meal to bring tomorrow."

"Oh, that sounds wonderful, Tia. Do you want to?"

"I'd love to. Does Roland still love cannelloni?"

"He often says that no one makes it like you do." Julie made a mock frown. "Not even me."

Tia patted Julie's shoulder. "Well, that's what I'll bring."

"In the meantime, I'll check with his doctor. If there's a problem, though I can't imagine there would be, I'll let you know."

Tia realized she'd need to do some grocery shopping. "Do

you still have your bike?" she asked. "The one I borrowed that summer?"

"Yes. Feel free to use it. But you could also use Roland's car. That reminds me." Julie reached into her purse, extracting a set of keys. "These are Roland's keys, but you keep them for now." She pointed out the various house keys, the mailbox key, and Roland's car key. "Be sure you put the emergency key back under the flowerpot, in case you accidentally lock yourself out. That happened to me once when the front door shut. Not fun."

"Good point." Tia dropped the keys into her bag.

"Really, feel free to use Roland's car."

"Yeah, thanks." Tia didn't want to admit it, but the last thing she wanted was to drive Roland's pristine Beemer around the busy streets of San Francisco.

Julie let out another long sigh.

"Are you going to be okay?" Tia asked with concern.

"Oh, that wasn't for Roland." She made a sheepish smile. "I suppose it should be. But quite honestly, and just between you and me, that was for Leo."

"For Leo?" Tia suddenly felt anxious again. "What do you mean?"

"I can't believe he's engaged to Natalie."

"Do you know Natalie?"

"Not very well."

"She actually seems very nice."

"How do you know her?"

Tia explained about dinner the night before and then at the dock that day. "I mean, she's not someone I can exactly relate to, but she really does seem nice. And she seems to truly love Leo."

"No doubt." Julie put her napkin over her unfinished soup bowl.

"You don't like her?"

"I don't like her for Leo."

Tia didn't know what to say.

"Not that anyone cares what I think." She made a forced laugh. "And not that I don't have enough other things to worry about. I should probably keep my nose out of other people's business." She stood up. "I feel like we need to go back."

"No problem."

"Visiting hours end at nine. That only gives you half an hour to entertain him with your ukulele."

As they walked to the elevators, Julie turned to look at Tia. "If Leo didn't bring you to the hospital, how did you get here?"

"A taxi."

Julie shook her head with a dour look. "I don't like that. Lone girl riding a taxi into the city at night."

"It was just fine," Tia assured her. "Don't worry."

They were nearly to the elevators when Julie pointed across the lobby. "Well, look who's here." She waved with enthusiasm. "Captain Leo!"

By the time Tia turned around, Leo had swept Julie up into a big hug. "Sorry to be late. And sorry for all you're going through. I was going to bring flowers, but I—"

"Better that you brought yourself," Julie told him. "If you can give Tia a ride home, I won't feel so worried. I was just lecturing her about girls alone in taxis at night in the city."

He smiled at Tia. "Happy to take you home."

"I hear you've gone and gotten yourself engaged, Captain

Leo." Julie shook her head as if she was skeptical. "Is it really true?"

He looked uneasy. "Yeah . . . it's true," he said quietly.

"You don't sound very enthusiastic or eager," Julie challenged him as they got in the elevator. "You sure you know what you're doing?"

"It seemed like a good idea at the time."

Julie's grim expression melted into an apologetic smile. "Sorry to rain on your parade. I guess I just feel protective of my captain." She reached out for his hand. "I should be telling you congratulations. Natalie seems like a very sweet girl."

"Thanks." He nodded as she squeezed his hand.

"When's the big date?" Julie asked as they went up.

"Natalie wants it to be this summer, but she's having a hard time finding a good venue." He brightened slightly. "So I suggested the *Pacific Pearl*."

Julie clapped her hands. "Wouldn't that be fun? I'd love for our first wedding to be for the captain. What does Miss Natalie say about that?"

"She was opposed at first, but I think she's coming around. She even suggested that maybe we could have the wedding ceremony on the boat and then hold the reception somewhere else—you know, where we could dock and let the wedding party out to go to the festivities. That way she could accommodate all her friends. Kind of the best of both worlds."

"How was your dinner?" Tia asked as they walked down the hall toward Roland's room. "I'm surprised you finished this early."

"It was okay," he said with what seemed like uncertainty. "Good view from that restaurant."

"Living pretty high for a boat captain," Julie teased as she paused by Roland's door. "Le Bernard one night and Plouf the next."

"Don't remind me."

"Look what the cat dragged in," Julie announced as she led the way into Roland's room. "My sea captain."

"Leo." Roland smiled, extending his hand. "I hear congratulations are in order."

"Thank you." Leo shook his hand. "How are you doing?"

"I've been better." Roland pointed to the chairs. "Have a seat. We're just about to have a little concert."

"A concert?" Leo looked puzzled, and Tia felt like crawling under the bed.

"Tia's going to play her ukulele for me," Roland explained.

"You play the ukulele?" Leo asked.

She made a sheepish nod as she reached for the case.

"I should've brought my guitar," he told her. "We could've had a duet."

"Really?" Julie looked surprised. "I didn't know you played guitar."

"I try to keep it a secret," he teased.

"Me too," Tia confessed as she did a quick tune-up, humming *my dog has fleas* in her head. "But Uncle Roland has a penchant for ukulele music," she explained. "So here goes." Fighting her self-consciousness, she started out by playing "Better Together."

"Come on," Roland called out. "You have to sing along to it."

She complied, singing quietly at first but with more enthusiasm as the others joined in where they knew the words. Next she played "The Lazy Song" and then "Soul Sisters."

"Do you still know 'Let It Be'?" Roland asked.

"Of course." She played it and they all sang along.

Then she played what she knew was Roland's favorite, the Hawaiian version of "Somewhere over the Rainbow," and seeing that visiting hours were over, she finished with "Amazing Grace" to the tune of the *Gilligan's Island* theme song, which made everyone laugh.

"We better go," she said as she put her ukulele away. "Before we get kicked out."

"Tia is bringing us a meal tomorrow," Julie told Roland. His eyes lit up. "Really?"

"It should probably be at midday," Julie told Tia. "I'm guessing he'll be eating light for dinner. Then nothing after that until . . . well, after the surgery."

"Lunch it is," Tia said. "Or should I say Sunday dinner?"

"Yes," Julie eagerly agreed. "Sunday dinner. How about if you bring it around 2:00?"

"You got it." Tia went over to say good-bye to her uncle.

"My mouth is already watering," Roland said as Tia kissed his cheek.

Leo grasped his hand. "Good to see you."

"You guys take care," Tia told them both.

"Tomorrow, bring your ukulele," Roland called out. "I want you to play 'Gilligan's Island' again, only this time we'll sing the original words too."

"Will do." She blew them both a kiss as she backed out the door. It wasn't until she was going down the hallway that she realized she was tearing up. Embarrassed at her emotion, she wiped the tears with the back of her free hand.

"Are you crying because of Roland?" Leo asked quietly as they waited for the elevator.

"Yeah." She sniffed. "I mean, he's probably going to pull through just fine, but seeing him like that . . . you know, sort of helpless . . . well, it just got to me."

"I know."

They went inside the elevator where several other people were already standing, and as they went down, Tia attempted to get control of her emotions. The last thing she needed to do right now, when she was already tired and feeling broken-hearted, was to lose it over Roland. Leo would probably think she was a real basket case.

"You okay?" he asked as they stepped outside into the cool evening air.

She took in a deep breath and nodded. "I guess I'm just tired."

"Yeah, it was a long day." He led her through the parking garage.

"I hope you didn't cut your celebration dinner short just to come here," she said as they walked. "I mean, I know they appreciate it, but they would've understood."

"To be honest, I cut it short because we were getting no-where."

"Getting nowhere?" Once again she felt that unexpected spurt of hope inside.

"Apparently I don't understand women too well."

"Oh."

He turned to peer at her. "Maybe you can help. You're a woman."

She shrugged but controlled herself from debating this fact. Yes, she was a woman, but she was nothing like Leo's woman. Still, she decided to play along, simply out of curios-ity. "What's the problem?" she said as they got into the Jeep.

"Apparently, I was expected to bring a ring to dinner tonight. To present it to her and to properly ask for her hand."

"Okay . . . ?"

"And apparently, I botched it. Badly."

"What happened?"

"We were about midway through the meal when Nat started hinting. It seemed she had done some ring shopping today. Both online and in a couple of shops. Apparently she sent some photos and details to me, on my phone, which I wasn't keeping very close track of."

"Yeah." She nodded. "Today was pretty hectic."

"Anyway, there we are at the restaurant and I thought, fine, let's see what these rings look like." He blew out a long, slow sigh. "The prices were just ridiculous. Of course, being a guy, I told her I couldn't afford a ring like that."

"Hmm." Tia tried to imagine how that must've gone over.

"Yeah. Nat wasn't too happy. Oh, she was polite about it, and even somewhat understanding. She even suggested that it was okay to buy the ring with credit." He turned to Tia with a puzzled look. "An engagement ring that you don't really own? Does that make any sense?"

"Well, not to me, but I'm a pretty practical person." She made an uneasy smile. "Almost to a fault, according to some of my friends." She shook her head. "Frugality, I mean."

"Here's my question, Tia. If I'm the one buying the engagement ring, shouldn't I be the one to pick it out?" He stopped the Jeep at the end of the line waiting to pay to exit.

"I, uh, I'm not so sure that's right. I mean, to be fair, different girls like different sorts of things. It seems like you'd want to be sure your fiancée wants what you pick out, wouldn't you?"

"I guess."

"I mean, if it were me, well, I wouldn't want a big flashy ring. But then I'm not really into jewelry."

"What about the ring you're wearing?"

She looked down at her right hand, surprised that he'd even noticed the small silver ring. "My claddagh?"

"Claddagh? What's that?"

"It's an Irish ring. My mom gave it to me . . . before she left. Her parents were from Ireland. It's one of the few things I have from her, and it's pretty special." She looked at how the heart was pointing away from her, the symbol that her heart was available for love. Not that it mattered.

"You do like some kinds of jewelry, then," Leo pointed out.

"Sure. But I don't really care for diamonds."

"A girl who doesn't like diamonds?" He eased the Jeep forward a bit, then turned to peer curiously at her. "Not even for an engagement ring?"

"It probably sounds silly, but I always had a very specific idea of what I'd like for an engagement ring. Just like Natalie—except that she is looking forward to a nice big diamond. It should be about what your fiancée wants and expects. Don't you think?"

"Maybe. But now you've made me curious. What kind of diamondless ring would you go for? Just a plain band of gold?"

"I've always imagined a ring that would have my birthstone and my husband's birthstone in it. They'd be sort of entwined together with either white gold or platinum, since I'm not crazy about yellow gold."

"Interesting." He moved another space forward.

She continued, "Of course, it could be problematic if my

husband-to-be had a birthstone I didn't like. I mean, like if he was born in the wrong month. Like October or November. I'm not really fond of those colors—pink and yellow—they wouldn't look very good with my stone."

Leo laughed as he pulled up another space. "You wouldn't marry someone born in the wrong month? Kind of like astrology?"

"No, that's ridiculous."

"So which months *do* you prefer?"

"Well, because my stone is aquamarine, which is this pale blue, I really like how the blue topaz looks with it. That's December's stone. The two blue tones remind me of ocean and sky." She laughed. "I probably sound totally insane."

He didn't respond as he moved up to the booth, paying the attendant and then pulling out onto the street.

Tia felt embarrassed for sharing this much. What was she thinking? Or was she simply too tired to think straight? "Okay, I realize that's probably not much help with you and Natalie. But my point is that Natalie *should* have a say in what kind of engagement ring you give her. I mean, she'll have it for a lifetime, Leo. She should love it, don't you think?"

He slowly nodded. "Yeah. You're right."

Once again, she felt a contradictory mixture of relief and regret. But she reminded herself she was simply taking her medicine. Times like this with Leo were like getting a painful shot—it would protect her later . . . right?

10

On Sunday morning, just as she was making espresso, Tia received a text from Leo inviting her to call him if she wanted a ride to church. Although she thought it seemed a little odd—shouldn't he be taking Natalie to church?—she decided to give him a call.

He greeted her, then explained that Julie had texted him late last night. "She suggested you might like to visit her church this morning. She and Roland recently started attending the same church where my family goes. If you're interested—"

"Sure," she eagerly said. She wasn't sure if her enthusiasm was more about church or more about Leo. Perhaps it didn't matter. "That'd be nice."

"Great. I asked my sister, Melinda, if she'd mind picking you up, and she said she was happy to. She'll be there a little after 9:00."

"Oh—okay. Thanks."

Tia felt a sense of letdown as she took her coffee out to the back deck. At the same time she felt foolish for even reacting. What was wrong with her? She knew that Leo was engaged, so why did she allow her hopes to elevate like that—only to be plunged back down to the ground again? She gazed out toward the shimmering blue bay, soaking in the amazing view of the Golden Gate Bridge and the city on the other side. With the faint remnants of last night's fog, the filtered light made the scene perfect for a watercolor. She momentarily considered pulling out her art kit and making an attempt, but she knew there wasn't time. Instead, she took several photos with her phone, promising herself she would play with the painting later.

Tia wasn't quite sure how to dress for church. Back home in Norton, she usually just wore jeans. But this was San Francisco. She decided to try out a summery dress she'd gotten on her shopping spree, topping it with her faded jean jacket since it was still cool outside.

Melinda rang the doorbell at 9:15. With her sandy hair and blue eyes, she reminded Tia of a female version of Leo. "It's nice to meet you," Melinda said politely as they walked down the driveway. "Leo says you're going to be the chef on the *Pacific Pearl*."

"That's right," Tia said as they got into the car.

"I love the idea of dinner cruises. Especially on a smaller boat. So romantic."

"Yeah, hopefully."

"Hopefully?"

Tia explained about Roland's condition. "If he doesn't pull through, I can't imagine Julie wanting to proceed."

"Oh, I hadn't heard about that. I just got home from college a few days ago. I'll be praying for him." She stopped at an intersection. "So much going on lately . . . it's hard to keep up."

"Were you surprised about Leo and Natalie's engagement?"

"Are you kidding? You could've knocked me over with a feather over that one."

Tia wasn't sure how to respond.

"I mean, sure, I realize they've dated off and on for, well, like forever. But I never in a million years thought they'd really get married."

"Why not?" Okay, Tia knew this was like opening a can of emotional worms, but she couldn't help herself.

"Well, it's not that I don't like Natalie. I actually do. She's been kind of like a big sister to me. My parents like her too. In fact, they're pretty much over the moon about the engagement. But I'm just not sure they're right for each other. I mean, they're such opposites."

"They say opposites attract," Tia pointed out.

"Yeah, I know. I've been telling myself that very thing. But I can't help thinking that opposites can pull each other in opposite directions too. I'd hate to see that happen to Leo." She chuckled. "I guess you can tell that I feel protective of my older brother."

"What's the age difference between you guys?"

"Leo's six years older. It seemed like a lot growing up. But he was always so good to me. So protective. As I got older, we've gotten pretty close. If I have a problem, I usually go to Leo for advice." She hit her hand on the steering wheel. "I wish he'd do that with me."

"You think he's got problems?" Tia knew she was fishing, but it was too late to pull back her line.

"Oh, sure, he's got problems. Who doesn't?"

"Natalie?"

Melinda laughed. "Well, I suppose her life looks pretty perfect to the casual observer. But although I love Nat dearly, I'm aware that she's got challenges too."

Tia wanted to ask what they were but already felt overly nosy.

"I'm sure you've noticed that she's kind of a type A personality. Very smart and motivated and detail-oriented. She'll be a fabulous attorney."

"If I needed legal representation, I'd certainly consider her."

"Maybe I'm making a mountain out of a molehill," Melinda said as she pulled into a parking lot situated next to a handsome stone building. "Maybe they'll be perfectly happy together."

"Hopefully." Tia pointed at the building. "Is that your church?"

"Yeah."

"What lovely architecture." Tia imagined doing a pen and ink drawing of it.

"Pretty sweet, huh? It was built in the 1880s."

"I don't think there's anything that old in my hometown." As they walked up to the charming building, Tia snagged some quick pictures on her phone. "I'm surprised Natalie doesn't want to get married here."

"I guess the sanctuary is too small." Melinda pulled one of the big, heavy, wooden doors open, lowering her voice. "It doesn't even seat two hundred."

Before long they were seated on an old wooden pew directly behind Leo and Natalie, flanked by two older couples that Tia assumed might be the parents. They all looked very nice together, almost like the poster family for prosperity and perfection. Both men were going slightly gray, but both still had a full head of hair. And the women, without a trace of gray hair, both looked stylishly classic. Tia's only consolation was this was a picture she definitely didn't fit into. She was relieved she'd worn a dress, but with her old jean jacket, she felt slightly out of place, although Melinda looked fairly casual in her jeans and a white silk shirt.

As the music started, Tia realized that Leo's tidily together family looked nothing like hers. It wasn't that Tia would call the D'Amicos "messy" exactly, but they were definitely loose and laid-back and slightly noisy. As pointless as it seemed, she found comfort in this. She and Leo were from two different worlds. Meanwhile, Leo and Natalie were from the same world. Sure, they might have some blips along the way, but in the long run, they would probably be just fine.

When it was time to greet the people around them, Leo and Natalie turned around and welcomed Tia and Melinda, also taking the time to introduce Tia to the two sets of parents.

"Poor Roland has been in my prayers," Leo's mother told Tia. "I sent flowers and planned to go visit, but Jim said I should wait until after the surgery. I suppose that makes sense. But how is he holding up?"

Tia gave Mrs. Parker the lowdown on Roland, promising to take greetings from the Parkers when she went to see him again today. Before they could visit further, it was time to turn their attention to the pulpit.

Tia paid close attention to the sermon, and to her relief, it was good and solid and encouraging. She realized that even if some of the congregation were dressed more formally, many of them looked just as casual as she—and she thought she might even be comfortable here. Well, except for the Leo and

Natalie factor. She promised herself that if she came back, she would simply find a seat well away from them.

After the service, Melinda invited Tia to go downstairs for "coffee hour." "But don't worry, we won't stay an hour. We'll just grab some cookies and joe, say hey, and go." True to her promise, they were ready to leave after just a few minutes, but Leo stopped them.

"I know you plan to take lunch to Roland and Julie," he told her. "Do you need a ride to the hospital?"

"I'll just take a taxi," she said lightly.

"That's no good," he said.

"Maybe I can take you," Melinda offered. "I have something this afternoon, but when do you plan to go?"

"I promised to be there by 2:00."

Melinda looked disappointed. "That's not going to work for me. Sorry."

"I'll take you," Leo declared.

"But I—"

"No arguing," he told her. "I'd like to see Roland again anyway. You know, to wish him well before his surgery tomorrow."

"Well, uh, okay." She glanced over to where Natalie was chatting with some women her age. Probably telling them the exciting news of her recent engagement.

"I'll come by a little past 1:00. Give us time to load things up."

She thanked him, and then she and Melinda left. "Do you need to pick up anything at the grocery store?" Melinda asked as they got into her car. "There's a Whole Foods nearby."

"That'd be great," Tia told her. "I'd planned to ride Julie's bike, but this would be a real time-saver."

Tia and Melinda had fun grocery shopping in Whole Foods. Melinda seemed to have a strong interest in cooking, asking lots of good questions. "Maybe you'll let me volunteer to help on the *Pacific Pearl* someday," she said as they carried the bags out to the car. "Let me work with you in the galley to see how it's done. I think it would be fun."

"Watch out, I might hold you to that offer." Tia set her bag in the backseat.

"Seriously, I hope you do."

Tia tried not to think about Leo as she tied on one of Julie's aprons and started to prepare her uncle's favorite Italian dish, cannelloni. Of course, trying *not* to think about something was as good as obsessing over it. As she rolled the freshly made pasta dough into tubes, she let her mind wander. She was curious as to Natalie's reaction to Leo's offer to give her a ride today. Most likely, Natalie would see this as a friendly gesture of goodwill for his boss's husband. Nothing more. But Tia wasn't sure she'd be that generous if she were in Natalie's shoes. Not that there was any chance of that. For starters, she couldn't afford Natalie's fancy shoes—she frowned down at her bare feet—and they wouldn't look right on her anyway!

To help get her mind off Leo and what she knew could never be, she turned on the Bose player in the kitchen. She wasn't surprised to discover a Beatles CD already in it—her uncle's favorite. As she chopped fresh oregano, basil, onions, and mushrooms, then browned Italian sausage and mixed eggs and cheeses and cream, she cranked up the music and danced to the old tunes.

She was just grooving to "All My Loving" while chopping a lemon cucumber to go into the fabulous green salad she was creating when a sound behind her made her jump. Holding the chef's knife like a weapon, she whipped around.

"Sorry!" Leo held his hands up like a criminal. "I rang the doorbell but no one answered. Then I knocked and—"

"How did you get in here?" she demanded, still wielding the knife.

"The key under the flowerpot." He held up the key. "Sorry to startle you." His serious face broke into a big grin. "Although I have to admit I enjoyed the show."

She rolled her eyes as she laid down her knife, wiping her hands on the apron. "Just how long were you standing there?" she demanded.

"Long enough." He laughed.

She reached for the knife again, waving it menacingly at him. "You obviously are unaware of how feisty we Italians can be. Particularly in the kitchen. And particularly when we're being spied upon."

"Sorry." He held up his hands again. "Wow, something in here smells amazing."

"It's cannelloni," she said in a testy tone, turning back to her salad. "And since you nearly gave me a heart attack, I'll let you be the pack mule to get everything loaded into the car while I freshen up."

"You look pretty fresh to me," he said as he snatched a missed cucumber slice, popping it into his mouth.

She glared at him as she turned off the music. What would Natalie think if she could hear her fiancé talking like this? Probably nothing. Tia sighed. She was probably making it into much more than it really was.

"Sorry to come early." He pulled up a stool at the island. "But I was in the neighborhood and figured I'd just stop by."

"In the neighborhood?"

"Yeah. My parents live just a few blocks from here."

"Oh. I didn't know." She wedged a small vase of flowers that she'd picked from the yard into a corner of the picnic basket she'd unearthed in the garage.

He gazed out the window. "But their house doesn't have this stunning view."

"It is pretty, isn't it?" She paused to look out. "This morning it looked so magical with the fog sort of melting away. I took some photos on my phone."

"Nice." He pointed to the bag of carrots. "Mind if I have one?"

"Help yourself. I assume you weren't at your parents for a meal then?"

He laughed. "More like a meeting."

"A meeting?" She snapped the lid onto the salad bowl, setting it in the cooler along with several Ziploc bags of ice.

"Wedding planning." He scowled like a six-year-old tasting brussels sprouts for the first time.

"Oh." She returned to filling the picnic basket with place settings.

Leo went to the stove where she'd set the cannelloni and took a deep whiff. "What did you say this is called?"

"Cannelloni," she told him.

"Looks like lasagna."

"It's similar. Instead of layers of pasta and sauce and cheese, it's tubes that are filled and then baked."

"It looks amazing."

"Do you plan to join us for lunch at the hospital?"

"Am I invited?" he asked eagerly.

"There's plenty."

"Count me in."

She added another place setting, then covered the hot cannelloni with foil, using several kitchen towels and a tablecloth to insulate it before she nestled it on top. "Why don't you take the basket and cooler out to your Jeep?" She pointed to the key still in his hand. "And put that back where it belongs."

"Aye-aye, Captain."

She frowned. "I thought *you* were the captain."

"Of the boat. You're obviously the captain of the kitchen."

As he headed out with the basket, she went to her room for a quick cleanup, exchanging her sloppy cooking outfit for a crisp white shirt and a pair of khaki capri pants. But as she was brushing her hair down from her ponytail, she couldn't help but second-guess her invitation to Leo. *Why did I do that?* Clearly she was a glutton for punishment.

11

"My sister really likes you," Leo said as he drove them to the hospital.

"I like her too." Tia knew this wasn't exactly conversation fodder, but she didn't really care, and for a short spell neither of them spoke at all. Tia pretended to be absorbed with the passing scenery as Leo navigated his way through the city. She was determined not to fall into her previous trap—attempting to fill the empty spaces with precarious conversation. That kind of chatter usually got her in much deeper than she intended to go. She knew better, but it was the way she was wired. Unless she kept her mouth closed, she tended to be an open book. Useless in poker and never very good at keeping secrets either. For whatever reason, Leo seemed to amplify these traits in her. Today she would be on her guard. She would put some boundaries into place.

"You're being awfully quiet today." Leo glanced her way. "Everything okay?"

"Sure." She nodded.

"I hope you're not still offended at my breaking in on your kitchen disco."

She made an exasperated sigh. "No, of course not."

"Oh, good." He looked her way again. "So you're really okay? Not mad at me? We're still friends?"

She gave him her brightest smile. "Of course we're still friends."

"Good. So you're just in a quiet mood?"

She nodded but felt guilty. It was as if she'd trained him to think she was quite the conversationalist and now she was shutting him down. And really, for what reason? She let another minute pass before she decided to speak.

"Did you make a decision about Natalie's engagement ring?" She knew she was probably foolish to go there again, but the truth was, she was curious.

"No . . . not exactly. Although I did give serious consideration to what you said last night. It makes sense." He sighed. "The problem is, I really can't afford a ring like that. And to get it—especially with credit—feels like I'm setting us up for failure, you know? Like making her think she can keep up this lavish lifestyle that just doesn't match up to what a boat captain earns."

"That's a good point. Does Natalie understand that? Does she have a realistic picture of what it will be like, I mean, after the wedding? My church back in Norton offers premarital classes to anyone getting married. My best friend Anna took them with her fiancé last year. I think it helped them a lot. Maybe your church has something like that."

"Not that I know of, but it sounds like a good idea."

"I'm no expert, Leo, but it seems like you need to have

a realistic idea of what it will be like on your end too. I mean, how do you feel about Natalie being a successful attorney?"

"I'm okay with that."

"Because some guys resent it when their wives . . . well, you know . . ."

"Make more money?"

"Yeah. Maybe it's something that bothers older people more. Like my parents. It unraveled their marriage. Well, sort of."

"What happened?"

"It's a long story . . . but in a nutshell, my parents worked for the same accounting firm, but my mom got promoted to a managerial position. As it turned out, it wasn't because she was more qualified, though. It was because she was involved with the boss."

"That's not good."

"No. It was a big fat mess." She sighed as she remembered how they'd been in the thick of it when she'd come down to San Francisco that summer.

"Are your parents still together? Did they work it out?"

"No. They've been divorced for about ten years."

"That's too bad. I assume you stayed with your dad since I've heard you mention him more than your mom."

"Yeah. My mom and her new husband moved to Tampa. They had a couple of kids."

"So you have half siblings?"

She nodded. "But I've never met them. My mom and I have pretty much lost touch."

"Are you mad at her?"

"I was mad at first. But I've gotten over that. I realized a long time ago that my lack of forgiveness was hurting me more than it was hurting her. Back then I'm sure I wanted to hurt her . . . for the way she hurt my dad and me."

"Man, that must've been tough." He turned onto the hospital's street. "You said ten years ago. Wasn't that about the same time we went to sailing camp?"

"Yeah. Aunt Julie brought me down here because she'd hoped my parents would work things out."

"Wow, that was a heavy load for a girl your age. To come down here knowing your parents were about to split up. Maybe that explains why you were so quiet that week, keeping to yourself in the galley most of the time."

"I suppose I was processing a lot of stuff. Plus I was just plain insecure. Most of the kids on the trip knew each other. I was odd girl out. Of course, I also felt more comfortable in the galley."

"I remember trying to get time with you that week. Unsuccessfully, I might add." He pulled into a parking space.

"Oh, right," she said sarcastically.

"It's true."

"As I recall, you were being pursued by every girl on the boat," Tia said as she reached for the picnic basket.

"Even if that were true, do you think that was my fault?" Leo got out the cooler as well as her ukulele case.

"Of course it was your fault," she teased. "You were so charming that the girls simply couldn't resist you."

He laughed. "Those were girls I'd known most of my life. We were just comfortable with each other. No big deal."

"Hey, why wasn't Natalie at that camp?"

"She was."

Tia blinked. "She was?"

"You don't remember the tall, awkward, skinny girl with braces and zits and mousy brown hair?"

Tia did remember a girl like that. In fact, she'd even felt sorry for her. She had liked that Leo was as nice to her as he was to the other girls. "Yeah, I do remember her, but not her name."

"She went by *Nattie* back then."

"No way!" Tia stared at him. "That was your Natalie?"

"Yep!" He laughed as they went into the hospital.

"I don't believe it."

"Well, then just ask her."

"That's crazy." Tia shook her head. "Does Natalie remember me from that camp?"

"She didn't at first. But I told her about you and then she got it."

"You told her about me?" Tia glanced nervously at him. "What did you tell her?"

"Just that you were the cook." He shrugged. "That's all."

"Oh." She nodded, feeling both relieved and curious. Why didn't he tell Natalie about the kiss? Was he embarrassed? But as they got into the elevator with several others, she knew this was neither the time nor the place for such questions. In fact, there probably never would be a time or place.

"Something smells good," a middle-aged man said as the elevator went up.

"It's cannelloni." Leo pointed to the basket. "She made it."

"Well, if it's as good as it smells, you kids should open a restaurant."

"That's exactly what we're doing." Leo quickly explained about dinner cruises on the *Pacific Pearl*. "Hopefully we'll start running them by midsummer." The doors opened on their floor. "Look for our website," he called as they exited.

"We have a website?" Tia asked.

"We will."

"You're quite the PR man," Tia said as they went down the hallway.

"Thanks. I do what I can."

Tia knocked lightly on Roland's door. "Room service," she called out as she cracked it open. "Sunday dinner for Mr. Sheffield."

"Just in time too." Julie waved them in. "Roland was starting to gnaw on the sheets."

Tia laughed as she unwrapped the cannelloni and took it to Roland's bed.

"Oh, my." He took a long, slow whiff. "I must've died and gone to heaven."

"Oh, Roland," Julie scolded as she opened the basket. "Please don't joke like that."

"Sorry, honey." He made an apologetic smile. "But what're we waiting for? Let's eat!"

While Julie set up the food on a side table, Tia laid a red-and-white checked tablecloth on Roland's bed table. She set out his silverware, a wine glass (which she planned to fill with sparkling cider), and the small vase of flowers.

"Very nice." He rubbed his hands together. "But where's the food?"

"Here you go." Julie set a salad plate before him.

"Ah, now that's a salad." Roland picked up his fork.

"How about if we ask a blessing first?" Julie suggested. She looked at Leo. "Care to do the honors?"

"Glad to." They all bowed their heads as Leo said a simple

blessing over the food as well as over Roland's surgery the next day.

"Amen," they all said together.

"Let's eat." Roland dove into his salad as the others filled their own salad plates.

"This is fun," Roland said as Tia filled his wine glass and set a generous slice of bread by his salad plate. "I should come to the hospital more often."

"Oh, Roland." Julie shook her head.

Before long, Tia began dishing out the cannelloni, putting the first plate in front of her uncle. "Ah, this is what I'm talking about," he said gratefully.

She refreshed his sparkling cider and added another slice of bread. "I just hope it's not too much." She suddenly felt concerned.

"Don't worry," Julie assured her. "He's only going to have chicken broth and Jell-O for dinner."

"Unless I sneak another portion of this under my pillow," he teased.

"You need to save room for dessert," Tia warned him.

"Dessert?" His eyes lit up. "Dare I hope that it's what I think it is?"

She stifled a smile. "Well, you used to like my tiramisu . . ."

"Ah!" He sighed. "What a wonderful last supper."

"Last supper indeed," Julie scolded. "That is not funny, Roland."

"Well, last supper before surgery," he said as he used a crust of bread to wipe marinara sauce from his plate.

"I can't remember the last time I had such a delicious meal," Leo said as he went for a second helping of cannelloni. "Thanks for letting me crash your party, Roland."

"Glad you could come," Roland told him.

"The last time I tasted Tia's cooking, it was good, but not this good."

"What do you mean the last time?" Julie asked.

"Oh, didn't Tia tell you that we went to sailing camp together about ten years ago?"

"You went to that camp?" Julie looked surprised. "So you two already knew each other?"

"Yeah." Leo exchanged glances with Tia. "Tia spend most of her time in the galley, but her efforts were appreciated."

"You never told me you knew Leo." Julie shook a finger at Tia.

"Well, I guess it never really came up." To distract them, Tia lifted the tiramisu from the picnic basket, removing the plastic lid and presenting it to her uncle. "How about this?"

"You are an angel," he told her. "But we really need an espresso to go with it."

"You're right," Tia said, "but I didn't think of that."

"I'll run to the Starbucks kiosk downstairs," Leo offered. "Four espressos coming up."

After Leo left, Julie turned to Tia. "You and Leo at sailing camp together? That is so interesting."

"Interesting?" Tia feigned ignorance as she cut into the tiramisu.

Roland started chuckling. "Your aunt thought she was going to play cupid," he told Tia.

"What?"

"But her plans got squelched," Roland lowered his voice, "when she learned that Leo and Natalie got engaged."

"Oh, Roland." Julie frowned at him. "Really!"

"You know it's true, sweetie." He poked Tia as she removed his empty dinner plate. "You should've heard your aunt complaining all morning long. Going on about her spoiled plans and bad timing."

"Oh, Julie." Tia gave her a dismal look. "I hope you never say anything like that to Leo."

"Of course not." Julie rinsed a plate in the sink. "I'm not an idiot."

"I'm sure you're happy for Leo and Natalie." Tia carefully set a square of tiramisu on a dessert plate, putting a sprig of mint beside it.

"Yes, yes." Julie set a rinsed plate aside. "I'm sure they'll be perfectly happy together." She shook a finger at Tia. "But I can't believe you never told me that you already knew Leo. I didn't think we kept secrets from each other, *dear niece*."

"I, uh, I just didn't think it was important." Tia turned her attention back to dishing out the dessert. She still remembered how she'd very nearly told Julie about Leo after sailing camp ended. How close she'd come to blurting out her excitement over her first kiss. But so much had been going on at the time. It had been the end of summer, and Tia's flight home had been the next morning. There just hadn't been time.

"Here comes the espresso express," Leo announced as he entered the room with the coffee carrier in hand.

"That was quick." Tia tossed warning glances at Julie and Roland. Hopefully they would have the good sense to put the kibosh on the previous conversation.

"There was no line at Starbucks." He set the coffees next to the tiramisu.

"Perfect timing." Tia set a dessert plate in front of Roland, and Leo followed her with a coffee.

"*Perfetto.*" Roland beamed at them as he picked up his fork.

The room got quiet, except for compliments to the chef, as they all enjoyed the chilled dessert. Tia glanced nervously at Leo, wondering if he had any idea what his boss had hoped to hatch with her invitation for Tia to come to San Francisco. Was that the only reason Julie had asked her to come down here? *No, that was ridiculous.* Julie had asked her here because she knew Tia was a good chef. At least Tia hoped so. Still, it was unsettling to think that Julie had hoped to make a match between Leo and Tia. It was time for Tia to start distancing herself from Leo. Not a moment too soon.

12

After the cooler was repacked with the leftovers and the ice packs, Tia got out her ukulele, and they held another impromptu singalong. But after a few lively songs she could tell that despite his smile, Roland was tiring. She slowed the tempo down and finally ended with Roland's favorite, "Somewhere over the Rainbow," Hawaiian style.

Tia put away her ukulele, then went over to kiss her uncle's cheek. "You get some good rest now. Don't forget that I'll be here with Julie tomorrow," she promised, "while you're in surgery."

"Thanks, honey. I appreciate it. Thanks for the unforgettable Sunday dinner."

"You're going to be just fine." She squeezed his hand. "I know it."

"You've got a lot of people praying for you," Leo assured him as he picked up the cooler.

"That's good to know." Roland sighed as he leaned back into his pillows.

"I hope we didn't wear you out," Tia said as she got the picnic basket.

"Not at all," he assured her. "You were good medicine."

"See you tomorrow," Tia told both of them as she went out the door. Once again she felt a hard lump in her throat as they walked to the elevator, but to her relief, she didn't cry.

"He's going to come through this," Leo said as he pushed the down button.

"I think so too."

Leo held up the cooler. "That was an awesome lunch, Tia. Seriously, I can't remember the last time I had such a great meal. Thanks!"

"Thank you." She smiled at him. "I'm really glad you joined us. I think Roland appreciated it too."

"It was my pleasure." He grinned as they went into the elevator. "Now I know firsthand that Julie didn't make a big mistake in hiring you after all."

She narrowed her eyes at him. "You thought it was a big mistake?"

"To be honest, it seemed like a bad idea. I mean, I had no idea who her niece was when Julie said she planned to ask you down here. I pointed out how a chef could make or break the dinner cruises, and I warned her that she shouldn't hire you just because you were a relative. To be honest, it seemed a formula for disaster."

"Disaster?" She frowned.

"Well, what if you hadn't been such a fabulous cook? What if you were lousy? It would be hard to have to fire a relative. Don't you think?"

"I guess so." As they went into the parking garage, Tia tried not to dwell on Roland's disturbing revelation about Julie's failed attempt at matchmaking. What if she'd called Tia a week sooner? Would Leo have still gotten engaged? Of course, she knew it was pointless to obsess over it. Just move on already!

"You seem kind of quiet again," Leo said as they got into the Jeep.

"Oh?" She leaned back and sighed. "I think I'm just a little tired."

"Well, you had a long day yesterday. And all that cooking today. You're probably due for some R&R."

"Yeah."

"You're going to keep watch with Julie tomorrow?"

"That's the plan."

"Do you need a ride to the hospital?"

She turned to look at him. "It's really nice how helpful you've been, Leo. But it's not like you have to take care of me. I'm not helpless."

"Ouch." He chuckled. "Is that a rejection?"

"Sorry. I guess I worry that Natalie might not appreciate how much time you've spent with me lately."

"She understands. After all, we're co-workers. Julie is our boss. And we both care about Roland. It's only natural we spend time together. We are friends, aren't we?"

She slowly nodded. "Yes, I hope so."

"A friend helping a friend—what's wrong with that?"

"In that case, yes, I would appreciate a ride tomorrow. Julie said they'll take Roland to surgery around 10:00. I wanted to get there just a little before that. Not too early so that they can have their time together, you know?"

"Yeah. That makes sense." Leo turned on his radio, adjusting it so that a jazz song was playing.

"I'm surprised your radio works in the parking garage," she said absently. "But I like the music."

"It's connected to my iPod," he explained. "That's Miles Davis."

"Nice."

"You seemed like a jazz person to me." He pulled up to the pay booth, handing the attendant the parking stub and some cash.

As they emerged from the parking garage, Tia blinked into the bright sun overhead. "It's still a nice day out here," she said absently.

"Very nice." He glanced at her before pulling onto the street. "Is there anything you'd like to do in the city? I mean, while we're here. I realize you're kind of stuck over at Roland and Julie's. No car or anything."

She explained that she actually had permission to use Roland's car. "The truth is, although I do have a driver's license, I rarely drive anywhere. I've never owned a car. I'd be really uncomfortable driving Roland's BMW around."

"Interesting."

"I plan to start riding Julie's bike. That's how I'll get back and forth to the boat. I'm actually looking forward to it."

"That's cool."

"I know, you probably think it's dumb. My own dad calls me an 'earth muffin' because he assumes I don't drive a car because of environmental concerns. I suppose that was part of it at first, but it's mostly because I don't really enjoy driving." Okay, now she really did feel stupid. Why had she just confessed all that?

"I don't think it's dumb. To be honest, I think most of us rely on our cars too much." He laughed. "If I could get everywhere by boat, I would."

"Well, that still uses fossil fuels," she pointed out.

"Not when it's a rowboat or a sailboat."

"Yeah, that's true."

"Anyway, back to my question. While we're still in the city, is there anywhere you need to go? Anything you'd like to do or see?"

"You know what I'd really been wanting to—" She stopped herself. "Never mind."

"What?" he demanded. "You have to tell me."

"Oh, it's nothing. Something I can do anytime. Maybe even ride the bike—"

"Come on, Tia, tell me. What is it?"

"Oh, it's no big deal. I just wanted to see Golden Gate Park again. I remember going there with Julie, but we never made it farther than the Japanese Tea Gardens. I know there's a lot more to see. I'm sure I didn't see half—"

"Great idea." He made an abrupt turn at the intersection, then pointed down at her feet. "Those look like good walking sandals. Wanna see how much area we can cover before the fog rolls in? The forecast was for late afternoon fog."

"Oh, I don't know—"

"Come on, Tia. This will be fun. I haven't been there myself for quite a while. Let's do it!"

"Uh . . . okay . . ."

"Since you already saw the east section of the park, I'll park on the west end and we'll start there."

She suppressed the urge to protest and backpedal. What on earth was she thinking by agreeing to this? Seriously, she did not *need* to stroll through the park with Leo. How was that going to help with her new resolution to distance herself from him? What would his fiancée say?

However, the look on his face was so earnest and hopeful—and surprisingly boyish—as if he was really looking forward to this. How could she burst his balloon? So she said nothing.

He found on-street parking on the west side of the park, and they entered near the Murphy Windmill. Despite her earlier reluctance, Tia felt a surge of excitement to see the beautiful gardens. She began taking photos with her phone. "Do I look like a tourist?" she asked.

"Not too much." He chuckled.

They paused to watch some teens playing soccer, then slowly strolled past a playground crawling with kids. "I nearly forgot it's Sunday," Leo said. "That and this weather have really pulled the people out."

They crossed over to the Chain of Lakes where Tia took some more photos, then continued on down John F. Kennedy Drive, pausing to get photos at the Bison Paddock.

"This was always my favorite spot," Leo said as he pointed to a pond where kids of all ages were operating remote control boats. "It's the Model Yacht Club."

Tia knelt down to get a photo of a tow-haired boy getting ready to launch a sailboat. Taking several shots, she could imagine adapting a scene like this into a pleasant watercolor. They went all around Spreckels Lake, where she got even more pictures.

"This is really fun," she admitted as they continued along. "Thanks for bringing me."

"Hey, I'm having fun too."

By 5:00, Tia was concerned that she was using up too much of Leo's time. "We should probably turn back," she told him.

"Why?" he demanded.

She tried to think of an excuse. "The leftovers in the cooler," she said suddenly. "I'm afraid that ice pack will start melting before long."

"Oh, good point. It would be a shame to waste that fabulous food."

"Besides"—she pointed toward the west—"the fog's coming in."

They walked a bit more briskly on the return trip and even more so as the cool damp fog rolled in to meet them. "Some people don't like the fog," she said as they turned onto Martin Luther King Jr. Drive. "But I think it's kind of—" She stopped herself from saying *romantic*, because she didn't mean *that* kind of romantic. "It's sort of mysterious and dramatic. You know?"

"Yeah, I kind of like it too. Well, unless I'm out on the ocean. That can be a pain. But if I'm just hanging in my house, I kind of like seeing it surrounding everything. It's sort of cozy and comforting."

"Yeah," she agreed.

Before long they were back in the Jeep and driving over the Golden Gate Bridge again, heading for Sausalito. Tia didn't want to admit it—even to herself—but this had been an almost perfect day. Oh, she knew that was a major overstatement. Especially considering how many things were actually wrong with it. Just the same, she felt a deep down sort of happiness. However, she knew that it was only a temporary state.

"I hope the leftovers are still okay," Leo said as he pulled into the driveway.

"I'm guessing they're still cold. But speaking of leftovers, why don't you take them home with you?"

"Seriously?" He looked like he'd just won the lottery.

"Absolutely." Before he could get to it, she grabbed the picnic basket and ukulele case. "Just bring the cooler and stuff back sometime. You know, when you're in the neighborhood. You can just leave it on the front porch."

"You're sure you don't want it?"

"I'm positive. It's my thank-you for taking me to the park."

"Well, you are very welcome!"

With the basket and case in hand, she hurried up to the house with a sense of nearly perfect bliss. But as she went inside, a small wave of guilt washed over her. Like she was being blamed for stealing something valuable. Happiness perhaps? Or perhaps she was guilty of something more . . . something she wasn't really ready to own up to just yet.

13

It was a little past 9:00 when Leo showed up to take Tia to the hospital. But first he brought the cooler into the kitchen. "I'm embarrassed to say that I polished off all the leftovers last night." He set the cleaned food containers on the counter. "Ready to go?"

"I am." She reached for her backpack.

"Does that mean you plan to camp there?" he teased as they went outside, where last night's fog was still socked in. She noticed he'd put the top on the Jeep.

"No, it means I don't like hospital food. Neither does Julie. I decided to pack a few things in case we get hungry."

His brows arched. "Nice thinking."

"Well, it's not a feast like yesterday."

As he drove through the fog, neither of them spoke much, but it didn't seem like an awkward silence. More like they were both comfortable enough not to fill the air with idle chatter. Like, she told herself, they were friends. At least she hoped so. That's what she'd been trying to convince herself last night as she was preparing food for today. It was her way to deflect unwanted feelings of guilt and to distance herself emotionally.

"We made good time," Leo said as he parked the Jeep. "Missed the commuter traffic."

Tia pointed to the clock. "Roland won't be going into surgery for about fifteen minutes."

"Gives us time to say a quick prayer for him." Leo turned off the Jeep.

"Yeah?" she said hopefully. "That'd be nice."

Sitting in the Jeep in the parking garage, they both bowed their heads and took turns praying that Roland's surgery would be a success, that everyone helping him would do their best job, and that he would come out of it healthier than ever.

"Thanks," she told Leo as they walked through the parking garage. "I really do believe prayers help. Our family in Norton is praying for him today too." She wanted to say how much she appreciated him bringing her here today but didn't want to go overboard. Really, her intention was to maintain this relationship as a friendship. She didn't want to feel guilty the next time she crossed paths with Natalie.

Julie wasn't yet in the waiting area where she'd told Tia to meet her, but they settled in just the same. "How about if I get us coffees?" Leo offered.

"Wonderful. Julie and I both like lattes with a little cinnamon on top."

"You got it."

Shortly after he left, Julie showed up. "They just took him in," she said as she sat down. "He seemed pretty relaxed." But her hands were shaking.

"He's going to be okay." Tia reached for her hand, and Julie immediately broke into tears.

"I—I know," she blubbered. "But I'm still scared. I don't know what I'd do without him. And I'm just so tired." She paused to blow her nose. "My emotions are probably going to be all over the place."

"I've asked everyone I know to pray for him," Tia said. "Leo and I just said another prayer ourselves."

"Thank you!"

"Maybe we should pray again right now."

"Yes." Julie nodded. "I'd like that."

Once again, Tia prayed for her uncle, and by the time they finished, Julie's hands had nearly stopped trembling and Leo was coming with their coffee.

"Oh, you dear boy!" Julie exclaimed as he handed her a latte. "Just what I needed. You both are just what I needed. Thank you for being here."

As the three sat together, Julie explained that some of her friends had offered to come sit with her, but she didn't really feel that close with any of them. "I suppose that's my own fault," she admitted, "because Roland is truly my best friend."

"I think that's how a good marriage should be," Tia told her. "You're lucky."

"You know Roland's quite a bit older than me," Julie said. "I'd never really given it much thought until recently, when he started having problems with his heart. That was sort of a reality check."

"He's not that old," Tia pointed out. "Besides, you said his father was pretty elderly when he passed on. I'm guessing Roland will be around a good long while too." In an attempt to change the subject, Tia decided to talk about the boat. "I was just thinking about the *Pacific Pearl* this morning," she said. "I'm so eager to get back to it and back to work."

Julie's eyes lit up. "Really?"

Tia nodded. "Yeah. It's like that boat has gotten under my skin. I can't wait to see it renovated. It was so fun to rip out all that horrible eighties décor. I can't even imagine what Roland's mother was thinking."

Julie smiled. "To be fair, it wasn't completely her doing. She had a good friend who was a decorator, and for some reason, Lucille just gave her carte blanche with it. Roland's dad put his foot down when it came to the stateroom, though. Said he wouldn't be able to sleep with all that froufrou."

"Good for him," Leo said.

"Yeah, the stateroom is what first gave me hope," Tia confessed.

"Speaking of the stateroom, I've decided it should be a multiuse room." Julie started sharing her ideas for making it serve as an office, an infirmary, or just a quiet area. "Of course, sometimes it will be a stateroom too." She pointed at Tia. "When the demo in the rest of the boat is done—well, as much as you guys can do before the carpenters come— I'd like you to give the stateroom a thorough cleaning, clear everything out, and replace the linens and whatnot. Just make it nice."

"Sure," Tia said eagerly.

"When do the carpenters come?" Leo asked.

"When I called Murray Brothers a couple of weeks ago, Jack Murray promised to be there by this Thursday." Julie sighed. "At the time I was disappointed they couldn't come sooner. Now it feels too soon."

"We'll have the demo done by then," Leo told her.

"Really?" Julie's brows arched.

"Based on the progress we made Friday, I really think so," he said.

"I promised Jack it would be done by then." Julie sounded relieved. "But I was ready to call him to postpone it."

"I've been thinking a lot about the new galley," Tia told her. "I've got some ideas that I'd like to put down on paper."

"Great. I can't wait to see them." Julie glanced down at her watch with a furrowed brow.

Tia suddenly drew a blank on how to distract her aunt from worrying. "Oh, yeah," she said quickly. "Uncle Tony and Dad send their love. I talked to Dad last night for almost an hour. Guess what?"

"What?" Julie asked.

"Dad told me he's considering marriage."

"Seriously? Vince getting remarried?" Julie's dark eyes grew wide. "Wow . . . do you think he'll really do it?"

"I think he's serious." Tia felt a little guilty for sharing this. "Although he did ask me to keep it under my hat." She giggled, knowing she'd have to come clean with him. "Dad knows I'm not good at keeping secrets. Besides, I don't think he meant you, Julie. Just people in Norton. You know how gossipy it gets at D'Amico's."

"This is Deanna, right?" Julie asked.

"Yeah. They've been together for a while."

"I've never met her in person, but she sounds nice. Do you like her?"

"I actually do. I mean, I sort of didn't at first. Mostly because she's so different than I am. She's kind of a girly girl, if you know what I mean."

Julie chuckled. "I saw her photo on Facebook. She's very pretty."

"Yeah. Dad would agree. I think now that I'm sort of out of the picture, well, maybe they're taking it to the next level."

"I'm happy for Vince," Julie said.

As they continued visiting, Tia attempted to distract Julie by giving her updates on everyone in the family, going into great detail and trying not to glance at the clock behind the nurses' station. Finally, out of topics, Tia took a break, sipping the last of her lukewarm latte.

"I have a question," Leo said. "I've been hearing all these Italian sounding names as you talk about your family, Tia. Is your name Italian too?"

Tia smiled. "Well, my real name is."

"Christina Louise," Julie informed him. "Isn't that pretty?"

He nodded but still looked uncertain. "Tia is short for Christina?"

"It was because of my cousin Marcus," Tia explained. "That's Uncle Tony's son, and he's about three years older than me. His mom, Aunt Karen, used to babysit me when I was an infant. As the story goes, Marcus couldn't say Christina, so she told him to call me Tina. But he always said Tia instead. Pretty soon they were all calling me Tia." She shrugged. "It kind of stuck."

"Well, it's a nice name," Leo said. "It suits you."

"I like its simplicity," she admitted. "I'm basically a simple sort of girl."

Julie laughed. "Simple in a complicated, beautiful sort of way."

As the conversation continued, Tia could tell that Leo was trying to take his turn at keeping Julie preoccupied. During these times, Tia would sneak a glimpse at the clock. Finally, when it was past 1:00, she asked if Julie was hungry.

"I don't think I can eat a thing," Julie told her. "Not until they're done."

"You need to keep your strength up," Leo said.

"How long is the surgery supposed to take?" Tia asked nervously.

"Three to four hours." Julie frowned at her watch. "That means it could be another hour."

Leo pointed to Tia's backpack. "Well, I happen to know that Tia has something edible in there."

"You guys go ahead," Julie said.

"I'd rather wait," Tia told her.

"Me too," Leo agreed. He confessed to how he'd pigged out on the leftovers last night. "I didn't realize your niece was such a talented chef," he told Julie. "You obviously knew what you were doing when you brought her down here."

Julie glanced at Tia, then smiled. "Yes, well, I did ask my brother about her. Just to make sure she was really up to the task."

"You did?" Tia was surprised.

"It's not that I didn't think you were capable," Julie said apologetically.

"That's okay. I'm actually glad you asked Uncle Tony. That makes me feel good. Like you went for real references."

Leo told Julie about the people in the elevator yesterday. "I think they were about to mug us for the cannelloni."

Tia laughed. "You should have heard Leo promoting dinner cruises on the *Pacific Pearl*. What a natural PR guy."

"That reminds me—we need to get a website up and running. I even texted my sister about it. Melinda's majoring

143

in graphic design, and she's already built some pretty cool sites."

"Excellent idea." Julie slowly nodded. "But maybe we should wait until . . . well, after we see how Roland's recovery goes."

"Yeah. No problem." He nodded. "I mostly just started the conversation with her."

"Thanks."

It was getting close to 2:00 when a woman in green scrubs approached them. Tia couldn't read her rather somber expression but suddenly felt worried. Had something gone wrong?

"Mrs. Sheffield?" the woman asked.

"Dr. Moore!" Julie eagerly stood. "How is he?"

The doctor smiled. "The surgery couldn't have gone better. Mr. Sheffield is on his way to ICU."

"Can I go to him?"

"He's still groggy from the anesthesia. They'll need some time to get him settled in."

"Okay." Julie nodded. "But he's going to be fine?"

"It all went very well. No complications." The doctor smiled wearily.

"How long will he be in ICU?" Julie asked.

"Two days. Then five or six more days in supervised care after that. We'll give you some material to read regarding his recovery. But really"—she placed a hand on Julie's shoulder—"it's time for you to take a deep breath and relax now."

"Thank you." Julie's voice choked. *"So much!"*

To celebrate the successful surgery, Tia unzipped her backpack, pulling out a bundle that contained the lunch she'd prepared this morning.

"That looks like it could contain a baby," Julie said.

"Now that's scary." Tia chuckled as she peeled the kitchen towel insulation away from the brown paper bag. "That was to keep them cool." She extracted three hoagie style sandwiches that she'd wrapped in parchment and tied with raffia.

"This looks interesting," Julie said as Tia handed her one. "What is it?"

"Just ham and avocado with a little Dijon mustard on a baguette."

"Yum!" Leo exclaimed when she handed him one.

She also pulled out three bottles of water and a container of sliced veggies that she'd sprinkled with herbs and balsamic vinegar. Before they started to eat, Julie said a quick thank-you prayer—not so much for the food as for her husband. Feeling relaxed and relieved, they enjoyed their picnic lunch together. When they were done, Tia brought out a Ziploc bag of snickerdoodle cookies.

"My favorite!" Julie exclaimed.

"I know." Tia grinned.

Tia could tell that Julie was feeling antsy as they were throwing the picnic remains into the trash. "Why don't you go check on him?" Tia suggested.

"Yes, I think I need to." Julie gave them both a big hug. "Thank you guys for coming. It was a real comfort. But I'm sure you have other things to do." She held up her phone. "I'll keep you posted on how he's doing. And I'll let you know if I plan to come home tonight or wait until tomorrow."

"Sounds good." Tia nodded. "Give him our love."

"Will do."

This time when Leo drove her home, Tia felt like they'd reached the end of a very short season. Although she wished it didn't have to end, she knew that it was for the best. So when he turned onto her street, she knew it was time to seal the deal.

"I appreciate you giving me rides lately." She started to recite the lines she'd rehearsed in her head. "But from now on, I'll be perfectly comfortable using Julie's bike to get around. I already checked the distance from her house to the docks on my GPS, and it's an easy ride."

"Well, if you ever do need a ride, just let me know. It's no big deal."

"I really enjoy the freedom of biking," she said as he pulled into the driveway. "It sounds like Julie will come home today or tomorrow. So if I do need a ride, I'm sure she'll be able to help."

"Okay." He gave a crooked smile. "Thanks for lunch."

"You're welcome." She grabbed her backpack from the backseat. "See you around. I plan to be at the boat first thing in the morning to keep working on the demo."

"Great. See you then."

As she went into the house, she knew that she hadn't been completely honest when she'd said she'd be at the boat first thing in the morning. The truth was, she planned to ride her bike to the boat as soon as she had time to change her clothes. She just didn't want him to know it.

14

Tia hadn't been exaggerating when she told Leo how much she liked the freedom of riding a bike. It felt so right to go zipping down the street, the cool air whooshing past her. She was in her element. And despite feeling gloomy about cutting some ties with Leo, she felt very nearly happy.

She locked her bike to the Dumpster, which appeared to have been recently emptied, then pulled out the makeshift gangplank and made her way onto the boat. Fishing the key from her backpack pocket, she let herself into the main cabin and looked around. Even stripped of the hideous wallpaper and carpet and furnishings, it still looked somewhat dismal. But what she really wanted to look into was the stateroom. Julie had given her the green light to tear into it, and that was just what she planned to do.

She'd poked around the room a bit last week, enough to discover there was stuff that needed to go. Musty old linens and clothes and personal items that had been left behind in the cabinets and drawers. Nothing of value or importance as far as she could see. She was eager to clear it all out. She grabbed up a couple of trash bags and started to fill them. As always, she was careful to separate what might be reusable to donate to a thrift shop and what truly was destined for the landfill.

By 5:30, she had removed everything except the mattress, a few cleaning supplies, and a couple rolls of toilet paper. Because the mattress appeared to be in good condition, she went ahead and pulled out a set of white queen-sized sheets and blue lightweight blanket she'd found in the cupboard and neatly made the bed. Feeling pleased with herself, she decided to try it out. Not bad. She told herself as she stood up and straightened it again that it might be a nice place to sneak in a quick nap during a long day of work on the boat.

Satisfied that her work for now was done, she took the bulging trash bags out, and after tossing a couple in the Dumpster, she left the recyclable one on a covered area of the deck. Still not ready to leave, she retrieved her backpack from the cabin and locked the door, then settled down in one of the wooden deck chairs, situating it to look out over the boat-filled docks. She pulled out her sketch pad and pencils, and after gazing at the peaceful scene for several minutes, she started to sketch.

Feeling inspired, she worked quickly for nearly an hour. Noticing how the light was changing and worried she'd soon be in shadows, she paused to take some photos on her phone, then returned to her sketch.

Nearly two hours had passed when she finally stood and stretched. If she wanted to make it home in daylight, it was time to leave. But for a moment, she considered just spending the night here. Why not sleep in the stateroom? That way she'd be ready to get back to work in the morning. Except that she was hungry. She was just about to close her sketch pad when she heard a loud clunking sound on the starboard side. Curious to see if something had collided with the boat, she hurried over to peer down the side.

"*Leo!*" she exclaimed when she recognized the occupant of a small rowboat. "What on earth are you doing down there?"

He grinned up at her. "Same question back at you." He tied his boat to a ladder that was suspended from the *Pacific Pearl* and quickly scampered up.

"Is that your boat?"

"One of them." He hopped onto the deck.

"One of them?"

"Yeah. This is my exercise boat. Manpowered." He scratched his head. "Seriously, what are you doing here?"

She explained about cleaning out the stateroom, pointing to the trash bag still on deck. "It felt good to get it done."

"Nice work." He picked up her still opened sketch pad, studying it closely. "Did *you* do this?"

She shrugged. "Yeah . . . I mean, who else would've done it? I'm the only one here. Or I was."

"This is really good, Tia."

"Oh, well, it's okay. More like exercise." She smiled. "Like your little boat."

He looked at her with a curious expression. "For someone who calls herself 'simple,' you're not."

She frowned. "No, I actually am simple. As in, I like simplicity. I prefer a simple lifestyle. Uncomplicated, you know?"

He laid her sketch pad down and nodded.

"I told you what I was doing here," she said. "How about you?"

"Oh, I like to pop over sometimes. You know, after being away for a day. Just to be sure everything's okay."

"But you came by rowboat?" She peered out toward the foggy bay. "From where exactly?"

"From my house."

"You *rowed* from your house?"

He chuckled.

"Seriously?"

"You don't believe me?"

"No, I believe you. I just can't quite wrap my head around it." Did Leo really have a bayside home? If so, he was obviously wealthier than she realized. That would be a good thing where Natalie was concerned. Perhaps he could afford that big diamond after all. "You live on the waterfront?" She could feel herself fishing.

"You could say that."

She remembered some waterfront condos she'd noticed on her bike ride down here. That was probably where he lived. Not that they looked inexpensive. As far as she knew, nothing was inexpensive in this area.

"You're not curious about my house?" He had a mischievous gleam in his eyes.

She picked up her sketchpad and pencils, slipping them into her backpack. "Sure, I'm curious."

"I can show it to you if you'd like. It's only a short boat ride away."

She looked out over the bay with the fog steadily creeping in. "You won't get lost in this fog?"

"Oh, this is nothing. Besides, I have my GPS."

The idea of taking a rowboat ride was actually rather appealing. And yet . . . what about her resolve? "I, uh, I have my bike here. And it'll be dark in an hour. I should probably go—"

"Come on," he urged. "Besides, I want to show you something."

"What?" She studied him, trying to determine his true motives. But it seemed like he wanted nothing beyond good honest friendship. And remembering his generous support with her and Julie today, what right did she have to judge him?

"I've been working on that coffee table we rescued last week. It's looking pretty good."

"Okay," she said suddenly. "If you're sure it's just a few minutes away from here."

"Yeah. If I row fast." Just like that, she was sitting in the bow of his rowboat, watching as he put his shoulders into the oars, rapidly cutting through the water.

"Do you feel like you've been kidnapped?" he asked.

"Sort of," she admitted.

"Arr, matey, I'm hauling you off to me pirate ship," he said in a good pirate voice. "Where I'll shackle you to me galley. And there you will cook for me scallywag chums."

She laughed as she unzipped her backpack, pulling out her hoodie sweatshirt to fend off the damp air. Leo seemed to be steering the rowboat toward the houseboat section of the bay. Tia studied the varied and interesting architecture of the floating homes coming into view. "Don't tell me you live on a houseboat," she said as he continued on into this area.

"Something wrong with that?"

"Of course not. But it's just not fair. You get to be a boat captain and live on a houseboat too? I'm getting seriously jealous."

He laughed. "Sorry about that."

"Really, you live on a houseboat?" She stared up at a tall white multistory houseboat with lots of windows and a big brown dog watching them from an upper deck.

"I do."

"Wow. Being a boat captain must pay better than I imagined."

He laughed. "No, I'm sure you imagined it about right."

"These homes are gorgeous," she said as he continued rowing past well-maintained and interesting structures. No two were alike. Unless she was mistaken, they were not inexpensive either. She even pulled out her phone, snapping a few pics and hoping that none of the homeowners minded. It was so picturesque. She could imagine doing a watercolor of this.

"Here we are." He slid his boat beside a modest houseboat. It was single story, covered in weathered cedar shingles, with fresh white trim framing the numerous windows. Very attractive. Everything looked spick-and-span and inviting. He tied the rowboat to the small dock and gave her a hand as she stepped out. "Home sweet home," he declared.

"Very nice." She nodded with approval as he led her past a couple of white Adirondack chairs and up to a door painted in glossy royal blue paint. "Well-maintained too."

"You should've seen it a few years ago. Back when my grandmother let me start living here." He slipped his key into the door. "It was in serious need of help."

"It's your grandmother's house?"

"It was then. But she passed on a few years ago." He opened the door, waving her inside. "She left it to me."

Tia entered the surprisingly open space. "Wow, this is nice, Leo." With one quick glance, she took in the hardwood floors, the windows that looked out onto the bay, a small stone fireplace with a woodstove insert, and a kitchen with creamy white cabinets and some sort of stone countertop. "It's really lovely."

"Thank you." Leo pointed to a wall that was painted in a very pale aquatic blue. "Remember I told you about removing wallpaper? All of these walls were covered in big bold stripes."

She suddenly noticed the round coffee table in front of a tan corduroy couch. "Wow, this looks great. You got the whitewash off." She went over to touch the rich, dark surface.

"Yeah. All it took was a stripping product and some steel wool, along with a lot of elbow grease. The good news was that the whitewash came off without ruining the original finish. They must've used spar varnish back when it was made, because it was pretty tough. I'll apply one more finish coat and call it good."

"It looks perfect in here." She shook her head in wonder. "Aren't you glad you salvaged it?"

"For sure." He pointed at her. "You should get some credit. You're the one who spotted it."

"Mind if I check out your kitchen?" she asked. "I kinda have a thing for kitchens."

"Not at all. I'm afraid it's pretty modest."

She went over to look more closely. He had a decent-looking propane stove and good-sized fridge. He even had a dishwasher. "I wouldn't call this modest," she said. "It's well laid out and quite functional looking."

"Thanks. The cabinets were already here. They were painted in what I can only describe as electric blue. I decided to go with white to brighten it up in here."

"They look great." She ran her hand over the pale gray countertop. "Is this quartz?"

"Yep."

"Well, as a cook, I approve of your kitchen. Natalie should be perfectly at home here."

He nodded with an uncertain look. "You really think so?"

"Of course. The whole place is delightful, Leo. Inside and out. You've done a beautiful job and it's a wonderful place to live." She pointed out the window. "And that's a million-dollar view. Well, when the fog's not so thick. I can't imagine why she wouldn't love living here after you guys are married."

"She's only been here a couple of times," he admitted. "It's been sort of weird . . . She never wants to stay long. It's almost like she doesn't like it. Or else it just makes her uncomfortable."

Suddenly Tia felt uncomfortable too. Not that she planned to show it. That would almost be like admitting she was still into him. "Maybe it's being in a bachelor's house." She made a nervous laugh. "I mean, that probably sounds silly. But I was raised that way. Since you guys were dating and all, maybe it was just awkward, you know?"

He seemed to get this. "Oh, yeah, that makes sense."

"Anyway, thanks for showing your houseboat to me. And the coffee table too. But we should go." She peered out into the gray mist, which seemed to be getting thicker by the minute. "Wow, it's turning into pea soup out there."

"Yeah. I think I better take you back in the Jeep."

She looked around the great room one last time, trying to soak it all in, wanting to memorize this sweet space. Mostly because she felt fairly certain she wouldn't be back here any-time soon. Unless it was to visit Natalie and Leo—after they were married. To help her to accept this difficult image, she tried to envision Natalie standing in the kitchen right now. She pictured her looking lovely as usual, but wearing a chef's apron and stirring a steaming pot of fisherman's stew. Leo would be standing nearby, tossing a salad. Yes, the happy newlyweds . . . that helped some.

"It's a really special house," she said as they were leaving. "You should feel very thankful."

"I do." He locked the door. "I was always close to my grandparents. But it's not like I'm their only grandchild. I started helping out around here after my grandfather died, when I was a young teenager. I got the use of my grand-father's rowboat, and I'd help my grandmother with tasks that were too much for her. Stuff like painting or cleaning or easy repairs. To be honest, it was partly because I loved her and partly because I loved being here on the water."

"I'm sure she appreciated it." She took in each houseboat they passed as they walked the long dock. Some of them were tiny and funky, and others looked like mansions.

"Definitely. But she got too old to keep it up and moved into a retirement place. She invited me to come live here, just to maintain it in exchange for rent. That was a no-brainer for me. I'd work on it whenever I had spare time—painting, reroofing, repairing, whatever. And I'd bring my grandmother out here every so often, just to enjoy it. She loved seeing what I'd done. I figured she planned to sell it. But when she died, I found out that she'd left it to me." He led her to where the Jeep was parked.

"Lucky you."

"Well, yeah. Except there was a little hitch in her will." He unlocked the Jeep and they both got in. "My grandmother

155

said the houseboat was mine as long as I lived there. But if I moved out, it was to be sold and the proceeds split evenly between her six grandchildren."

"Interesting."

"I think that's fair."

"How did your sister and cousins feel about it?"

"There was some squabbling at first. Fortunately, she'd left them all a little something. But the houseboat was her biggest asset."

"Well, she obviously knew you loved it," Tia said as he drove. "It must've made her happy to think you'd have it and to know that you'd care for it. I think that's nice."

As he drove back to the dock, Tia realized that she'd blown it again. Despite her resolve to distance herself, to establish firm boundaries, she'd fallen for his charms again. She'd allowed him to talk her into a boat ride and a visit to his lovely houseboat home.

She sternly reminded herself that it was the home he would share with Natalie after they got married. She retrieved the image she'd created earlier: Leo and Natalie in the kitchen, living happily ever after.

15

For the next two days both Tia and Leo worked like dogs getting the *Pacific Pearl* ready for the carpenters who were supposed to arrive on Thursday morning. By Wednesday evening, the boat's interior cabins were completely stripped of carpet, wallpaper, and furnishings. They'd even removed most of the doors to be salvaged and a lot of the hardware. The galley had been gutted, and only one head (bathroom) was still functional. The only untouched interior space was the stateroom and its bath, which Tia had been slowly turning into her own temporary space, with her aunt's approval.

"Well, it looks like we're ready for the carpenters," Leo said as they lugged the last trash bags down the gangplank. "Nice job." He opened the Dumpster and tossed his bag into it.

"Yeah." She hoisted her bag in after his. "Glad that it's done." She brushed her hands on her jeans.

"You know, for a small girl, you're pretty strong."

She shrugged as she adjusted the red bandana she'd tied

over her hair. "You have to be strong to be a chef. It's very physical. Chopping food, lifting heavy pots, bending and reaching and constantly moving. Not to mention you're on your feet all day. Wimps just can't cut it."

"Well, good work."

Tia heard her phone chiming with a text and, thankful for the distraction, checked to see who it was. "That's Julie," she told Leo as she started texting an answer. "She says Roland's back in his private room now. Sounds like he's feeling pretty good too."

"Great news."

Tia finished her text, then pocketed her phone, pointing to the galley pieces that were still sitting on the dock. "Wasn't Jake supposed to be here by now?"

"Yeah." Leo frowned at his phone. "But it's after 6:00. And I'm supposed to pick Natalie up at 7:00."

"Just take off," Tia told him as they went back on board. "I'll wait here for Jake."

"You sure?"

"Positive. Julie said she won't be home until after 8:00 anyway."

"Okay. I'll give Jake a call to make sure he didn't forget." Leo was already going down the ladder to his boat.

"Have a nice evening," she said as he untied his boat. She didn't know what he and Natalie were doing this evening, and for that she was grateful. The less she knew about Leo's personal life, the happier she would be. She was also grateful that they hadn't had a chance to really talk much in the past couple of days. It helped her to maintain the boundaries she was establishing.

"See you tomorrow," he called as he started to row.

She waved, then turned away with a feeling of dismay. She had assumed that with the demo completed, there would be no reason for Leo to spend so much time here. Just last night, Julie's first night at home, Tia had asked her about assigning specific roles for this renovation time.

Julie had clearly specified that Tia was to supervise the interior work (with Julie's off-site approval, of course) and Leo was in charge of the exterior. It seemed simple enough. But as Tia went into the stateroom—which she'd made more homey with some of her personal things, more linens, several scented jar candles she'd gotten at Whole Foods, some books, and even a small vase of flowers that she'd brought with her this morning—she wasn't so sure. Leo seemed pretty comfortable taking the lead. What if he assumed he was supposed to oversee the carpenters tomorrow?

Tia got out her phone, this time calling Julie. "Sorry to bother you," she said quickly. "I'm still at the boat. Waiting for Jake to pick up a load of recyclables. Anyway, I know the carpenters are supposed to be here by 7:00 in the morning and I got to thinking, what if I just stay overnight? That way I'll be here."

"You really want to?"

Tia explained how she'd outfitted the stateroom. "It's really pretty swanky."

Julie laughed. "Well, good for you! Of course you can stay there. I've heard the security is really good there, so I'm not worried. Just be sure to lock up."

"Absolutely."

"Call me if you need anything."

"For sure."

"Okay then. Enjoy your first night on the *Pearl*."

"Thanks!" It wasn't until Tia put her phone away that she realized she didn't have any food there. She'd have no way to prepare anything with the galley gutted either. But if Jake got here soon enough, she'd still have time to make a run to the little fisherman's market next to the Fish Shack, where she could grab a few things before they closed at 7:00. Their prices were high and their food selection was a bit dodgy, but it would be okay for now. They even had Styrofoam coolers there too, probably for fishermen. She went outside to the foredeck, peering down the dock to see if the green pickup was anywhere in sight.

She considered just making a quick run to the market but didn't want to risk Jake getting there and having no help to load up. Instead of getting irritated like she was tempted to do, she got out her ukulele, sat down on a deck chair, and started to play. If Jake didn't get there in time, she would just ride the bike home to Julie's and spend the night there. No big deal. She put her feet up on the starboard gunwale and, gazing out over the beautiful bay, started to play "Don't Worry, Be Happy" on her ukulele.

She was just getting into it when she heard someone calling, "Ahoy!"

She jumped up to see Jake boarding the boat. "Hey, Jake."

"Don't stop playing," he said. "That sounded great."

"Oh?" Still holding her ukulele, she pointed to the junk all over the dock. "Don't you want me to help you get that stuff loaded on—"

"The thrift store is closed now anyway."

"But we can't leave it on the dock overnight. Julie will get fined and—"

"I plan to load it up and take it." He pulled up the deck

chair next to hers. "But I'll have to let it sit in my truck overnight and drop it off in the morning. No big deal."

"Yeah . . . okay." She pulled out her phone to check the time.

"You have someplace you need to be?"

She explained her plan to make a quick run to the market for provisions for the night. "They close in about fifteen minutes."

"You'd really eat food from there?" He made a face. "And here Leo's been bragging up what a fabulous cook you are."

She made a sheepish smile. "Well, it's not exactly my first choice. But all I have is a bike and my feet, and I—"

"Here's an idea." Jake stood up. "You help me load my truck, and I'll take you out for a real meal. I know a place that—"

"Look at me." She pointed to her dirty work clothes and the bandana still tied around her head. "I'm filthy. Not fit to be seen in public."

He grinned. "Well, excuse me for disagreeing, but I think you look great."

"Thanks." She rolled her eyes. "But I wouldn't be comfortable going out like this."

"You said you're spending the night. Don't you have some clean clothes or something?"

"Not really. I mean, just more work clothes."

"I have another idea." Jake nodded. "Even better than the first."

"Yeah?"

"We'll load up my truck and then I'll run out to get us some takeout food. You stay here and relax or clean up or whatever."

"That's nice of you, but I still won't have anything for breakfast," she protested. "I should just go ahead and go—"

"I know. How about if I grab you something for your breakfast while I'm waiting for takeout?"

"Really?" She frowned. "You want to go to that much trouble for me?"

"Sure." His smile looked genuine. "Maybe you'll return the favor by cooking me a meal someday. Not that I'd hold you to it—although I just happen to have a legally binding contract in my back pocket."

She laughed. "It's a deal."

As they worked together to load his pickup, Tia wondered if Jake had asked her to dinner for a "date" or simply as a gesture of friendship. Because she was getting so used to keeping her relationship with Leo on the level of "just friendship," she decided it might be best to keep things that way with Jake as well. Because if he was really asking her out on a date . . . well, she'd probably have to say no. Not because he wasn't a nice guy, but simply because her heart wouldn't be in it.

"Okay then." He closed the tailgate. "I should probably ask if you have any food allergies or strong dislikes or anything."

She waved her hand. "I'm a foodie, Jake. Besides that, I'm ravenous. I doubt I'd find fault with anything you bring."

"That's right." He chuckled. "You were willing to eat something from the fish bait market."

"Fish bait market?"

"That's what we called it as kids. A place to get fish bait and soda and chips. Anything else and it got a little scary."

"Good to know." She waved as she went back on board.

She went to the stateroom, took a quick shower, and put on a pair of gray sweatpants, old flip-flops, and her worn Seahawks shirt. As she did, she wondered what it might've been like to have met someone like Jake a few weeks ago—back before Leo Parker had stepped back into her life and shaken things up.

Returning to the deck, she arranged a pair of deck chairs on the starboard side, facing the bay. Then she set a small round table between them. Realizing that it was getting dusky out there, she went back to the stateroom to get a couple of her candles, as well as the small bouquet of flowers. By the time she had it set up, it looked rather nice. Hopefully not romantic, though. She looked down at her frumpy casual clothes and decided she was safe on that account.

While she waited for Jake to return, she got out her ukulele and started to play again. It was one of those incredibly beautiful evenings. No fog, no wind, and it was beginning to look like a gorgeous sunset.

The sky was just starting to get rosy when Jake returned. To her delight, he had brought Thai food. "I got you some bagels and orange juice and stuff for your breakfast," he said as he set the bags on a cabinet in the covered area of the deck.

"I thought we could eat outside," she said as they loaded their plates.

"Perfect."

"This smells delicious," she said as she led him over to her makeshift dining area.

"This is nice," he said as he sat down. "Great view too."

"But of course," she teased, "I arranged for the sunset."

"You know, this is nearly summer solstice," he told her. "Almost the longest day of the year."

They visited companionably as they ate. Tia decided that Jake was definitely an easy person to be with. In a lot of ways, he wasn't so different from Leo. Perhaps a bit more of a jokester. She could understand why the two guys were such good friends.

"Your dinner has hit the spot," she announced after she finished her last bite. "Thank you."

"Thanks for letting me share it with you."

"Don't forget that I owe you one now." She looked out at the sky, which still had some color in it. "What a gorgeous night."

"How about that ukulele?" Jake asked as he picked up their paper plates and dropped them in the carryout bag. "I didn't hear much of you playing, but it sounded like you know what you're doing." He pulled a harmonica out of his shirt pocket. "Want to do some jamming?"

She laughed as she picked up her ukulele again. "I don't think I've ever jammed with a harmonica, but it's worth a try."

They were just getting going when Tia heard a clunking sound down where the Jacob's ladder hung. "Sounds like visitors," she said.

"Huh?"

She pointed to where Leo's head was just emerging above the gunwale. He looked even more surprised than they were. "What're you doing here?" he demanded as he stepped onto the deck.

Something about his tone made her want to challenge him, but instead she answered calmly, "Having dinner. What are you doing here?"

"I was taking Natalie for a boat ride and I thought I'd check to see if—"

"Help me aboard," Natalie called out in a weak-sounding voice. "Before I fall in."

Leo whipped around, going over to pull Natalie up and onto the boat and helping her to stand.

"Oh my." Natalie was swaying slightly. "I don't feel too well."

Tia could tell something was wrong with Natalie. Maybe she'd been drinking.

"Tia!" Natalie stumbled over to her, holding on to her. "Please, help me to the bathroom."

Tia glanced at the guys, but they looked just as lost as she felt. Without saying a word, Tia rushed Natalie through the gutted main cabin, to the stateroom, and into the head there. They were barely in the little bathroom space when Natalie fell down in front of the toilet and started to vomit violently.

Feeling sorry for her, Tia held Natalie's hair back, telling her it would be okay. Finally she dampened a washcloth for Natalie to clean her face with as she sat on the closed toilet lid.

"Are you better now?" Tia asked with concern.

"I, uh, I dunno." Natalie looked up with running mascara.

"Did you drink too much at dinner?"

"No." Natalie barely shook her head. "That's not it."

"Do you think it's food poisoning?" Thanks to culinary school, Tia knew that food poisoning was a real threat to any restaurant.

"No, that's not it." Natalie's voice was so soft Tia could barely hear her.

Tia took the washcloth, rinsed it out in cool water, then gave it back.

"Please, don't tell," Natalie whispered.

"Don't tell that you got sick?" Tia was confused.

"No." Natalie looked at Tia with frightened eyes. "Promise you won't tell."

Tia didn't know what to say, but Natalie looked so pathetic, she agreed. "I promise. What's going on?"

"I got seasick."

"Seasick?" Tia blinked.

"On Leo's little boat. I could feel it coming, but I was trying to hold on." She started to cry now. "I've never been good on boats."

"But you went to that sailing camp."

"Yeah. I took so much Dramamine on that trip that I was sick for a whole week afterward. And the seasickness has gotten worse as I've gotten older." She put her hand to her head. "In fact, I feel it coming on now. Is this boat moving?"

"We're at dock," Tia told her.

"I gotta get off." Natalie threw down the washcloth and stood. "Help me."

As Tia put an arm around Natalie, she could feel her shaking. She hurriedly escorted her through the main cabin, down the gangplank, and onto the dock. "Here you go," she said quietly. "Just take some deep breaths and try to calm yourself."

"Thank you," Natalie gasped.

With an arm still helping Natalie to stand, Tia waited until she calmed down. "Better?" Tia asked.

"Yes. I think so." Natalie looked at her with grateful eyes. "You're a good person, Tia."

"Thanks."

"Please don't break your promise. Do not tell Leo about the seasick thing, okay?"

"Okay." Tia nodded.

"I'll just let him think it's food poisoning."

Tia wasn't sure what to say now.

"Will you go get him for me?"

"Yeah. But how are you going to get home? I mean, you guys came by boat."

Natalie glanced over to where Jake's pickup was parked. "I'll handle that. You just get Leo and tell him that I'm pretty sick, okay? That's not a lie either."

"Okay." Tia went back to the boat, finding the guys seated in the deck chairs, enjoying the last streaks of color in the sunset. "Natalie's really sick," Tia told them. "She's on the dock now."

"On the dock?" Leo jumped to his feet and took off.

Jake turned to Tia. "What happened?"

"She was throwing up," Tia told him.

"Uh-oh."

"Yeah. It wasn't pretty." Tia tried not to remember the stench in the stateroom head. She would sanitize it later.

"Had she been—"

"Jake?" Leo was calling. "Can you help us?"

Jake and Tia ran over to the other side where Leo was helping Natalie to Jake's truck. "Hey, Jake," Leo said. "Do you mind giving Nat a ride home? We think that would be quicker than rowing back across and getting my Jeep and driving her. I'll go too."

"Uh, yeah, sure." Jake gave Tia an apologetic look. "Sorry to—"

"No, I understand," Tia said. "Thank you for the lovely dinner. Remember, I owe you one now."

Jake grinned. "That's right."

167

"Get better," Tia called to Natalie as they all got into the pickup. She watched as they drove away, then returned to the boat to clean up the dinner things and put her ukulele away. It was sort of a strange and abrupt way to end what had been a surprisingly pleasant evening. She didn't mind much, though. Not that she was glad Natalie had gotten ill. But the whole thing with Jake, while enjoyable, was a little unsettling. Although she knew the reason why, she didn't really want to think about that right now. Besides, unfortunately, she needed to clean the head.

16

By the time Tia got everything shipshape and herself ready for bed, she realized that something was thudding against the starboard side of the boat. It was clunking loudly enough to keep her awake all night. Guessing that it was Leo's rowboat, which probably hadn't been properly secured for the night, she forced herself out of bed and went to investigate. Sure enough, it was only tied from the bow, and the rest of the boat was getting bounced around with each movement of the water.

Climbing down the Jacob's ladder, she noticed that the wind had picked up and wished she'd thought to pull a sweatshirt over her tank top and shorts. Hopefully this wouldn't take long. But getting the rowboat aligned with the big boat, with the soft bumpers arranged as padding between the boats, and tying the whole thing off took longer than she expected. Plus, as she leaned over to fuss with the ropes and bumpers, she was getting splashed by the water until she was damp and cold.

Finally, feeling like it was safe and sound and like she might be able to get some sleep, she scaled the ladder. She was barely to the gunwale and shivering from the cold when she saw the shadow of a man hovering over her. Startled by the intruder, she lost her grasp with one hand so that she dangled from the ladder, then slammed into the side of the boat. She hit so hard that she tumbled from the ladder and plunged into the bay.

Hitting the cold water was a shock, but more frightening than being in the bay was the thought that a stranger had boarded the *Pacific Pearl*. She was about to swim around the boat, planning to climb onto the dock and scream for help, when she heard someone calling her name.

"Tia!" he yelled. "Over here."

She looked up to see Leo leaning from the rowboat, holding out his hands. "Come on."

She reached out in relief, allowing him to pull her up out of the water like a big fish and flopping down into the boat with a big thud.

"What on earth are you doing out here?" he demanded.

"Besides freezing?" she said through chattering teeth.

"Let's get you up that ladder." He helped her to her feet, positioning her on the ladder.

"My hands are so cold, I'm not sure I can hold on," she said as she started to climb.

But Leo was right behind her, using his arms and body weight to support her as she slowly made her way up to the deck, standing there in a dripping, freezing mess. "Let's get you inside." He put his arm around her shoulder, walking her through the main cabin and pushing her into the stateroom. "Get into something dry," he commanded.

She hurried inside, stripping off her soggy clothes, pulling on her sweats, and wrapping her hair in a towel before she went back out to check on Leo. "You're pretty wet too," she said. "Let me get you a towel."

"That's okay."

Ignoring him, she returned to the cabin for another towel. By the time she got back, she realized he'd brought a couple of deck chairs into the main cabin, and he'd turned on the heat. "Here." She handed him the towel.

"Thanks." He used it to absorb some of the water from his shirt, then finally just wrapped it around his shoulders like a shawl and sat down. "Now, tell me, what are you doing here? And why were you down there on my boat?"

She explained her plan to stay overnight and how the boat was clunking and keeping her awake.

"Sorry about that. I knew it wasn't tied down well. But my plan was to come back and row it home."

"In the night?"

"Sure. I've got my GPS. And it's not far."

"How did you get back here?"

"Nat drove me."

"She's better?"

"Yeah. She really snapped out of it. Whatever she ate must've fully exited when she lost her dinner here. By the time we got to her apartment, she was just fine."

"Oh . . . good." She was curious when that was but at the same time didn't care. It just felt so good to be sitting here with him. Except that . . . well . . . she didn't want to think about it.

"Natalie really appreciated how helpful you were, Tia. She thinks highly of you."

"That's nice." Tia looked away with a frown.

"I was pretty surprised to see that you and Jake were on a date."

"A date?" Tia turned back to glare at him. "Says who?"

"Well, it looked like a date," he said. "I think Jake was hoping it was a date. He's really looking forward to when you fix a meal for him. Isn't that the same as dating?"

She scowled. "I guess it depends on how you define dating."

"A couple having a meal together? Doesn't that equal a date?"

"I've had a meal with you before," she pointed out. "I wouldn't call that a date."

He chuckled. "You seem a little defensive."

"I just don't like you insinuating that Jake and I are dating."

"Do you have something against Jake?" He almost sounded hopeful.

She considered her answer. "The truth is, I think Jake is very nice. I actually like him a lot. And he's a good harmonica player."

"Yeah, he is," Leo agreed in a glum tone.

"But I wouldn't say that we were dating. Not yet anyway."

"Aha. So it *is* a possibility in the future then?"

Tia stood up. "I don't know what time it is, Leo, but I know it's getting late. The carpenters will be here bright and early. I need to call it a night."

"Yeah." He stood too. "Sure."

"Will you be warm enough?" she asked suddenly.

"I'm fine. Thanks." He handed her back the towel.

"I hope it's not too hard to untie your boat."

"I'm sure I can manage." He reached for the door. "Don't forget to lock up after me."

"Don't worry." She sighed. "You scared me so badly when I was on the ladder, I'll be very careful about security."

"I'll pull the gangplank in," he said as he opened the door.

"Anything else I need to know?" she asked. "I mean, about staying on the boat?"

"Well, if you hear a rumbling noise, like an engine, it's just the generator down below."

"Generator?"

"Yeah, for the electricity. That and some batteries keep your lights and water pumps and things running."

"Right."

"You sure you're okay spending the night here?" he asked with a concerned brow.

"I'm fine."

"Goodnight then." He tipped his head, backing away.

"Bon voyage," she called out before she closed and locked the door. She didn't envy him rowing through the fog in dampened clothes. Hopefully he wouldn't get lost.

As she returned to the stateroom, locking that door as well, she wondered at Leo's reaction to her sharing a meal with Jake. It was quite possible she was delusional—especially after her unexpected dip in the bay—but it almost felt like Leo was jealous of Jake. However, that seemed pretty unlikely. Not to mention unfair. Especially considering he was engaged!

Despite her late night, Tia was up bright and early in the morning. As she munched on her bagel and juice and banana, she went over the notes she'd made with Julie the other day. By the time the carpenters, the two Murray brothers, arrived, she was ready for them.

She was finishing walking them through the boat, showing them what walls needed to go and what needed to be done, when she heard Leo's boat clunking against the starboard side. She was handing Jack Murray copies of the hand-drawn blueprints that she and Julie had worked on together by the time Leo came on board. Tia quickly introduced everyone, pointing out that Leo was the captain. "He's in charge of everything on the exterior," she told Jack. "I'm in charge of the inside."

"Well, unless you're talking about the bridge. I'm in charge of that." He grinned at Tia. "And the engine room. Those are both on the inside."

"Of course." She made a stiff smile. "But the galley, dining area, heads . . . those are all my responsibility."

"Speaking of the galley." Jack looked at a page in his hand. "Do you have final blueprints for that yet?"

"Those are the general dimensions," she explained. "Showing how we want it opened up. The plan is to keep the propane stove and the plumbing in the same place. But I'm still getting specs on the appliances. I think I'll have it figured out by the end of the day."

"Great." He nodded. "Sounds like you know what you're doing."

"Well, it's sort of learn as we go. I'm a professional chef, though, so I do have certain expectations for the galley. Plus my aunt has a kitchen consultant friend on speed dial. She's done a lot of galleys."

"Then we'll get started," he told her.

"I'll be aboard most of the day," she said. "If you have questions."

"I'm here to lend a hand if you need it," Leo said.

"Great." Jack pointed to the biggest wall in the main cabin. "I think we'll start removing that first."

While the guys were making a lot of noise in the main cabin and down below, Tia focused her attention on the galley blueprints and the appliance catalogues, slowly figuring out what would work best, then calling Julie for approval before she called in her orders. "It's really coming along," Tia assured her.

"Great." Julie sounded tired. "I'm looking forward to getting over there in the next day or two. In the meantime, it's really reassuring to know you're on it. By the way, how was your night on board last night? I thought about you."

"It was fine," Tia said. "I love the feel of the boat gently moving in the water. It sort of rocked me to sleep."

"You're a sea person, Tia."

She laughed as she remembered plunging into the bay. "Yeah, maybe so." She told Julie to give Roland her love and promised to send new pictures of today's demolition.

By the end of the day, the main cabin was completely opened up, and Tia could envision how it would look with tables throughout. Julie's plan was for twelve small round tables, six on each side. They would be fixed to the floor and big enough to seat two comfortably and four if people wanted to be squeezed together. In the middle would be six slightly larger square tables that could seat four or be combined into larger tables to accommodate groups. No doubt, it would be pretty cozy. There would be additional seating out beneath the covered deck area, although the weather would factor in.

"What do you think?" Leo asked as he returned to the boat after tossing some last bits of debris into the Dumpster.

"I can almost see it." She showed him the scaled drawing with the tables. "It's going to be a little tight, though."

"You'll have to hire skinny wait staff."

She rolled her eyes. "Right."

"What about the galley? Do you have it figured out yet? Jack was asking before they left."

She pulled out the drawing that showed the layout of the commercial appliances, workspaces, and storage areas. "I already put in orders for the stovetops and ovens, dishwasher, and refrigerator. Julie has a cabinet guy coming out on Monday."

"Cool." He pointed to the stairwell to the lower level. "Jack asked if you'd figured whether the appliances would fit down that or if we will have to cut a hole in the side of the boat."

"Very funny." She glowered at him. "Julie reminded me of that, and the appliances I ordered are specifically designed for ships. The salesman assured me they would fit."

"Okay." Leo held up his hands. "Just checking."

She pursed her lips, looking at him and wishing he was not so attractive. "FYI, Julie put me in charge of the interior spaces. Remember?"

"I remember." He made his charming smile. "It's just that we're together in this. I want to be helpful."

She softened. "Yeah. To be fair, that was a good question. I didn't honestly think about that myself until Julie pointed it out."

Leo's phone was buzzing now. "Oh, yeah," he said as he checked it. "I forgot to mention that Natalie made plans for you for tonight."

"What?" Tia asked sharply.

"Sorry. She asked me to tell you that she'll pick you up at 7:00. She's taking you home with her. Uh, she's fixing you dinner."

"Why?"

"I don't know. I guess she wants to thank you for something."

"But I—"

"Look, if you want to bail, just call Nat and tell her. I don't want to be in the middle of this."

"But I—"

"Hey, don't shoot the messenger." He made an apologetic smile. "Here's the truth. Nat doesn't really have a lot of girl-friends, Tia. For some reason she feels a real connection with you. Now, obviously, you don't have to go if you don't want to. But I think it's sweet that Nat wanted to have you over."

"It is sweet." Tia frowned. "Why doesn't Natalie have very many girlfriends?"

"She didn't have many friends in high school. Like I told you, she was sort of an ugly duckling. Shy and insecure and totally into academics. You probably know the type. Later on, in college, she kind of blossomed. Then, it seems, the girls in her sorority resented her. Apparently it was a pretty academic sorority and they weren't much into appearances. And suddenly Natalie was. It's like she's always been a misfit, you know?"

"Yeah, that makes sense."

"Maybe you should just go with your gut and tell her you can't come." Leo looked torn. "But if you have room in your life for another friend, you might want to go."

Tia felt selfish. "Okay, I'll go. Just for the record, I don't have a bunch of friends either. I'm pretty selective."

He grinned. "Then I'm honored if you consider me a friend." His smile faded. "You do, don't you?"

"Being that you fished me out of the bay last night—that is, after you nearly scared me to death, which made me fall in the first place." She rolled her eyes for drama's sake. "Yeah, I suppose you're a friend. But if Natalie's coming by 7:00, I better get myself cleaned up now."

As Tia changed into her cleanest pair of jeans and a fresh shirt, she became increasingly curious as to why Natalie was trying so hard to befriend her. It wasn't as if they had a lot in common. Surely there were young women in her workplace or neighborhood or church who would be more appropriate.

"I'm so glad you wanted to do this," Natalie said as Tia got into her pretty silver car. "Let me reassure you, I'm not cooking tonight. I ordered out." She giggled. "Or perhaps you haven't heard about my culinary skills yet."

"Not really." Tia mentally compared Natalie's chic navy suit to her own casual outfit, which looked downright slummy now. "Sorry I didn't dress up more." She explained how she was "camping" on the boat with only work clothes to choose from, though she didn't mention how even those were in need of laundering now. "I wanted to get more of my clothes from my aunt's house, but it's hard to carry much on my bike."

"We can stop by and pick up your things," Natalie said. "Let's do it on our way back, since our dinner should be delivered shortly after we get to my place."

"That'd be great. Thanks."

"You're actually *living* on the boat?" Natalie asked in a slightly incredulous tone. "Isn't it kind of lonely at night?"

Tia explained how Julie was still spending most of her time at the hospital. "She comes home to sleep and shower and change her clothes, but that's about it. We barely see each other anyway."

Tia figured that Natalie lived in the city but was surprised at the great location—right on Market Street. "This used to be a hotel," Natalie explained as they rode the elevator. "Built in the 1920s. It was remodeled into apartments about ten years ago."

"It's really nice," Tia said as they went into the apartment. "Very uptown."

Natalie laughed as she tossed her keys into a metal bowl atop a sleek glass-topped console next to the door. "I like modern style." She waved to the spacious apartment. "As you can see."

Tia looked around the somewhat spartan room. The floors were sleek, pale hardwood and the walls were painted a fairly stark white, with large pieces of brightly colored modern art here and there to break it up. A large white leather sectional dominated the space. Scattered about were spots of bright primary colors in the shape of throw pillows and area rugs. Even though it wasn't really Tia's style, it wasn't unattractive and would probably make a good cover for some modern home magazine. However, it was the city view from the oversized windows that made the room interesting. "This is gorgeous," she told Natalie as she gazed out.

"Thanks. I did the decorating myself. It's still not finished, though."

Tia didn't bother to correct the misconception as she looked toward the kitchen, which was another sea of white and stainless steel. Very contemporary, and in Tia's opinion, not very warm or welcoming. She pointed at the glass-topped electric stove. "Do you like this?" she asked.

"I've rarely used it," Natalie confessed. "But it works okay. And it stays nice and clean."

"Everything looks nice and clean," Tia said as she ran her hand over the white countertop.

"Leo probably told you I'm not much of a cook," Natalie said. "But I do want to learn. I'm thinking, maybe if you and I become good friends, well, perhaps you'll help me develop my culinary talents. Or you might at least rub off on me." She laughed as she opened an upper cabinet. "As you can see, I've been collecting cookbooks. I'm particularly interested in Asian and Indian foods. Are you very adept with those?"

"I know a few dishes, but I wouldn't call them my strengths. I'm more into European cuisine. Obviously Italian, although I really like French and Spanish food too."

"But you do like Indian food?"

"Oh, sure." Tia smiled. "I like most any ethnic food. And I'm always interested in trying something new."

"Good. I ordered Indian for us tonight. We have a really good Indian restaurant downstairs." She looked at her watch. "They should be here soon. In the meantime, want to see the rest of the apartment? Although there's not a lot more to see."

Tia agreed and was shown a powder room painted a jarring shade of red. "It's only a one-bedroom." Natalie opened a door to reveal a good-sized room. The floors were the same pale hardwood and the walls were a deep shade of fuchsia. The bedding and linens were a mixture of other purple and lavender shades. "I know these colors aren't exactly guy friendly." Natalie laughed. "I suspect we'll have to make some changes after the wedding."

"You guys are going to live here?" Tia tried to keep the concern from her voice.

"Absolutely." Natalie sighed. "As you can probably imagine, I wouldn't last a night on that houseboat of Leo's. I usually get sick within half an hour of being there. Unless I take Dramamine."

"Leo has no idea? He doesn't know about this seasickness thing?"

"No, of course not. It's like I told you yesterday. Please, I'm trusting you not to tell him, Tia."

"I haven't. And I won't."

"This is my wonderful closet." Natalie opened up two doors, exposing one of the biggest closets Tia had ever seen. It looked completely full, but not a messy sort of full. It looked more like a small department store.

"Wow."

"Yeah, I'm kind of a clotheshorse." Natalie giggled. "I think it's because I spent so many years not caring about how I looked. I guess I've been making up for it since then. And of course, I'm a career girl. I need business outfits."

"Where will Leo's things go?"

Natalie's mouth twisted to one side. "I'm working on that. I suppose I'll have to make room. Or maybe he can take over the hall closet. Hopefully he doesn't have too much stuff." Just then the doorbell rang. "I'll bet that's dinner." Natalie hurried off to get it, and Tia let out a long sigh as she closed the big closet and followed.

Did Leo have any idea what he was getting into? Not that it was Tia's job to stick her nose in his business. Although he'd seemed pretty comfortable playing busybody last night when he'd questioned her relationship with Jake.

Even so, she had no intention of going there. No way. Oh, she might encourage Natalie to be more open with her fiancé, in the form of a friend's advice. Or she might simply bite her tongue and butt out. Although she did feel sorry for Leo, and Natalie too for that matter. It seemed those two had a lot of obstacles ahead. Hopefully their love was strong enough to keep them afloat—although Natalie would not appreciate that metaphor.

17

The Indian food was surprisingly good, but Tia was glad when they were done and relieved to be dropped back at the boat. Although she sensed Leo was right—Natalie really did need some girlfriends—Tia was not planning to sign on for the task. It wasn't that she didn't like Natalie, because she actually did. It wasn't that she couldn't relate to Natalie either, because in some ways she could. Oh, not when it came to things like money and fashion and citified style. But underneath it all Natalie seemed like a kind person with a good heart. She was extremely intelligent, and it was obvious that she cared greatly about her job and her clients. And she cared about Leo. Tia lost count of how many times Natalie referred to Leo as her best friend. In Natalie's eyes, Leo was a real-life hero.

Therein lay the problem: *Leo.* Being good friends with Natalie would make Tia's relationship with Leo even more precarious, and she just couldn't afford that right now. As she put away the clothes that she'd picked up from Julie and

Roland's—thanks to Natalie—she was just grateful that the evening with Leo's fiancée was over and done. For the next invitation, if there was one, Tia would have to come up with a really good excuse to decline.

Tia wasn't oblivious either. She knew that part of Natalie's plan in having Tia over tonight had been to ensure that "mum was the word" in regard to her seasickness secret.

"To be honest," Tia had begun as she was getting dropped off, "I'm trying to keep things strictly business between Leo and me. We're co-workers, and I feel it's important to be professional. For the sake of the business. So, really, we don't talk about much besides work. You know?" Okay, she knew that wasn't exactly how it had gone down in the past, but it was what she wanted in the future.

"You're probably right. Friendships in the workplace can be problematic." Natalie had placed her hand on Tia's shoulder. "But you can still be friends with me."

Tia had simply nodded and, gathering up her things, thanked Natalie for an enjoyable evening, despite how confused and conflicted she felt now. Still, she reminded herself as she got ready for bed, this was not her problem. Not really.

Friday was similar to Thursday with more demolition, this time on the lower level, and lots of noise. Once again, Leo was on hand to help. Although the Murray brothers seemed appreciative, Tia couldn't help but think Leo was overstepping his bounds. Especially when he started suggesting a change in the floor plan for the galley.

"I just thought it made sense," he told Tia as they were "discussing" this with Jack Murray.

"I have to agree with him," Jack said.

"That's fine, but I'm the chef," Tia reminded them. "I had reasons for drawing it out the way I did."

"I get that," Leo told her, "but you can at least listen to what I'm thinking."

"Look." Jack pointed to where Leo had sketched in pencil over her floor plan. "You'd actually gain more space if you relocated the heads to this side."

Tia took in a deep breath and stared down at the revision. "Okay, you guys might be right. I was trying to save money by keeping the plumbing for the bathrooms in the same place."

"It's not as big a deal as you think," Jack assured her. "For the little extra it will cost, it'll be worth it."

"See," Leo continued, "it makes a little holding area right here. You know, in case the heads are all occupied and it's standing room only."

Tia nodded. "Yeah, I was a little concerned over the lack of facility. I mean, I've seen restaurants with fewer toilets, but being that we're out on the water . . . well, it could get awkward."

"Especially if the waves got rough and people got seasick," Jack added.

Tia glanced at Leo.

"Anyone who gets seasick needs to hang on deck," he said. "They can ralph over the gunwale." The guys laughed.

"Okay," Tia conceded. "I'm fine with it. Let me check with Julie over the additional expense." As she left them, she knew her aunt would agree. Really, the revision made perfect sense. Maybe she was just jealous she hadn't thought of it herself. Or else she was simply aggravated that Leo seemed to have no sense of boundaries.

After a quick chat with Julie, Tia texted Leo from the stateroom, giving him the go-ahead. It was just easier that way. Then she went back to menu planning. Her goal was to come up with a selection of menus that would be rotated, giving the feeling that every day was a completely new menu. That would streamline shopping and storage as well. Even though she'd never cooked on a boat before, she had a strong feeling that the restaurant would be more successful if she kept the menu simple but elegant.

She was just finishing up a menu when someone knocked on the door. Thinking it was Leo as usual, she opened it with a slightly irritated expression. Couldn't he just let her be for a change? But to her surprise it was Leo's sister, Melinda.

"Sorry," Melinda said. "Am I disturbing you?"

Tia smiled. "No, I thought it was your brother."

Melinda laughed. "Yeah, he can be a pest sometimes."

"We were arguing over some blueprint changes earlier. I was probably still feeling grumpy about it." Tia opened the door wider. "Come on in if you want. It's not exactly roomy in here, but—"

"I really didn't want to interrupt your work." Melinda picked up one of the menus. "Mmm, this looks good."

"You'd like that?"

"Are you kidding?" Melinda continued skimming. "I'm getting hungry already."

"I've been trying to keep most of the selections on the lighter side, but I want to offer some hearty fare too. I'm not really sure what people feel like eating on a boat."

"Have you looked into what the other dinner cruises offer?"

"I did peek around online. The most popular line seems to

serve more small plates, and that's why I started wondering if I should offer a lighter selection."

"You should probably go on a spying mission." Melinda set the menu down.

"That's a great idea." Tia wondered why she hadn't thought of this sooner.

"If you need a date, I'm game." Melinda pulled out her phone. "In fact, I'll do a quick search on it right now."

"We'd probably have to book it well in advance."

"Maybe . . . but remember this is a big line. I doubt they run it full every night."

"That's true." Tia knew from crunching numbers that the *Pacific Pearl* would have to be at least half full to make any profit.

"Wow, there's availability *tonight*," Melinda told her.

"Cool." Tia nodded eagerly. "I'm in. This will be a great way to see what the competition is up to."

"Count me in."

"Count you in where?" Leo poked his head around the door.

"Tia and I are going on a date tonight," Melinda told him.

"A date?" Leo looked confused.

"On a dinner cruise. We're going to spy and—"

"I want to go too." He pushed the door fully open. "You can't leave me out."

"Yeah, you and Nat should come along." Melinda held up her phone. "We can reserve a table for four if we do it right now."

"All right." Leo's enthusiasm seemed slightly diminished.

"You guys want me to book it?" Melinda looked from Tia to Leo.

"I do." Tia gave Leo an uncomfortable glance. "But maybe you should check with Natalie first."

"Nah. She already informed me she wanted to go out tonight. This will make for a good surprise."

Tia had to bite her tongue. He had no idea just what sort of surprise it would really be if Natalie didn't take a solid dose of Dramamine first.

"Okay, I'm doing it. Reserving a table for four," Melinda announced. "For tonight."

"Here." Leo pulled a credit card from his wallet, handing it to Melinda. "Go ahead and secure it with this for now."

"Thanks." Melinda sat on the end of the bed as she filled in the information.

"You're really going to surprise Natalie with this?" Tia asked hesitantly.

"Yeah." He nodded. "We've never done anything like this before. It'll be fun."

"But she might need to know more . . . like how to dress. You know, like maybe she should bring a sweater because it could be chilly out on the water."

"Good idea. I'll tell her that."

"All right." Melinda stood. "It's a done deal. We're supposed to be at the dock by 7:00. That's when they start loading. The boat sails at 7:30 and returns by 10:30. Food and soft drinks and coffee are included, but they tack on tax, tips, and landing fee."

"Landing fee?" Tia asked Leo.

"Well, they obviously want to get you coming and going." He chuckled. "Maybe Julie can handle that differently on the *Pacific Pearl*. I like the idea of including everything in the ticket price. No hidden fees to jack it up."

"I agree," Tia said. "People should know the cost up front. Of course, anything from the bar will be separate."

"It'll be interesting to see how the other dinner cruises are done." Leo went back into the main cabin, followed by Melinda.

"This is going to be fun," Melinda said eagerly.

"Fun and productive." Tia closed the door to the state-room.

"I can pick you up if you'd like," Melinda told Tia. "Probably around 6:45. That should be plenty of time."

Tia thanked her.

"What are you doing here anyway?" Leo asked his sister. "I mean, besides trying to date Tia?"

"Ha ha." She poked him in the ribs. "I just came over to see how Tia's doing and to check on the progress. I wanted to see if my big brother was driving her crazy yet." She winked at Tia. "Sounds like I got here just in time too."

"Meaning I'm driving her crazy?" Leo asked.

"If the shoe fits."

Leo made a disappointed face. "And here I thought I was helping."

Tia smiled. "You are helping, Leo. I guess I was just getting cranky today. I don't exactly like people revising my plans. But as it turned out, you were right. I was wrong."

Leo nudged his sister. "Got to admire a woman who's willing to admit she was wrong."

"Yeah, that quality's even rarer in a guy," Tia quipped back.

"By the way, I came up here to ask if you want to see how it's going below," Leo said to Tia. "I think you're going to like how spacious the galley is going to be."

Tia reluctantly followed him below with Melinda trailing

behind her, but when she saw the opened-up galley, she was convinced. Leo really had been right. "It looks great," she told him. "Good call."

"The Murray brothers are done for the day. I'm just cleaning up."

"Need any help?" Melinda offered.

Soon all three of them were gathering wood shards into trash bags, sweeping up sawdust, and wiping the woodwork clean. The whole while, Tia was worried about Natalie's "surprise." If no one warned her to at least take some Dramamine, she was going to be miserable for three long hours. In all likelihood that would mean they would all be miserable. As soon as they finished the cleanup, Tia hurried to her phone. Instead of texting, to avoid leaving a trail that Leo might discover later, she called Natalie.

"Hey, Tia," Natalie said cheerfully. "What's up, girlfriend?"

"I'm giving you a quick heads-up," she said quietly, just in case Leo was still on board and into eavesdropping.

"What is it?"

Tia quickly filled her in about the dinner cruise plan. "I tried to dissuade Leo. And I told him he should at least give you some warning—"

"Warning? You didn't tell him about—"

"No, not at all. I simply said he should tell you about the boat, you know, so you could bring a jacket or something. But Leo's plan is to surprise you."

"Oh no."

"I just thought you should know. You can take Dramamine, right?"

"That's still pretty iffy. Sometimes it works, sometimes it doesn't."

"Sorry. Anyway, I'm sure you'll figure it out."

"Thanks for the heads-up."

"Just don't tell Leo I tipped you off."

"Don't worry." Natalie made a nervous laugh. "Isn't it fun sharing secrets?"

"I guess." But the truth was, Tia didn't much like this game.

As Tia took a nice long shower, she tried to decide what was appropriate to wear on a dinner cruise—especially when your "date" was a girl. She suspected that Natalie would show up dressed to the nines as usual. Hopefully she'd be well set with plenty of Dramamine running through her bloodstream. Finally Tia decided to go with comfort, choosing her favorite faded denim skirt and a white shirt topped with a vintage cardigan in a tomato shade of red. Since her hair was still damp, she decided to just go with a loose ponytail tied with a blue bandana. She knew she'd probably look plain and boring next to Natalie and Melinda, but she really didn't care. This was a spying mission, not a date.

To her surprise it was Leo's red Jeep she saw parked at the end of the dock when she strolled that way looking for Melinda. Leo got out, waving toward her. "Slight change in plans," he called.

Tia peered into the passenger side. "Where's Natalie?"

"She opted out. Seems she has a horrible headache and wanted to spend the evening in."

"You're not staying in with her?"

"There's no refunding tickets with such short notice," he pointed out. "I'm hungry. Plus this is research, remember?"

"Yeah."

"Anyway, Melinda and Jake will meet us at the dock."

"Jake?"

He nodded toward the Jeep. "I'll explain on the way over there."

As he drove, he told her about inviting Jake after Natalie bailed. "I already paid for a table for four. I called Melinda first, asking if she had some friends to replace Nat and me. She didn't, so at the last minute I called Jake. Since he was closer to Melinda, he offered to get her. I was closer to the dock here, so I picked you up. Make sense?"

Tia wasn't sure, but she simply nodded. "Sorry about Natalie."

He frowned. "Yeah. Me too. She sounded fine when I talked to her earlier today. I guess it just hit her all of a sudden."

"Yeah."

"It's too bad," he said. "We were supposed to finalize some wedding plans tonight. I wanted to let her know that I've decided we'll have the wedding on the boat after all. She sort of offered that to me as a concession a while back. In exchange she gets to have a big reception wherever she likes. She can invite as many people as she and her family feel is appropriate. But I'm digging in my heels. I want the wedding itself to be small and personal. Anyway, I hoped that we could settle this stuff on the dinner cruise. I thought if she really enjoyed the evening, it might help to solidify the on-board wedding. You know?"

"That makes sense." *Especially if you're totally oblivious*, she thought, *and clueless to the fact that your fiancée despises being on the water.*

"You seem a little somber tonight."

"Sorry." She tried to insert cheer into her voice. "We've been so busy with the boat demo. I guess I'm more worn out than I realized."

"Natalie said you girls had a great time last night."

"Oh, yeah. That was really sweet of her to have me over. And her apartment is so nice." Tia felt her voice going flat again. Did they have to keep talking about Natalie?

"Kind of modern for my taste."

"Yeah." She looked out the window, trying to think of another topic. "Julie said Roland is coming home this weekend."

"That's great. Isn't that sooner than the doctor had told her?"

"Maybe. But apparently his recovery is moving right along."

"I'll bet he can't wait to get out of there."

"Julie said he's getting pretty stir-crazy."

"Poor Roland. But I'm glad he's on the mend."

"I forgot to ask, are the Murray brothers coming tomorrow? I know it's Saturday, but I thought they might—"

"No, they don't work on weekends."

"Can't blame 'em for that." She was trying to think of something else to say. Something to keep the conversation streaming along when all she could think of was that Natalie had missed out on tonight because of her seasickness challenges. For some reason that made her feel guilty, like she could've said something earlier. But what?

"Oh, yeah," she said quickly. "Julie mentioned that the guys are coming to install the new propane fire pit tomorrow."

"Great. I assume it goes in the same spot the old fireplace was in?"

"Right. Out on the foredeck. Just beyond the covered area."

"That'll be nice. Does Julie want me there to supervise?"

"No, no, I can do that." She wished she'd kept her big mouth closed, because the last thing she wanted was Leo hanging around tomorrow. She'd actually been looking forward to having the boat completely to herself.

"Except that the deck is my domain, remember?"

"Oh, yeah."

"But you'd prefer to handle it yourself?" he asked.

"No, that's okay. If you feel the need to oversee it, of course you should come. I just figured you might enjoy a day off. I mean, you probably have things to do. You and Natalie might have wedding planning stuff to take care of. Settle on the location. Natalie told me last night that you guys still haven't settled the whole engagement ring business either." Tia wanted to kick herself now. Why, oh why, had she gone *there* again? Probably because she was curious. Curious and stupid. And she would probably get exactly what she deserved too—more pain.

18

Jake and Melinda were waiting on the dock, and to Tia's relief, they were dressed fairly casually too. Leo, wearing navy slacks and a pale blue dress shirt, looked slightly out of place with the three of them. Tia knew he'd probably dressed like that for Natalie's sake. He'd left his sports jacket in the Jeep, and as they boarded the boat, he rolled up his shirtsleeves, revealing his tanned forearms.

"This boat's so much bigger than the *Pacific Pearl*," Tia observed as the four of them strolled along the deck, taking it all in. She lowered her voice. "Feels very impersonal to me."

"I agree," Melinda said. "But it's still fun."

"Looks like that's a popular spot." Leo nodded to where a lot of passengers were crowded around a long, curved bar on the foredeck.

They hadn't been aboard long when the bell rang signaling that the boat was preparing to depart.

"I want to go up to the bow," Tia said eagerly. "I think it feels more exciting up there." They all hurried to the front, watching as the boat slowly set out on the water. "What a gorgeous evening," Tia said as the gentlest breeze caressed her face.

"Looks like it'll be a good sunset." Melinda pointed to the clouds on the western horizon.

Before long they were out on the open water, and as much as Tia wanted to stay right there in the bow, she knew this was supposed to be a mission. "I guess we should look around," she said. "At least I should since I'm here to spy."

"Spy?" Jake looked confused.

"Checking out the competition," Tia explained. "The *Pacific Pearl* will definitely be different than this line, but it's good to know what we're up against. You know?"

He nodded. "Absolutely."

"Let's start sleuthing around," Melinda said with a mischievous smile.

"Where do we start?" Tia asked.

"How about if I pretend to give you guys a tour of the boat?" Leo offered.

"Perfect." Tia nodded. "Lead on."

"They have a DJ," Jake pointed out as they walked across the foredeck. "And a dance floor."

"Dancing might be a challenge if the water is rough," Melinda said.

"Might be a good excuse for stepping on toes," Jake added.

"I think live music would be nicer," Tia told them. "I mean, on the *Pearl*. I wonder if we could reserve a corner of the restaurant for live music."

"What about piano?" Melinda suggested. "I really love piano music in a restaurant."

"A grand piano would eat a lot of space," Tia told her.

"Why couldn't you have an upright?" Jake suggested.

"Maybe so." Tia made a mental note to mention this to Julie.

They wandered all around the boat, allowing Leo to play the tour guide as he pointed out the highlights, even taking them to the bridge where they met the captain. Of course, no one confessed the real reason they were so interested. Tia was enjoying the tour simply for the fun of it too. She just happened to love boats.

"I'm hungry," Melinda declared after they finished a complete round of the boat.

"Me too," Jake told her. "Show me the grub."

As the four of them waited to be seated at a table, Tia critiqued the quality of their customer service. If she were grading them, they wouldn't get more than a C- so far. Not only were their uniforms unimpressive, but their expressions revealed that they would rather be someplace else. And the dining room was disappointing as well. Instead of feeling like an elegant night out, this place felt more like a diner or cafeteria.

"Impressed?" Leo asked her with a twinkle in his eyes.

"Not much."

"Me neither."

"But it's encouraging," she quietly admitted. "Makes me believe that what we offer will be unique enough to draw a following."

"I know."

"Taking notes?" Melinda asked Tia.

Tia pointed to her forehead. "In here."

Eventually they were seated at a table in the center of the dining room, well away from windows. After they assured their waiter that they did not want to order alcohol, something he seemed insistent that they reconsider, they were handed some dog-eared menus with a limited "small plate" selection.

"How about if we all order something different?" Melinda suggested. "That way Tia can get a good idea of what she'll be up against."

"So far, I can't imagine that Tia couldn't bury this chef," Leo said quietly. "This menu is pretty sad."

"I can't believe it cost so much," Melinda added. "Of course, that's probably mostly for the boat ride."

"I was going for the roast beef plate," Jake told them. "Sounds like there might be more food involved."

"I was thinking the same thing," Leo admitted.

"You guys get what you want," Tia said. "I think I've got a pretty good idea of what's going on in the kitchen."

"You mean galley?" Leo said.

"Yeah." She looked across the room to the small windows. "I almost forgot we were on a boat."

After a disappointing dinner, everyone agreed the dining room was stuffy and noisy. They decided to go outside for some air and to enjoy the view and music.

"Anyone want to dance?" Melinda asked hopefully.

"Sure," Jake told her, but then he looked uneasy, glancing at Tia as if she might feel left out.

"You guys go for it," she told them. "I just want to enjoy the view." She looked out to the glowing city skyline, painted in shades of gold by the last rays of the sun. She pulled out her phone and took some quick pictures.

"Should we snag that table?" Leo pointed to a spot that was vacating.

"Good idea." They both hurried over to claim it.

"Care for something to drink?" he asked as they sat down.

"I wouldn't mind an Arnold Palmer," she told him as she took some shots of the Golden Gate Bridge with the peach-colored clouds behind it.

His brow creased in a confused way.

"That's basically just lemonade and iced tea," she explained. "No alcohol."

"Oh, right." He nodded. "Sounds good. Two Arnolds coming right up."

After a couple of dances, Melinda and Jake got soft drinks, then came over to join them at the table. "I just overheard something interesting," Melinda told Tia.

"What's that?"

"Apparently this particular boat isn't known for having the best dinner cruises."

"I think we already figured that one out," Leo said.

"No, what I mean is that this is more of a party boat."

Tia glanced over to where the bar was still crowded. "That makes sense."

"If you want a more elegant meal, you choose one of the other boats. Apparently it's spelled out on their website if you look more carefully." She glanced at her brother. "Sorry about that."

"That's probably why it wasn't that hard to book a table for four," Tia said.

"Guess we'll have to do this all over again," Jake teased.

"Maybe I'll just study their website," Tia told them.

"But being on this boat gives me an idea," Melinda told Leo. "What if you have the wedding on the *Pacific Pearl*, like you want, but you have the reception on one of these boats?

I heard you can reserve the whole boat if you get the right day. I'm sure it'd be a small fortune, but Natalie's parents might be willing."

"That would be fun," Leo told her. "We could probably rig up a railed gangway to allow the wedding party to go from the *Pearl* to the bigger ship."

"You think Natalie would go for it?" Melinda asked.

Tia turned away, pretending to watch the dancers, but she really just didn't want anyone to see her face—to read her hopeless expression. She glanced at Jake. "Seemed like you had a pretty good time out there on the dance floor."

"Too bad you're not into dancing."

"I never said that," she told him.

His eyes lit up. "You are then?"

"You bet."

"Come on." Jake reached for her hand. "You haven't lived until you've danced on a boat. I'll apologize in advance for my own lack of fancy footwork. *Dancing with the Stars* isn't exactly beating down my door these days."

As it turned out, Jake was a decent dancer. Probably better than Tia, who was so grateful to escape that conversation that she actually started to enjoy herself. Dancing on the sea was surprisingly fun. The cool ocean air and the slowly setting sun, combined with the rocking motion of the boat, was a delightful combination. But after a couple of dances, she noticed Melinda looking their way and suddenly felt a little guilty.

"I'll bet Melinda would like to dance again," she told Jake as the song ended.

"You don't think she can dance with her brother?" Jake teased.

"I'm sure she could, but she might enjoy it more with you." Tia smiled as she grabbed his hand, leading him back to the table. "Your turn with Fred Astaire," she told Melinda.

"You girls are gonna wear me out," Jake said sarcastically. He pointed to Leo. "What's wrong with you, man? Got a bunion on your big toe or something?"

"Come on," Melinda told Jake. "A good song is starting."

Tia felt awkward as she sat back down. No way did she want Leo pressured into taking her out on the dance floor. To avoid this possibility, she decided to keep the conversation stimulated by sharing some of the ideas that she'd started to hatch since they'd come aboard. Fortunately, Leo got into the spirit of it, and the prospect of the two of them hitting the dance floor together seemed to evaporate.

"Beautiful sunset," Tia said absently.

"Yeah." Leo looked out on the horizon with interest.

Tia pulled out her phone to take some shots of the sunset through the Golden Gate Bridge. "These are going to be stunning," she told Leo. "Don't you want to take some too?"

He laughed. "If you knew how many times I've taken shots of that bridge at various times of the day, including about a thousand sunsets, you'd understand."

"Oh, right." She pointed at him. "Hey, how about if I get a shot of you with the view behind you—we can send it to Natalie? Might cheer her up."

"That's a thoughtful idea." Leo cooperated by striking some poses as she took a couple of shots. She immediately sent them to Natalie with the caption "Wish you were here."

"You should let me get some of you," Leo said. "You could send them to your dad or your family at the restaurant."

201

"Thanks." She handed him her phone.

"We should do a selfie too," he told her as he stood beside her, holding her phone at arm's length as she smiled happily.

He handed her phone back, and she took a quick peek at the last photo and was about to put it away when she heard the chime for a text. "Natalie wrote back," Tia said. "She loves the photo. Says she's going to frame it for her desk at work."

"Thanks for doing that." Leo leaned back with a long sigh. "I actually thought this might be my big chance to get Natalie on a boat." He shook his head. "I know it sounds kind of crazy, but sometimes I almost get the feeling she doesn't like boats."

"Oh." Tia looked out over the water.

"To be honest, I was worried she might balk at taking a dinner cruise tonight. That's why I decided to keep it a surprise. But Nat surprised me by announcing she was under the weather without even knowing what was up."

Now Tia felt guilty . . . and she felt something else too. Remorse? Or maybe just regret. Like she should've just stayed out of Leo's business altogether. She should've just let Natalie come along like Leo had planned. Even if poor Nat ended up hanging over the gunwale all night, heaving her guts out into the bay, at least the cat would be out of the bag by now, and Tia would be out of the liar's loop.

Except that it had seemed so mean to subject Natalie to that kind of torture. Not something a friend did to a friend. Tia knew that Natalie considered her a friend. How would she have reacted when she discovered that Tia had known ahead of time and not warned her? Besides that, Tia had assumed that Natalie would just take her seasickness meds and make the best of it tonight. Feeling torn and confused, Tia stared blankly out toward the dance floor. It seemed there were no easy answers.

"I'll bet you'd like to dance," Leo said suddenly.

"Oh, no, I was just think—"

But it was too late. Leo was out of his chair and reaching for her hand. Before she could think of a gracious way to decline, he was leading her onto the crowded dance floor, and just like that they were dancing. Thankfully it was a fast song, but it was also coming to a fast end. When it ended, Leo insisted they stick it out for a full-length one this time. Of course, as fate would have it, the next song was a slow, romantic one. Although Tia was about to excuse herself, the words got stuck in her throat as Leo took her in his arms, slowly dancing to the rhythm of the music.

She felt lost. Lost in his arms. Lost at sea. Lost, lost, lost. When he asked her to dance again, she didn't even bother to argue with herself. Instead, she just gave in. Really, what did it matter?

When a fast song came on and they switched partners so that she could dance with Jake and Leo could dance with his sister, she attempted to convince herself that it was the same as when he'd danced with her. He was simply treating her like his sister and his friend. No big deal. But when they switched back for another slow song—because Melinda said it was creepy to slow dance with her brother—Tia forgot about all that friend and sister nonsense. Because Leo did not feel like a brother to her. Not in the least.

Bittersweet, she thought as they danced the last dance before the boat slowed down for the dock. This was bittersweet in the truest sense of the word. If she were to be completely honest, it was more bitter than it was sweet. It was like showing a child a beautiful birthday cake on her birthday and then saying, "Sorry, it's not for you." *Bittersweet.*

19

On Saturday morning, Tia felt torn. The brave side of her wanted to dig in her heels and stick around while the new fire pit was being installed. After all, the boat was sort of like her home for the time being. She had every right to be here. But the chicken side of her wanted to hightail it out and avoid any more interaction with Leo.

The chicken side won. As soon as she heard Leo calling out "Ahoy!" as he boarded the boat, she grabbed her backpack and hurried out. "See you later," she called as she went down the recently replaced gangway. Instead of the wobbly board, this one was solid and sound. Quite an improvement.

"Where you going?" Leo asked.

"To welcome Roland home," she explained. "I'm going to do some cleaning and stuff and fix them a welcome home dinner. Lots to do." She forced a smile as she unlocked her bike. "Thanks for being here for the fire pit installation." She hopped on the bike and took off. Free as a bird—well, maybe a chicken.

It was true that she wanted to do something special for Roland and Julie. She'd started hatching the plan early this morning. First she'd ride her bike to Whole Foods and pick up some things. Then she'd slip into the house while Julie was gone to the hospital. She'd do some quick cleaning and sprucing up, and she'd put together another cannelloni with instructions for how to heat it, as well as the things to go with it. Then she'd slip back out before they got home, which Julie was predicting would be around 4:00 in the afternoon.

As it turned out, it was a good thing she got an early start, because everything seemed to take longer than she planned. Then when she texted Julie at the hospital to see how it was going, she discovered that Roland was getting released an hour sooner than expected. She threw herself into high gear and managed to get out of the house at a little past 3:00.

By the time she was pedaling back to the docks, the fog had already rolled in. She welcomed its coolness. She imagined spending the remainder of her afternoon curled up in the stateroom with a good book. A chance to just relax. Because she felt bone tired. Not to mention grubby and hungry.

To her dismay, Leo's red Jeep was still in the parking lot. That meant either the fire pit guys weren't finished yet or he had decided to stick around and work. *Well, fine,* she thought as she continued on down the dock. She would politely ignore him, go to the stateroom, take a quick shower and change her clothes, and then, since she hadn't had a chance to do her own grocery shopping to refill her "larder," which was actually a small cooler and a cupboard, she would sneak off the boat and run down to the Fish Shack for some fish and chips. It seemed like a good plan.

To her relief, a big yellow truck was parked next to the

boat. That meant that Leo should still be occupied. As she slipped onto the boat, she spied him on the foredeck with a couple of guys. At least the fire pit was installed and appeared to be running. As much as she wanted to see it up close, she really wanted to avoid Leo today. She felt she owed it to her heart to steer clear of him. Really, how much could a girl take?

She made it to the stateroom without being noticed. Despite being ravenous, she decided to take her time showering and dressing. Hopefully Leo would be long gone by the time she emerged. Eventually, though, her hunger got the best of her and she ventured out.

She peeked out the main cabin windows to see that the yellow truck was gone. It seemed quiet out on deck. Feeling assured she was alone, she slipped out, locked the main cabin door, and was just heading for the gangway when she heard Leo calling out.

"Hey Leo, I'm just on my—"

"Come check it out," he said cheerfully.

She reluctantly went over, ready to make a polite excuse, but something about those dancing orange flames and Leo's welcoming smile made her swallow her words. Instead, she found herself warming her hands by the flickering fire.

"The fire pit looks really nice," she said quietly. "Such a great idea."

"Yeah. Perfect for those less than sunny days that are so common in these parts."

"I'll bet you could roast hot dogs on this," she said.

"For sure. The guys even left a metal rack that fits on top." He pointed to a large flat cardboard box. "They said you can cook on it." He chuckled. "But probably not enough for fifty guests."

"Probably not." Her stomach rumbled noisily.

"Sounds like someone's hungry."

She gave a weak smile. "Actually, I was just about to run down to the Fish Shack."

"Great idea. Mind if I join you? I'm starving."

She shrugged. "Sure, but I'm going right now."

"Me too."

"Do you need to turn that off?"

"The guys said to let it run for an hour to 'season' it."

"Oh. Is it okay to leave it unsupervised?" She nodded toward the bay. "It feels like a breeze is kicking up. It won't catch the boat on fire, will it?"

"I know. You stay here and keep an eye on things, and I'll run and get our food. We can eat by the fire."

She agreed, telling him what to get her and handing him her money. He started to refuse, but she gave him a stern look, and to her relief, he didn't argue. "I'll be as quick as I can." Relieved to be away from him for a few minutes, she pulled a deck chair up to the fire and sat down facing the bay.

She sighed as she leaned back. Really, she couldn't think of a better place to be right now. Even if she did have to share it with Leo. Besides, she reminded herself, they were just friends. She needed to beat that into her brain. Just friends. She decided that when he returned, she would play the role of a friend. She would ask him how Natalie was doing and whether they'd agreed on a wedding date . . . or location . . . or settled on a ring.

Okay, she knew that her questions were dual-purposed. First of all, she was simply curious—as any friend would be. Second, she wanted to put him on the spot a little. In fact, the more she thought about it, the more she felt he deserved to be put on the spot. Because unless it was her imagination, Leo was dragging his feet. And if he was dragging his feet, perhaps he needed to talk about it with someone.

By the time Leo returned with two bags of scrumptious-smelling fish and chips, Tia was ready for him. Instead of jumping right in, she focused on her food and small talk. As they were finishing up, she tossed out her first question.

"How is Natalie doing today? Did her headache go away?"

"Yeah. She just called an hour ago. She sounds fine."

"Oh, that's good. Are you guys going to get together to solidify your wedding plans?"

"Natalie's parents are having us for dinner tonight." He made a slight grimace.

Tia pointed at the big chunk of fish in his hand. "And you're eating that now? How will you be hungry in a couple hours?"

"You've never tasted Natalie's mom's cooking, have you?"

Tia laughed. Apparently it was a case of *like mother, like daughter*.

"But the purpose of this dinner isn't food," he confessed. "I'm pretty sure Nat's mom wants us to nail down a date. Apparently she's found several reception venues that are available in August."

"August . . . That's not far off." As Tia bit into a fry, she gazed at the bay and reminded herself she was talking to her friend . . . not her crush.

"I know. For some reason Nat is not backing down. She's determined to be married this summer."

"And you're good with that?" Tia turned to look at him. Leo didn't answer as he slowly chewed.

"Sorry," Tia backpedaled. "I'm probably being too nosy."

"It's okay." He wiped his mouth with a napkin. "That's a good question. Probably the kind of question Nat's parents want to ask."

"You're still planning to have the wedding on the boat?" she asked.

He nodded firmly. "That's what *I* want."

"And Natalie?"

He frowned. "She's agreed to it . . . but reluctantly."

Tia knew she was on shaky ground now. To attempt to dissuade him from a boat wedding could tip her hand. Besides, Natalie could always drug herself with Dramamine. To change the direction of the conversation, she asked about the ring.

"Yeah, I still need to figure that one out." He shook his head. "I know you said that a girl should love her engagement ring. And I get that. But shouldn't a guy like it too?"

She considered this. "That seems fair enough."

He wadded up his bag with a frustrated expression. "I just don't think weddings are meant for the guys."

She chuckled. "It probably seems that way."

"I'm half tempted to just throw up my hands . . ." He held up his hands as if someone was holding a gun on him.

"What do you mean?" Tia was almost afraid to ask—afraid to hope. Was he having second thoughts about marrying Natalie? Did she really want to be the one to make him admit it?

"I don't know." He lowered his hands. "I guess it would be easier to just let them do it how they want. They tell me when and where and I'll show up. You know?"

Her spirits sank. "Yeah. I know."

He looked at his watch. "Well, that's been about an hour. Guess I can turn it off now."

"Great." She tried to sound cheerful as she stood. "I want to see how it works so I can turn it off and on too."

He bent down to show her the mechanism, turning off the flame and then the pilot light. "Simple."

She nodded. "Thanks."

"Thanks for listening to me." He looked into her eyes. "It helps to talk about these things. With someone who's uninvolved, you know?"

"Sure." She nodded stupidly as the word *uninvolved* kept reverberating through her head. "That makes sense."

Despite her earlier longing for solitude, she now felt sad and lonely watching him leave. Still, she knew she'd gotten just what she deserved. She kicked her toe at the stone fire pit. *People who play with fire should expect to get burned.*

The next week felt like a three-ring circus on the *Pacific Pearl*. Craftsmen that Julie had scheduled weeks ago started to arrive. Electricians, painters, plumbers, carpenters, floor installers, cabinetmakers, and so on—some showing up when they had promised, and some showing up when they liked. It was Tia's job to make sure the workmen didn't step on each others' toes as well as to ensure they got their tasks done.

Although Leo was usually on hand to help, it seemed their paths were crossing much less than usual. Probably because they were both so busy, but possibly because they were both avoiding each other. Tia suspected that their last personal conversation, when she had grilled him about his wedding plans with Natalie, had left him cold. She had probably crossed some invisible line. But for that, she was grateful.

At the end of each day, after the workers and Leo were

gone, Tia would walk around and take pictures of everything and send them to Julie. A little later, she'd call her aunt to discuss the day's accomplishments and go over tomorrow's work schedule.

Another project that was taking off was the creation of the *Pacific Pearl* website. Although Melinda was responsible for building the site and taking photos, she called Tia in the middle of the week for help with food photos.

"I could use stock photos, but wouldn't it be cool if the website had pics of real food that you actually prepared, served on the same kind of plates and things that you plan to use on the *Pacific Pearl*?"

"This is a pretty busy week," Tia told her. "The galley isn't even close to being ready for cooking yet, and the dining room tables aren't scheduled to arrive for another week." She remembered the boxes she'd stored along one wall of her stateroom. "Although the monogrammed plates and linens just got here yesterday."

"I knew your kitchen wasn't ready yet, but I figured you could come over here to cook at my parents' house. Then we could set up a table and cover it with your dishes and linens and flowers or candles or whatever. We could set it outside for really good light, and take some really enticing food photos. The shots would only have the tablecloth in the background, so no one would know they weren't taken on the boat."

"That does sound like a good idea." Tia looked over to where Leo was conversing with a carpenter. "I suppose I could ask Leo to cover for me. He's here most of the time anyway."

"Great! Is tomorrow afternoon too soon?"

Tia checked the work schedule to see that it was only electricians and plumbers tomorrow. She could probably go over everything with them in the morning, and if Leo was around he could follow up at the end of the day. "Okay," she agreed. "It should be fun. I'll have to do some grocery shopping first."

"I'll pick you up at the boat and we can make a stop at Whole Foods again," Melinda told her. "If it's okay with you, I'll ask my mom to cover the food cost, and you can just leave it here when you're done." She laughed. "I'm sure no one would complain."

"Sounds like you've got it all figured out."

That evening Tia went over the menus she'd been working on, selecting several dishes that she felt were photogenic, and made a shopping list. She was actually looking forward to some time off from playing contractor. It would be fun to put on her chef's hat again.

The next day, she didn't mention her plans to Leo when she asked him to cover for her in the afternoon. Why should she? But when Melinda arrived to pick her up, Leo got curious. "What're you girls up to?" he asked as they were leaving with a couple boxes containing place settings and linens.

"Tia's cooking for me," Melinda told him.

"Cooking for *you*?" Leo's brow creased.

"Actually it's for the website." She explained about the photos. "But we get to keep the food at our house."

Leo's eyes lit up. "Tell Mom I'll stop by for dinner."

"Leo!" Melinda shook a finger at him.

"Hey, Mom has been bugging me for a week to come for dinner. Tonight's as good as anytime."

"Opportunist!" she called out at him as they left.

"Guess I better get extra food," Tia said as they walked down the dock.

"I can't blame him." Melinda laughed. "He doesn't cook much for himself. And Nat's not much of a cook."

"So I've heard."

"What do you think of Leo and Natalie?" Melinda asked unexpectedly.

"Huh?" Tia turned to look at her.

"You know, what do you think of them as a couple? You know them both pretty well now. At least you know Leo. According to Nat, you guys are pretty good friends too. By the way, did you know Nat is going to ask you to be a bridesmaid in her wedding?"

"*What?*"

"Don't tell her I mentioned it. I just thought you might need a heads-up."

"That's for sure."

"Natalie is a little short on female friends. I'm her maid of honor, but the truth is, I've never been really close to her. Not like that, anyway. It's all a little awkward."

"Oh." Tia felt slightly sick at the idea of being in Leo's wedding, wearing some silly gown. No, she would have to decline politely.

"But really, what do you think of them as a couple, Tia? I've told you before that I have my concerns. I'm curious to hear your take."

"I, uh, I'm not sure." Tia tried to think of a good response as they got into Melinda's car. "To be honest, I was taken aback when I heard they were getting married—I mean, because they seemed so different from each other. But opposites attract . . . so I suppose that's my answer."

"But you can't wrap your head around it either," Melinda declared.

214

"Well, not exactly. I mean, Natalie is sweet and gorgeous and smart. Any guy would probably feel lucky—"

"Yeah, yeah, you're preaching to the choir, sister. I've heard that over and over these past few years. Ever since Nat graduated from law school and went to work at the firm, my dad's been singing her praises. So much so that I've actually been jealous at times. But I'm over that now. I'm glad Dad loves her. But lately . . . it's made me wonder about something."

"What?"

"I wonder if Leo got engaged just to make my dad happy."

"Seriously?"

"You know that our dad's an attorney—a senior partner with Natalie's dad. Did you know that their dads—our grandfathers—founded Morgan and Parker, Attorneys at Law?"

"I thought your grandfather was a captain on a ship?"

"That's on Mom's side. Grandpa McAllister."

"Oh."

"It was pretty important to Dad that Leo follow in their footsteps. He expected Leo to finish his law degree and join the practice to make it third generation. The same way Natalie has done."

"I didn't realize the law firm was third generation." Tia thought about D'Amico's back in Norton and how important it was to her family that the restaurant stay in the family. She got that.

"When Leo gave up law school to become a boat captain, of all things, well, you can imagine how Dad took it."

"Not so good?"

"Not at all."

"Leo has kind of hinted at that."

"Right . . . Leo has been a little on the outside where Dad's concerned." Melinda gave an ironic laugh. "In fact, our dad went after me for a while, certain that I was the one meant to carry on the name. But I put my foot down. Anyway, I've been thinking that Leo might be doing this to appease our dad. If he won't be an attorney, why not marry one? Dad is certainly pleased about it. Sometimes he seems happier than Leo."

"Are you suggesting Leo doesn't love Natalie?"

"No, I'm sure he loves her. We all love her. I'm just not certain he loves her enough to be happily married for the rest of his life. I'm not even sure that he really intended to marry her. I happen to know that she's the one who pushed for it."

"Do you honestly believe your brother would allow someone to make him do something he didn't want to do?"

"No, probably not. He obviously didn't care to placate Dad by finishing law school. I guess it makes no sense he'd placate him by marrying someone he doesn't really love." She sighed. "Maybe I'm making too much of it. But something about this whole thing is disturbing. I'd never tell Leo, but I have a bad feeling about it."

Tia wanted to know why Melinda was confiding all this to her. Did she have any idea of what Natalie had shared with Tia? Or was this just a coincidence? Probably more likely she was just being open with Tia because they were friends. How could she possibly know how frustrating this conversation was to Tia? How torturous . . . how futile?

20

As she and Melinda brought the bags and boxes inside, Tia questioned the way Leo had described his parents' home to her. Hadn't he made it sound like it was modest? At least compared to Roland and Julie's home? This house was just as grand as her aunt and uncle's—maybe more so—and it looked a lot bigger. But when Melinda led her to the kitchen, Tia observed that the backyard, while pretty with its lush green landscaping and swimming pool, didn't have a bay view. Maybe that's what Leo had meant.

"This is a lovely home," Tia said as they started to unload groceries.

"Thanks," a woman said from behind Tia.

"Hey, Mom," Melinda said as Mrs. Parker came into the kitchen. She was dressed casually in an oversized chambray shirt and blue jeans, and once again, Tia could see that Leo resembled his mother.

"Tia the talented chef has arrived."

Tia smiled. "Hello, Mrs. Parker."

"Please, just call me Joy."

Tia nodded, suddenly feeling inexplicably nervous. "Okay."

"Melinda tells me that you're going to do some amazing cooking and we get to keep the results."

"It will be sort of a mishmash of entrees." Tia explained her plan to cook individual servings, plate and garnish them, then let Melinda get her photos. "It'll make kind of a grab bag sort of dinner. I hope you don't mind."

"Are you kidding?" Joy peeked into one of the bags. "Oysters?"

"Yes." Tia removed the plastic bag of oysters. "For appetizers."

"Wonderful!"

"Leo invited himself for dinner," Melinda said as she opened a box, removing a white plate trimmed in navy with the *Pacific Pearl*'s monogram in the center. "Pretty, huh?"

"Yes." Joy nodded. "It will be fun to see it all come together on the boat. I already told Jim that I expect him to take me for a dinner cruise on our anniversary in early August. You will be running by then, won't you?"

"That's the plan," Tia assured her. "Julie really wants us to be running by mid-July."

"Do you need any help in here?" Joy asked as Tia set out a package of scallops.

"I already volunteered," Melinda said quickly. "I figure it'll be sort of like one-day culinary school."

"I'm happy to lend a hand if you need it," Joy offered.

"We'll be fine," Tia assured her. "Thank you for the loan of your kitchen. It looks well equipped. You must be a cook."

"I enjoy cooking." Joy smiled. "If I wasn't in the middle

of a painting, I'd ask if I could just sit here and watch. But I should probably get back before my muse disappears."

"You're an artist?" Tia asked with interest.

Joy shrugged. "Well . . . I'm a painter. I have a hard time calling myself an artist. It feels a bit pretentious and—"

"Oh, Mom." Melinda rolled her eyes. "You're a really good artist."

"Thank you, but I expect my family to say that." She winked at Tia.

"What sort of painting do you do?" Tia asked. "I mean, what medium?"

"Mostly acrylics. I'm too impatient for oils."

"I know what you mean," Tia said. "When I tried oils it got pretty muddy."

"You're a painter too?"

"Not really. I just dabble. Mostly sketches. Pen and ink. Watercolor sometimes. I've been collecting a lot of photos here in San Francisco, a lot of shots of the waterfront and the boats. Should be enough to keep me busy for a while."

"I saw a beautiful watercolor of a boat in the stateroom," Melinda said suddenly. "Did you do that?"

Tia smiled self-consciously. "Yeah."

"Would you like to see my studio?" Joy offered.

"I'd love to." Tia glanced at Melinda.

"Go ahead," Melinda told her. "I'll unload the bags."

"I've always loved art," Joy said as she led Tia out into the backyard. "But I started getting serious about it around ten years ago. Probably about the same time my children started needing me a lot less." She laughed. "Anyway, I wanted a separate place to do art. Someplace I could hide myself away and know that no one would come poking around."

"That makes sense."

Joy pointed to a small cottage-like structure with lots of windows. Opening a set of French doors, she waved her hand. "Welcome to my studio."

"Oh my." Tia stared in wonder. "It's lovely."

Joy smiled as she crossed her arms in front. "It is nice, isn't it?"

"It's better than nice. It's absolutely perfect." Tia walked around, taking it all in. The shelves were filled with art supplies, and the generous counters were arrayed with various artifacts, glass jars, and interesting objects. But it was the large windows with sunlight flooding in that really won her over. "You must love being out here."

"I do."

Tia pointed at the backside of the easel. "Is that what you're working on?"

Joy nodded.

"May I look? I'll totally understand if you don't want me to. I mean, I never enjoy someone looking over my shoulder when I've got a work in progress."

"Because you are a fellow artist, I will let you have a sneak peek," Joy told her.

Tia went around to see, hoping that it wasn't something truly bad that she'd have to pretend to like. To her relief it was a lovely landscape. "Is that a vineyard?" she asked.

"Yes," Joy said with enthusiasm. She pointed to some photos that were taped to a board. "This is the inspiration. It's actually a consignment piece for a friend. It's her vineyard in Napa."

"It's beautiful." Tia studied the photos and the partially finished painting. "You really know how to capture the light.

Actually you more than captured it—it's like you've brought it to life."

"Well, thank you." Joy beamed at her.

"I'll let you get back to it, although I doubt your muse will be trying to run out on this. It's too lovely to leave."

Joy walked her to the door. "I hope you'll let me see your work sometime."

Tia grinned. "You'll see my work at dinnertime."

Joy laughed. "That's right."

As Tia returned to the house, she almost wished she hadn't liked Joy Parker so much. It just figured that Leo would have such a delightful mother. Of course, Tia reminded herself, she was Melinda's mother too. Why not just focus on that?

"Ready to rock and roll?" Melinda asked.

"Yep." Tia nodded as she reached for a bundle of asparagus. "Your mom's studio is amazing."

"She doesn't show it to just anyone. It's like her secret hideaway."

"I can understand that."

"Tell me what to do," Melinda said eagerly. "I'm your kitchen servant."

For the next hour, they worked together prepping the foods they would use for the plates, and then Tia began to cook. After creating one dish at a time, just like she'd do in a restaurant, Tia would hand them over to Melinda, who took them outside to the table she'd set up on the patio, complete with linens and a small crystal vase with flowers, and took lots of photos. When she was satisfied with the results, she returned the plates to the kitchen, where they wrapped them in plastic wrap and stashed them in the fridge.

By 5:30, they were done with the last food photos and Tia was cleaning up the kitchen and explaining how Melinda could warm up the various entrees to serve to her family at dinnertime.

"Where are you going?" Melinda asked as she turned on the dishwasher.

"Back to the boat."

"Not until after dinner," Melinda insisted. "You can't cook all that fabulous food and not eat some of it."

"Well, I—"

"Besides, I'm your ride, remember?" Melinda pulled out a pitcher of iced tea. "I think we should enjoy a nice break until dinner."

They went outside to relax, and since the sun was still beaming down warmly, they sat by the side of the pool, dangling their feet in the water and chatting congenially.

"I see this is where the party is," Natalie said as she joined them.

"What're you doing here?" Melinda asked.

"Leo said Tia was cooking dinner for everyone." Natalie grinned. "I sort of invited myself. I hope it's okay."

"Sure," Tia said. "There's plenty of food."

"Great." Natalie removed her suit jacket, kicked off her shoes, then sat down next to Melinda, dipping her perfectly pedicured feet into the water. "Ahhh, now this is just what I needed. Do you know it got into the low nineties in the city today?"

"It seemed pretty warm," Melinda said. "Hey, do you want some tea?"

"That sounds lovely."

"I can get it." Tia jumped to her feet. "I want to check on

something in the kitchen anyway." Before they could protest, she hurried off. It wasn't that she didn't want to be around Natalie . . . not exactly, anyway. But remembering what Melinda had said about the bridesmaid thing was unsettling. The last thing she wanted right now was to have to invent some believable excuse for declining.

"I took a peek at the plates in the fridge," Joy confessed as Tia went into the kitchen. "We usually don't eat until around 7:00, but I'm not sure I can wait that long."

"Do you like oysters on the half shell?" Tia asked.

"Are you kidding?" Joy's eyes lit up.

"I made mignonette sauce." Tia opened the fridge, removing a covered dish with oysters already shucked and on the shell, anchored on a bed of rock salt. As she removed the lid, Joy let out a happy sigh. "I won't tell if you won't tell," Tia said as she produced the container of sauce, watching as Joy stuck a little seafood fork into the oyster, dipped it in the sauce, then slurped it down.

"Oh my!" Joy's expression was just short of heavenly. "That sauce is fabulous. Mind if I have another?"

"You can have as many as you like." Tia held the dish out for her to take another half shell.

"Wow, that is really wonderful." Joy held up her hands. "But I'm going to control myself now—and wait for dinner."

"Okay." Tia re-covered the dish and returned it to the fridge. "I was just getting Natalie some iced tea."

"Nat's here?" Joy pulled out a couple of tumblers, dropping ice into both of them.

"Yeah. She's out with Melinda." Tia got the pitcher out, filling up the two glasses in Joy's hands.

"I better go say hello to my future daughter-in-law," Joy said as they went back outside. As they crossed the patio, Joy started singing "Here Comes the Bride," and to be a good sport, Tia joined in. But if anyone was really listening to her, they would hear the sadness in her voice.

21

Despite her misgivings about being a guest in Leo's parents' home for dinner, Tia ended up having a surprisingly good time during dinner. It seemed that tying her identity to being "Melinda's friend" and "Leo's co-worker" helped her to fit in. That actually felt pretty good. It didn't hurt that everyone raved over her random selection of meals. And although she hadn't felt a strong connection with Leo and Melinda's dad, Jim, he seemed to warm up considerably when she announced dessert.

"It's only bread pudding with rum sauce," she said apologetically. "We wanted to keep it simple. We do have vanilla ice cream if anyone wants it a la mode."

"Jim adores bread pudding," Joy told Tia as she ground some beans for coffee.

"I'll give him a generous piece," Tia said as she set a piece of bread pudding on a plate and drizzled it with sauce.

"We all love bread pudding," Melinda said as she dropped a dollop of ice cream on top.

"Except for Natalie," Tia pointed out. "She passed on it."

"Maybe she's watching her figure," Joy suggested. "I hear she's found the perfect wedding gown." Joy began describing a strapless gown of satin and beadwork. "She is going to make a gorgeous bride."

Melinda didn't say anything.

"Yes," Tia agreed as she carried several desserts out to where they'd dined on the back patio. "She'll be beautiful."

Once they were all settled around the table again, Joy spoke up. "I was just telling the girls about your wedding gown," she told Natalie. "Your mom sent a photo, and I won't go into the details with Leo listening, but it sounds lovely."

"It's not a hundred percent for certain," Natalie told her. "But I feel really good about it."

"How about settling on the date?" Jim asked a bit sharply. "Bruce said you kids haven't decided between the last Saturday of August or the first Saturday of September. I vote for August since the other date is on Labor Day weekend."

"I agree," Natalie told him, then pointed at Leo. "He's the one who was opting for later. If Leo has his way, it won't be until October."

"October?" Jim's brow knitted. "I thought you kids had agreed on a summer wedding."

"The *Pacific Pearl* will barely be up and running in August," Leo told him. "I hate to bail on Julie during what will probably be her busiest time of year. Taking a day off for the wedding in the midst of all that—"

"But aren't you having the wedding on the boat?" Joy asked. "So you're actually giving her business. That's not bailing, Leo."

"There's also the honeymoon," he said somberly. "She'd have to hire someone else to cover for me."

"That's probably beneficial for everyone," Natalie said. "Julie should have a backup captain. Don't you think?"

Leo's face fell as the conversation continued. Tia, seeing that most of the dessert plates were empty, quietly gathered some of them up and made her way back into the kitchen, wishing for a small hole to crawl into.

"You don't have to clean up another thing," Melinda announced as she joined her.

"I don't mind."

"No." Melinda put a hand on Tia's. "I'll take care of it later. And I'll package up the dishes and everything and bring it back to you tomorrow."

"Thanks."

"You seem a little tired. Do you want to go home?" Melinda asked. "I mean, to the boat?"

"My home is on the boat for now." Tia forced a smile. "I suppose I am tired."

They both told the others good-bye and headed out. As Melinda drove, they were both quiet. Finally Melinda broke the silence. "Do you see what I mean about Leo?"

"Huh?" Tia turned to look at her.

"He doesn't seem happy to me."

"Well, he doesn't really enjoy the wedding details. He's mentioned that before. To be fair, most guys aren't into wedding plans."

"I think it's more than that."

Tia didn't say anything as she turned to look out the side window. She actually agreed with Melinda, but she had no intention of saying so.

"He seems really frustrated to me."

"Well, there's a lot going on for him." Tia was trying to think of something different to talk about . . . *anything.* "Hey, I was thinking about having a weenie roast on the boat tomorrow night," she said suddenly. She'd been thinking about doing something like this all week. "We've got the new fire pit going, and I thought it'd be fun to have some friends over. Like you and Jake. And if Roland is up to it, maybe he and Julie could come. We'd roast hot dogs and make s'mores and sing around the campfire, you know?"

"That sounds great. Count me in."

"Feel free to invite friends," Tia told her. "The more the merrier."

"Cool. A boat party."

"If anyone plays an instrument, ask them to bring it. I'll have my ukulele, and I'll ask Jake to bring his harmonica."

"I can't wait!"

They worked out some more details and made a short shopping list that Melinda promised to pick up. By the time Melinda dropped her off, Tia's spirits had lifted considerably. This was going to be fun! Of course, she'd made no mention that Leo and Natalie should be invited too—since they were part of that group. But knowing Natalie would decline coming to a floating party, what would be the point?

On Friday afternoon, Julie left Roland home alone and dropped by the boat to check on the progress. "Wow," she exclaimed as she and Tia walked through the main cabin where the cork flooring had just gone down that morning. "This is beautiful."

"I love the way the border stripes make it resemble a carpet," Tia said.

"You say the lighting goes in next week?" Julie asked as she peered up to where the electrical boxes were waiting.

"That's what the electrician said."

Tia took her down to the galley, which had received its cork floor too. "It's such a great surface for a kitchen," Tia said. "Soft on the feet, but impervious to almost everything."

"It's so much more spacious than I imagined." Julie opened a food storage cabinet that had been installed the day before. "This is roomy."

Tia pointed out the lift-up rails on the shelves. "To keep things from slipping if we're on rough seas." She demonstrated how the doorknobs worked. "The cabinets won't just fly open, yet they're easy to open with one hand."

They completed the tour, stopping at the fire pit, which Tia turned on. "Nice, huh?"

"I love it." Julie stretched out her arms to hug Tia. "You are doing such a fabulous job. I honestly don't know what I'd do without you."

"Well, to be fair, Leo's been pretty helpful too."

"I honestly think you two are doing a far better job together than I could've done on my own. It almost makes me glad I've had to be away. Well, except for the reason. I would never have wished that on Roland."

"How's he doing?"

"He's been in a little slump the last couple of days. I have to prod him to stay on top of things and to do his physical therapy. But from what I've read, this is normal after open heart surgery. I wouldn't call it depression as such, but I'm keeping an eye on him. I try not to be away from him for more than an hour at a time. I know some might think I'm being overprotective, but it's probably as much for me as it is for him." She glanced at her watch. "I should probably get going. I still need to stop by the store."

"You're sure you guys don't want to stop by here tonight?" Tia asked her again. "For hot dogs and s'mores and music?"

"Not this time." Julie smiled. "But someday we'll do that. You kids have fun."

Tia followed her down the gangplank and then, linking arms, walked her down the dock. "Give Roland my love," she said when they got to her SUV.

"I will. I know I already told you how much he loved the welcome home dinner, but he's still talking about it. He'd love it if you popped in to say hello."

"Okay, I'm glad to. Maybe I can cook for you guys again."

"That wasn't a hint, Tia. But someday when you're not so busy here on the boat, I know he'd love it. In the meantime, just drop by to visit."

"How about tomorrow?" Tia offered. "The only workers scheduled for tomorrow are the plumbers. Maybe Leo can deal with them."

"As long as someone is here with them. If tomorrow doesn't work, maybe after church on Sunday. By the way, are you going to the big engagement party tomorrow night?"

Tia wanted to say no, but the truth was, she'd already answered the electronic invitation's RSVP in the positive. "Yeah, I guess so."

"Then we'll see you there."

Tia made a stiff smile. "You bet."

As she walked back to the boat, she toyed with the idea of "accidentally forgetting" about tomorrow night's big bash.

With all her responsibilities on the boat, it seemed believable that she might forget. It could happen.

Tia hadn't deliberately neglected to mention tonight's hot dog roast to Leo today, although she was grateful that their paths hadn't crossed much, so she hadn't had a good opportunity to tell him about it. Her reasons were twofold. First of all, it would be easier for her if he wasn't there. Second, it would be kinder to Natalie.

According to Melinda's latest text, between her friends and Jake's, there would be close to twenty guests on the *Pacific Pearl* tonight. Everyone had been informed that hot dogs, buns, and s'mores would be provided, but they were all expected to bring something to go along with the meal and musical instruments, if they had them, to play for a jam session singalong.

As Tia showered, she realized how much she was looking forward to this little impromptu shindig. People weren't supposed to come until after 7:00, which gave her enough time to get some things set up. She started by moving all the deck chairs onto the deck with the fire pit. Then she set out the cooler, which was already filled with a selection of bratwursts and hot dogs that Melinda had brought by when she returned the boxes of dishes and things. She set up one table with hot dog buns and condiments and another table with marshmallows, graham crackers, and chocolate bars. It was simple as can be, and yet it promised an evening of pure enjoyment.

Feeling festive and hospitable, Tia went to finish cleaning up. She'd already decided to wear the red-and-white checked sundress she'd gotten at home before coming to San Francisco. It was a little more feminine than her usual garb, but it felt like fun. If it got too cool, she'd top it off with her red cardigan. And instead of putting her hair in a ponytail as usual, she let it fall over her shoulders in loose waves. Since she planned to stay on the boat, she decided to go barefoot.

As planned, Melinda arrived early with a bag of sodas and a bunch of hot dog roasting sticks she'd cut from her parents' backyard. "You look pretty," Melinda told Tia.

Tia grinned. "It's kind of fun to look like a girl occasionally."

A little past 7:00, Jake and several of his buddies as well as a lot of Melinda's friends started to show up. It wasn't long until several of them, including Tia, were enjoying an impromptu jam session around the fire. Meanwhile others were roasting hot dogs and eating and basically just having a good time.

"This is so much fun," Melinda told Tia as they met at the condiment table to dress their dogs. "You should tell Julie to consider having casual nights on the boat sometimes."

"That's not a bad idea."

Tia and Melinda found a couple of empty chairs and sat down to eat. As Tia munched on her bratwurst, she couldn't remember the last time she'd had this much fun. Watching the others mingling, laughing, singing, and eating, she felt sure they were having a good time too.

"I'm going to tell Julie about your idea," Tia told Melinda as she finished up. "We should come up with a catchy name for a casual night. We could put it on the website and—"

"That reminds me," Melinda said suddenly. "I got an idea for the website. I already asked Leo and he thought it would work."

"What is it?"

"We'll do a faux dinner cruise."

"Faux?"

"We'll invite some of our friends. Like the ones here to-night. Everyone will dress up like they're going on a formal dinner cruise. Then Leo will take the boat out shortly before sunset, and I'll get a bunch of staged photos with backdrops of the cityscape and the bridge and the sunset."

"That's a great idea." Tia nodded. "It would be nice if you could get some shots of the boat too. It's so pretty."

"Yeah. Leo suggested taking his rowboat. I could go out in it and get some shots from there. Leo thought we should consider going on the Fourth of July."

"Really?"

"That way we could get some cool shots with fireworks behind the boat. That would be pretty spectacular."

"That's a brilliant idea."

"But that doesn't give us much time to plan. The Fourth is only a week away."

"Maybe we should make an announcement tonight," Tia said. "Invite everyone to do this again on the Fourth."

"Want me to do that?" Melinda offered.

"Sure. Thanks."

Melinda went over to the fire pit, making a loud whistle through her fingers until she got the crowd to settle down. Once she had their attention, she made the announcement. The response was positive. "There's a catch," she explained. "Everyone has to dress up. At least for the first part of the trip. After I get the photos, you can get casual if you want. We'll have food and drinks for everyone." They all let out a cheer, then returned to their fun.

"Hey, Tia, hurry up with that hot dog," Jake called out

from where the musicians were seated near the fire pit. "We need a ukulele for this next song."

Finished with her food, Tia went over to join the music makers. She was impressed that Jake was more than just a harmonica player. He'd brought along a banjo and mandolin. Like Tia, he was into folk music, so it wasn't too hard coming up with songs they both knew. To her delight, Jake was also a fan of her favorite folk group, Nickel Creek. The two of them led the others in some songs they both knew and loved, including "The Lighthouse's Tale," which was one of Tia's favorites.

"Who are you in that song?" Jake asked Tia when they were finished.

"What?" She peered curiously at him.

"You have to relate to one of the characters. Are you the beloved fiancée who was lost at sea? The devoted light-keeper? Or the lighthouse?"

She laughed. "Well, I'm the lighthouse, of course."

"So you still warn the sailors on their way?" It was Leo who asked this, and Tia turned to see he was lurking in the shadows.

"Hey, stranger, how long have you been here?" she asked lightly.

"Long enough." He made a crooked smile. "That was a nice song. Mind if I crash the party?"

"You're not crashing," she assured him. "It's for everyone. Did you bring Natalie along?"

He shook his head. "I tried to, but she was getting a headache so I took her home." He held out a guitar case. "But I did bring this."

"Well, what're you waiting for?" Jake demanded. "Get on over here, man."

"Are you hungry?" Tia asked Leo.

"No thanks. I already ate."

"We do have s'mores," she said temptingly.

"S'mores?" His eyes lit up. "Well, I don't suppose I can pass that up."

The party continued with s'mores and sunset and music and firelight. Even though Tia knew she shouldn't be enjoying herself as much as she was—at least where Leo was concerned—she just couldn't help it. When the two of them did a duet of Nickel Creek's "When You Come Back Down," she was grateful for the dim light because she had tears in her eyes.

"Excuse me," she said in a husky voice, standing. "I need to get a drink of water. I'm getting a little hoarse." She hurried inside, going directly to the stateroom, where she took some deep breaths and attempted to compose herself. She wasn't even sure why the lyrics to that song got to her, but she suspected it was related to Leo. Anything more than that and she really didn't want to think about it. Seeing her cardigan on her bed, she slipped it on. *Grow up*, she told herself as she went back outside.

The jam session went on into the night, and Tia quickly got back into the spirit of it, playing and singing with enthusiasm until her fingers got so sore she had to take a break. She went over to the gunwale, looking out over the bay where a three-quarter moon was just starting to go down.

"Having fun?"

She turned to see Leo had joined her.

"I am," she confessed.

"Me too. This was a great idea."

She told him about Melinda's idea for a casual night on the boat sometimes. To keep filling the space, she also mentioned how everyone seemed excited to participate in the July Fourth evening. "That was a great idea, Leo. Hopefully we'll get some great photos. Unless it's foggy that night."

"That could be interesting too."

"You're right. In fact, we should make sure that some of the photos on the website represent other types of weather, like fog. Just to remind people that life isn't supposed to be nothing but sunshine and blue sky."

For a couple of minutes neither of them spoke.

"What are you thinking about?" Leo asked quietly.

Without bothering to filter herself, she answered, "Just wishing that nights like this could last forever."

He slowly nodded. "Yeah."

The party was starting to break up now, and to Tia's surprise, someone announced that it was nearly 1:00 in the morning. "Yeah, we better call it a night," Leo said, "before someone complains about the noise."

"Who's going to complain?" Jake asked. "The fish?"

Leo laughed. "Hey, there are a few people who live on their boats. People who enjoy their peace and quiet."

"Like me," Tia reminded him. She thanked everyone for coming, and Melinda reminded them about July Fourth next week.

"We'll set sail at 7:30," Leo warned. "Don't miss the boat!"

Leo, Melinda, and Jake stuck around to help clean up, which didn't take long. As they were leaving, Melinda reminded Tia about tomorrow night. "The big engagement party," she said without real enthusiasm. "Be there or be square."

236

"Right." Tia was thankful that it was too dark for them to see her expression. She knew it was less than cheery, and as she waved good-bye, she wondered if there might be a graceful way to avoid going at all . . . like falling and breaking her leg, perhaps?

22

On Saturday morning, Tia rode the bike over to Julie and Roland's house for coffee. Although Roland was a little quieter than usual, he did seem glad to see her. "You look good," she told him as the three of them sat outside on the deck together. "The color's back in your face, and it seems like you're getting stronger too."

He rubbed his beard. "Yes, according to my physical therapist I'm progressing 'nicely.'"

"He's been a little down in the dumps, though," Julie told Tia.

"So *she* says," Roland said dryly. "But until you have someone cut open your chest, crack you open like a walnut, and work your heart over, you probably can't relate."

Julie patted his arm. "I'm just glad you're still around."

He gave her a weak smile. "Even if I am turning into an old curmudgeon?"

"You're not," Julie insisted.

"You just need to give yourself time," Tia told him.

"That's right," Julie agreed. "You can't expect to snap back to your old self."

"I'm sure you girls are right." Roland sipped his coffee. "I've just never been a very patient sort of fellow. I'm used to things moving quickly."

"Well, I like that life has slowed down for us," Julie told him. "I've enjoyed this time we've had together."

His bushy gray brows arched. "Really?"

"Absolutely," she declared. "In a way it reminds me of our early days together, taking the time to get to know each other all over again."

He slowly nodded. "Yes, I suppose that's true. But I still feel guilty for taking up so much of your time."

"Well, you shouldn't. Tia and Leo are handling everything on the boat so efficiently. It's almost as if they don't need me." Julie grinned. "Do I know how to pick a team or what?"

"Speaking of Leo, didn't you say his engagement party is tonight?" Roland asked.

"Yes. At 7:00." Julie pointed to Tia. "We'll give you a ride."

"Oh . . . yeah." Tia looked at Roland. "You're going too?"

"Julie said it's time for me to get out and socialize." He paused as if he was unsure. "I do like Leo . . . even if I'm not too sure about his choice in women."

"Natalie is a very sweet person," Tia said.

"Yes," Julie agreed. "We're going tonight to support Leo no matter his choice."

"I'm not sure what to wear," Tia told Julie. "I assume it's sort of formal-ish, right?"

"Well, I'm making Roland put on a tie, and I'm wearing a dress."

Tia figured as much. Natalie would probably be dressed to the nines. The three of them visited together for about an hour longer, then Tia, seeing that Roland seemed a little weary, excused herself. "Time to get back to the boat." She gave Roland a hug.

"You know we still have the guest room for you," Julie said as she walked her to the front door. "It's not like you have to *live* on the boat."

"I know." Tia smiled. "But I actually like it."

Julie laughed. "Then you might as well enjoy it. At least while the weather is good. I'm not sure you'd want to be there in the middle of a winter storm."

"Maybe not."

"And for the time being"—Julie lowered her voice—"it's probably for the best anyway. You know, until Roland gets back to his old self."

Tia nodded. "Right."

They arranged to meet at the dock parking lot fifteen minutes before the party, but as Tia rode back to the boat, she tried to invent a believable excuse to avoid going.

Back at the boat, Tia decided to call her dad. She thought it might be comforting to hear his voice, and it was—at first. Then he started talking about Deanna. "She wants to set a date," he told Tia. "Not for a *wedding* wedding, but for us to get married in Vegas."

"Vegas?" Tia tried to imagine her rather straitlaced father in Sin City.

"Deanna has always wanted to go and I'm thinking, why not?"

"Yes . . . why not?"

"Oh, I know what you're thinking, Tia. But I've been doing

some research online and there's a lot more to Vegas than gambling. They have some amazing restaurants and some really good shows. Deanna wants to see Cirque du Soleil. She has vacation time coming the first week of August. So I'm thinking maybe we should just do it."

"You should go for it, Dad," she said, feigning enthusiasm. "Really, you should."

"Yes, I think so. I'll let you know when we nail down a date."

"Give Deanna my love," she said cheerfully.

When she hung up, she felt anything but cheerful. Although she wouldn't admit it to anyone, she felt downright envious. Dad and Deanna were getting married—and soon. Julie and Roland were still blissfully in love. Leo and Natalie were celebrating their engagement tonight. Oh, she knew she should be happy for all of them—and on some level she was—but she was feeling a bit sorry for herself. Sorry and certain that true love would never come her way.

As fate would have it, she didn't fall and break her leg that day, and she didn't want to lie to her friends. Without any good reason to bail on the engagement party, she put on her little black dress and hoped to play the wallflower tonight. Due to Roland's low energy level, she figured they wouldn't stay too long. Maybe just an hour if she was lucky.

"I've only been to the Morgans' once before," Julie said as she drove through her own neighborhood and then up the same hill that the Parker house was on. "But I'll warn you, Tia, it's pretty swanky."

"Swanky?" Tia snickered.

"The Morgans are well off. Their money goes way back," Roland said. "I heard the great-great-grandfather was a

merchant during the gold rush—sort of like Levi Strauss—
or something to that effect."

"Anyway, it's pretty posh," Julie said as she turned into a
gated driveway at the top of the hill.

"Looks like valet parking," Roland observed as Julie
drove the SUV up behind several expensive cars already
lining up to approach the portico. "Told you we should've
taken my car."

"Oh, don't be such a car snob," Julie teased as she pulled
up behind a gleaming new Mercedes, glancing back at Tia.
"Roland thinks his Beemer would be more impressive with
this crowd."

"Right." Roland laughed. "Who do we want to impress
anyway?"

Tia looked around the grounds. Everything was manicured and beautiful. Next to the portico was a large pond
with a statue of a dolphin leaping through a fountain. The
house was made of stone with the sort of substantial appearance that suggested it had been there for quite some
time. But as they got out of the car, it was the view that
stopped her. Because the house was at the top of the hill,
it looked as if it had a 365-degree view of the city, the bay,
and the bridge.

The sound of live music greeted them as they went through
the tall double doorway which was fully opened in a generous welcome. Luxurious bouquets of flowers were placed
here and there. With its stone columns and marble floors,
the grand home resembled a small palace.

"Looks more like a wedding than an engagement party,"
Julie whispered to Tia.

Tia simply nodded.

They were barely inside the large, open room where guests were mingling when Melinda rushed up to greet them. "There's a problem," she said quietly to Tia.

"A problem?"

"The caterer—a friend of Natalie's—got called away on an emergency. Seems her young son was hit by a car."

"Oh dear!" Julie exclaimed.

"Is he okay?" Tia asked.

"I guess so, but he's in the hospital and the caterer had to leave. Natalie's mom is on the phone trying to figure things out. My mom told her what a whiz you are in the kitchen, Tia, and—"

"I'd love to help," Tia told her.

"Really?" Melinda looked relieved.

"Are you sure?" Julie asked her.

Tia made a genuine smile. "Absolutely."

As Melinda led her to the kitchen, Tia felt relief washing over her. It wasn't as good as skipping the party altogether, but being stuck in the kitchen seemed a good second place.

"Here she is," Melinda said as she presented Tia to a tall blonde woman who looked like an older version of Natalie. "The talented woman I told you about. I think you met in church."

Mrs. Morgan frowned slightly. "I don't recall."

"Tia D'Amico." Tia smiled nervously.

"Pleased to meet you. I'm Lesley Morgan," the woman told her. "Of course, I'm Natalie's mother. Did Melinda tell you about our unfortunate mess?"

"She did. I'm happy to help."

"Oh, you *are* a dear. Hopefully it won't be for long. I'm waiting for someone to return my call right now." She held up her phone. "I really don't want Natalie to know what's going on. I don't want to spoil it for them."

Tia was already examining the containers of food in the kitchen, trying to imagine what the caterer's plan had been. "How many guests do you expect?"

"It's not a big gathering. About fifty, I believe."

"How did you plan to serve the food?"

"It's only a buffet of appetizers—in the dining room," Lesley explained. "We have a bartender out by the pool to serve drinks, as well as a punch bowl. But the caterer was supposed to handle the appetizers and dessert. A friend stepped in and put out some food, but I'm afraid she wasn't very clever about it."

"Okay." Tia nodded. "Sounds simple enough. Why don't you go out and enjoy your guests, and I'll just take over in here."

"Bless you," Lesley said. "Of course, I'll pay you for your time. And if I can get someone in here on such short notice, believe me, I will."

"Don't worry about that," Tia said. "I'm happy to handle this as long as necessary."

"I'll stick around and help her," Melinda told Lesley.

"Well, I want you girls to get out there and enjoy the party too," Lesley said as she started to leave.

Tia immediately jumped into action, locating serving dishes and platters, arranging food, and showing Melinda how and where to set it on the long table in the spacious dining room. Soon everything was in its place—looking rather splendid—and guests began flowing in.

"Thanks for helping," Tia told Melinda. "From here on out, all I need to do is keep refilling the appetizers, and that's a one-person job. You go on out and celebrate your brother's engagement."

Melinda's mouth twisted to one side. "Maybe I'd rather stay in the kitchen with you."

Tia gave her a gentle push. "Don't be a party pooper, Melinda."

"Fine." Melinda rolled her eyes. "But you send for me if you need help, okay?"

Tia nodded then returned to the kitchen to put some of the perishable appetizers into the fridge. She did not want anyone getting food poisoning on her watch. She moved a kitchen stool to where she could keep an unseen post near the dining room door, watching as appetizers disappeared and slipping in to refill the platters when the room wasn't too busy with guests. She went back and forth, cleaning up spills and replacing clean plates, silverware, napkins. Her job was ensuring that it all looked attractive, enticing, and well maintained.

Almost an hour passed before she saw Leo filling a plate. Jake was with him, being his usual jovial self and even talking about last night's jam session on the boat. Leo seemed rather serious and wasn't saying much. Dressed in a suit and tie, he looked somewhat stiff and uncomfortable—and not necessarily happy. Or was she just imagining things? Whatever the case, she was thankful not to come face-to-face with him tonight.

It was about 8:30 when Melinda returned to the kitchen. "Julie and Roland just left," she told Tia. "I told them I'd give you a ride home later. Okay?"

"Yeah. Thanks."

"Need any help?"

"No, I've got it. It's slowed down a lot anyway."

"Why don't you come out and join the party?" Melinda asked. "There's dancing outside."

Tia shrugged. "That's okay. I'm fine here."

Melinda looked skeptical, but at least she went back out.

A part of Tia wanted to go outside to watch what was happening, but another part was digging in its heels, relieved to stay put on her little kitchen stool. She told herself that she was needed here, even if it was simply to refill the petit fours platter and put out more dessert forks. She had just returned to the kitchen when she heard Natalie's voice in the dining room. She was talking quietly, almost in a conspirator's tone. Tia assumed she must be conversing with Leo, but when she peeked out, she spied a tall, dark-haired guy instead. "Promise not to tell anyone, Conrad."

"Scout's honor." His dark eyes twinkled.

"Because it's meant to be a surprise."

"I don't know how you'll pull it off, Natalie, but if anyone can do this, I'd put my money on you."

"My dad and Leo's dad are helping too. Like you and me, they're both Stanford Law School alumni. But Dad's got the best connections. He's got it all worked out that Leo can return to school in the fall—right after we get back from Baja. By my calculations, Leo should earn his law degree shortly after he turns thirty. Then he can join the firm."

"He's willing to give up boats?"

"Well, he can still go boating for fun," she said. "But everyone has to grow up eventually." She laughed. "Now remember, it's a secret, Conrad. Do not spill the beans. Please give my dad your letter of recommendation as soon as possible. We need more than just family members' endorsements. Can you imagine Leo's face when I present him with the acceptance letter for a wedding gift?"

"Not exactly." He chuckled. "But I've never been able to figure old Leo out anyway."

Another couple entered the dining room, and Natalie and Conrad began chatting about something else with them. Tia was unable to listen to another word. Her ears, it seemed, were too full to contain anything else. Did Natalie seriously believe that forcing Leo to go to law school was a *good* wedding gift? Had Tia heard them wrong? She gave her head a firm shake, trying to make sense of it. *Poor Leo!*

Tia was standing at the sink, rinsing a platter, when Leo walked up. "What are *you* doing in here?" he demanded in what seemed an irritated tone.

She blinked as she nearly dropped the platter. "Huh?"

"What are you doing in the kitchen?" He stared intently into her eyes.

"I, uh, I'm helping out." She quickly explained about the caterer's son.

"I know about that. But why you?"

"Because I'm a chef." She wiped her hands on the apron she'd borrowed.

"But this isn't right, Tia. You're my friend. You weren't invited here to be a servant and—"

"Look, Leo." She narrowed her eyes. "I'm in here because I *want* to be in here. Okay?"

"Oh, there you are." Natalie came into the kitchen. "Jake said he saw you sneaking back this way." She put her arms around Leo's waist. "Didn't get enough to eat, babe?"

"There's plenty of food in the dining room," Tia said tersely.

"Oh, Tia." Natalie seemed to have just noticed her.

"Hi, Natalie." Tia could hear the coldness in her voice but seemed unable to help it.

Natalie peered at her with sympathy. "Don't tell me you've been stuck in here for the whole evening? Mom told me you were lending a hand, but I didn't think you were still—"

"Like I just told Leo, I'm doing this because I want to. I like helping." Tia turned back to the sink, focusing her attention on the platter she was rinsing.

"You are a saint." Natalie planted a kiss on Tia's cheek. "Thank you, darling girl!"

Tia made a stiff smile as she set the platter on the island with the others. "Just consider it an engagement present."

Leo was still glowering at her.

"Do me a favor," Tia said lightly. "Please, go back out there with your guests while I finish up some things in here."

"But you can't keep—"

"*Please!*" Tia locked eyes with Leo. "Just go."

"Come on, Leo," Natalie said in a teasing tone. "We don't want her going for the knives."

"Thank you," Tia said curtly as Natalie pulled Leo out toward the dining room with her.

Tia felt her Italian blood boiling as she returned to the sink. So many emotions were surging through her just now, she wasn't even sure which ones were the most upsetting. Instead of attempting to figure it out, she threw all her energy into cleaning things up.

"Hey," Melinda said as she found Tia vigorously scrubbing a marble countertop. "Lesley asked me to tell you not to clean up. She has a janitorial service coming in tomorrow to do that."

"*Right.*" Tia threw the dishrag into the sink, pulled off her apron, and tossed it onto a kitchen stool.

"What's wrong with you?" Melinda looked alarmed.

"Nothing," Tia growled.

"Sure . . ." Melinda tipped her head to one side. "Are you mad because you missed the party?"

"Hardly." Tia went to where she'd stashed her bag in a cupboard. "I just want to go home."

"Well, lucky for you, so do I. That's why I came to get you. Ready?"

"I'm more than ready." Tia nodded to a side door that led from the kitchen out to what appeared to be a service area of trash cans and recycling bins. "Can we go that way?"

"Makes no difference to me. I already said my good-byes and asked the valet to bring my car around."

"Good."

It wasn't until they were in Melinda's car that Tia began to relax a little.

"Tia," Melinda said gently, "what's wrong?"

Tia took in a deep breath. "I guess I'm just fed up."

"Because you had to work in the kitchen all night?"

"No." Tia firmly shook her head. "That was a blessing in disguise. Really. I didn't mind that at all."

"What then?"

"*Too many secrets.*"

"Secrets?" Melinda glanced at Tia as she stopped at an intersection. "What kind of secrets?"

"If I told you, they wouldn't be secrets, now, would they?" Tia folded her arms in front of her.

"Okay . . . then who are the secrets about?"

Tia pressed her lips tightly together, staring blankly out the window.

"Come on, Tia. You can't say you know secrets and just leave it hanging like that."

Still Tia said nothing. For several minutes neither of them spoke.

"I thought we were friends," Melinda said when she finally pulled into the dock parking lot. "But maybe I was wrong."

"Oh, Melinda!" Tia exploded as she opened the door. "It's so frustrating, and I want to tell you, but I feel disloyal, and it's such a mess—a big fat mess! Thanks for the ride." Tia got out of the car and took off down the dock.

"Wait!" Melinda came running after her. "You can't get rid of me that easily. Not after saying what you just said, Tia. *What is going on?*"

Tia kept walking. "Nothing."

Melinda reached over and grabbed Tia's arm. "Tell me what's going on. I know it must have to do with my brother. I have a right to know."

"Maybe I'm just making a mountain out of a molehill."

"Then it's no big deal if you tell me. Come on, what's happened?"

Standing there on the dock, Tia poured out the story of what she'd just overheard—how Natalie planned to send Leo to law school as a wedding present. When she was done, Melinda simply threw back her head and laughed.

"It's not funny," Tia insisted.

"I know it's not funny." Melinda suddenly grew sober. "In fact, it's downright aggravating. But think about it, Tia. How is Natalie going to force Leo to do something he doesn't want to do? In case you haven't noticed, my brother is pretty stubborn."

"Except when it comes to Natalie."

Melinda scowled. "Yeah, that's probably true. Now that I think about it, Nat kind of talked Leo into getting engaged, didn't she? And she's the one pushing for a summer wedding when Leo really wanted to wait a year or more."

"That's not all."

"*What?*"

Tia clapped her hand over her mouth. "Nothing."

"Come on, out with it."

"I can't. I promised Natalie I wouldn't say anything." Tia shook her head. "I've already said too much. I'm sorry, Melinda. Maybe I'm just tired or something." She let out a long, exasperated sigh. "Thanks for the ride. Sorry to act like such a drama queen just now. You're right. It's probably no big deal." She started walking again.

"I didn't say that." Melinda kept walking with her. "The truth is, I think it is a big deal. I think my brother has no idea what he's really getting into."

"I'm sure he can figure it out."

"Hopefully."

Tia stopped beneath an overhead light, forcing a smile. "Sorry to dump on you like that. It was wrong of me to eavesdrop on Natalie. I hope you'll keep what I said private. *Okay?*" She peered intently at Melinda. "Please, for my sake. I never meant to be a busybody, sticking my nose where it doesn't belong."

Melinda shrugged. "Can't see there's much point in me tattling to Leo anyway. It's not like he has to go to law school if he doesn't want to."

"That's right."

Melinda hugged Tia. "For the record, I think it's sweet that you care enough about our family to confide in me though. And I'm sorry you got stuck in the kitchen all night."

Tia attempted a smile. "Believe me, there are worse things in the world than doing KP." As she walked back to the boat, she tried not to think about them.

23

By Monday, Tia felt like she had put her concerns over Leo behind her. She had convinced herself that she'd overblown the whole thing. Melinda was right: Leo could deal with this himself. From now on, she was determined not to get pulled into their drama. Leo and Natalie could sort out their own problems. Tia needed to keep her full focus on the boat. She had to manage the various workers, track the numerous deliveries, and keep Julie in the loop. That was more than enough to occupy her mind.

To her relief, Leo seemed preoccupied too. Their conversations were limited to what was going on around them, what needed to be done, and who was doing it. In a way, they were like ships in the night. Except it was daytime.

But toward the end of a very busy week, Tia wondered if it was only the boat business that Leo was preoccupied with. On Friday afternoon, she caught him gazing out over the bay with such a glum expression she couldn't help but ask him if he was okay.

He gave a half smile. "Yeah . . . just thinking."

"About something sad?" she asked.

"Not exactly."

She wished she hadn't said anything. Why not let sleeping dogs lie? She changed the subject. "Anyway, I was wondering if everything is set for tonight's cruise. I mean engine-wise. Is the *Pacific Pearl* all ready to sail?"

"She's shipshape." His smile seemed to grow brighter. "Did you hear the engines running this morning?"

"I did. It sounded good."

"Can't wait to take her out."

"Me too. I've never been out on her before. I'm really looking forward to it."

"That's right." He nodded. "You weren't here yet when I took her out several times. For a somewhat clunky-looking old boat, she's smooth and sleek in the water."

"You think she's clunky-looking?" Tia demanded.

"No, I think she's a classic. But some might think she looks a little old-fashioned."

"I guess I like old-fashioned." She ran her hand over the railing. "Do you need any help tonight? I mean, like a crew?"

"I've got a couple of friends to act as my deck hands. Jake offered to play first mate this time."

"Is he good with boats?"

"Good enough. He knows how to take orders." Leo looked intently at her. "Jake is a really good guy, you know?"

She nodded. "Yeah, I can tell."

"You guys sounded pretty good last week when you were playing music together. That lighthouse song was amazing."

"I know. I couldn't believe how good Jake is on mandolin.

I didn't realize he was such a musician. I thought he only played harmonica."

"Jake's a man of many hidden talents." Leo sighed. "He's also good at hiding his feelings, if you hadn't noticed. He likes playing the clown."

"That does provide some good entertainment," she admitted.

"Did you know that Jake thinks you're pretty cool, Tia?"

She shrugged. "I think he's cool too."

"No, I mean Jake is *into* you, Tia. Were you aware of that?"

"Oh, I think he just likes me as a friend, that's all."

"I've known Jake for years. You can trust me when I say he likes you for more than just a friend."

"Oh . . ." She frowned.

"He's looking forward to you fixing him dinner sometime."

"That's right." Tia slapped her forehead. "I forgot all about that promise. I wonder how he feels about peanut butter." She chuckled. "That's what I had for lunch today."

"Well, he knows how busy you've been, so I think he's waiting patiently."

Tia pursed her lips. What was Leo getting at?

"I'm not trying to interfere," he said slowly, "I just thought you should know. Jake is interested in more than just friendship with you."

"Well, I appreciate the heads-up. I'll confess that I'm sort of surprised." She bit her lip. "I don't know what to do."

"What do you mean?"

"I mean, I wouldn't want to lead him on, Leo. Jake is a sweet guy. And a fabulous musician. I'd like to think he's a good friend too. But that's all. Really." She shook a fist at

Leo. "Now that you told me that, I'll probably feel uncomfortable and get all standoffish and everything. Why did you have to tell me that?"

He made a lopsided grin. "Sorry. Didn't mean to get you all fired up."

"Well, you did."

"Want me to drop him a little hint, let him know that you're not looking for that kind of relationship just now?"

"Thanks, but that's not really my style. I'll handle it. I'll just let him know that I would appreciate his friendship more than anything right now, at least for the time being."

"Meaning you might change your mind?"

"Meaning I don't really know." She shook her head. Guys could be so dense sometimes. "I still have a lot to do to get stuff ready for tonight."

"Need any help?"

She considered this. "Probably." She explained how she wanted to stage some of the tables inside the dining room to give the appearance that people were eating when Melinda took photos. "Let's arrange the deck chairs around the deck too."

"Just tell me what to do and I'll do it." He glanced at his watch. "At least until six. Then I need to make a run into the city to get Natalie, get her back here in time to change into my captain's uniform, and prepare to sail."

"She's coming?"

"Yeah." He gave Tia a curious look. "She was invited too, wasn't she?"

"Of course." Tia turned away. "I've gotta get busy."

With the two of them working together, it didn't take long to get things arranged and staged for Melinda's photo session. The plan was for everyone to pose and cooperate during the first half of the cruise. Then they would change into casual clothes to make the photos appear to be of another type of event, and they could enjoy another hot dog roast and jam session with the fireworks in the background.

As Tia got cleaned up and dressed for the evening, once again putting on the checked sundress, she wondered if Natalie would actually show up tonight. Or would she come up with another excuse? Tia told herself as she brushed her hair that she didn't even care. That was Leo's problem.

"Ahoy there," called a female voice from the main cabin. "Tia?"

She went out to see Julie carrying two grocery bags. "I brought the food for staging the dining room. It's kind of a hodgepodge. I hope you can make it look somewhat believable for the photos."

Tia peeked in the bags to see an assortment of cartons of salads and things. "Well, according to Melinda, the food on the plates will not be the main focus tonight. It will be the boat and the smiling faces and the scenery."

"Perfect." Julie set the bags on one of the tables that hadn't been staged for photos. "I can't wait to see the results. Have a wonderful evening."

"Aren't you coming?" Tia asked.

"Roland's not really up for such a long night. We weren't even two hours at the engagement party and he was worn out." She frowned. "Although I think it's more emotional than physical."

"Maybe it's both."

"Probably." Julie patted her cheek. "You look very pretty tonight. Have fun, okay?"

"We'll enjoy your boat to the max," Tia promised.

"I'm glad." Julie waved good-bye. "Someone should."

Tia felt sorry for Julie as she left. As devoted as she was to Roland, Tia suspected that Julie was missing out on a lot. Yet it was reassuring to think that true love was like that—it made a person willing to settle for less in some ways in order to have what mattered most in larger ways.

Melinda was the next to arrive. She took a few minutes to walk Tia through her plan, explaining the areas they would use for staging photos and the areas where guests could dump bags and musical instruments and the foods they'd brought for the weenie roast later.

By seven, the guests were starting to arrive. Dressed semiformally, they were a festive-looking crowd and in good spirits. Tia explained Melinda's plan and started assigning people to tables. "You don't have to go into the dining room until the boat leaves the dock," she told them. "I'll ring the dinner bell. The food on the plates is for photo purposes," she said apologetically. "But feel free to eat it if you'd like. Just don't hurry, so that Melinda can get some good pictures. If you don't like it, don't complain. It's just staging. Mostly you need to act like you're having a great time."

"Act?" one of the girls said. "We will be having a great time."

Tia noticed Leo walking by, already dressed in his captain's uniform and looking strikingly handsome. "Where's Natalie?" Tia asked, expecting him to say she'd come down with a sudden headache.

"She wasn't ready when I got there. She wants to drive herself down here."

"But she's coming?"

"Sure."

Tia just nodded. *Yeah, sure she's coming.*

It was almost 7:30 when Tia heard the boat's engines firing up. She looked around, curious as to whether Natalie had shown, but she didn't see her amongst the crowd.

"Just in time," she heard a guy calling out. "Come on, Natalie, we were about to pull in the gangway. Hurry up before you're left behind."

Natalie, dressed in a lovely pink dress that reminded Tia of the inside of a seashell, reached for the guy's hand as she slowly crossed the gangway. As soon as her feet touched the deck, a couple of guys pulled the gangway in.

"Welcome," Tia said as she went to greet her. "I'm glad you could make it."

"I took some Dramamine about half an hour ago," Natalie whispered as she waved to some friends. "I'm praying it works."

"Just try to stay on deck as much as possible," Tia advised. "Fresh air is supposed to be good. Sometimes it helps to be on the foredeck or bow. Facing the direction we're headed."

"Okay." Natalie smiled. "Thanks for the tips!"

"No problem. I've got to go get stuff ready in the dining room now. Leo's at the bridge. In fact, that might be a good place to be too. Especially if you open the windows to get the air flowing through."

"Good idea. I'll go join the captain right now." She smiled bravely. "I'm sure I'll be just fine."

Tia hoped so as she went into the dining room. Her plan was to arrange the foods that Julie had brought as artistically as possible on the *Pacific Pearl* plates. She would set the tables in a believable fashion before the "models" came in

259

to pretend to dine. As she felt the boat's motion, she wished she could go out on deck to watch the *Pacific Pearl* heading for open water, but she knew she needed to get things set up first.

"That looks really good," Melinda said when she came in to check on Tia's progress. "Almost as good as the food you prepared yourself." She leaned down to examine a plate. *"Almost."*

"Do you think we're far enough out to have a good background for the photos yet?" Tia looked at the windows next to the staged tables.

"Looks good. Go ahead and call in our guests."

"Don't you mean victims?" Tia teased as she went out to ring the bell.

Before long, Tia and Melinda got the boisterous crowd seated and the photo session began. Seeing that Melinda had things under control, Tia went out for some fresh air and to experience the sensation of the boat she'd grown to love now moving through the water. Leo was right. She was sleek and smooth. The engine wasn't very noisy either. Plus, because of the holiday and fair weather, the bay was crawling with all sorts of boats, which in her opinion made the excursion all the more interesting.

Tia went out to the bow, enjoying the feel of the breeze in her face and watching as the boat slowly moved toward the Golden Gate Bridge. It wouldn't be long until Melinda could get the bridge framed through the dining room windows, with the diners merrily enjoying their grocery store food in front of it. The western sky was growing peachy and golden, which would be a perfect backdrop behind the bridge.

"Tia!"

She turned to see Leo waving frantically at her from up on the bridge. "Help! Hurry!"

Feeling a wave of terror, she took off, sprinting across the deck. Was the boat in peril? Did they have sufficient lifeboats? Visions of the *Titanic* rushed through her head as she ran up the stairs, bursting in to find Leo with one hand on the helm and the other supporting Natalie. The small sunny room reeked of vomit.

"She's sick," he told her. "Can you get her to a head before she throws up again?"

"Yeah. Sure." Tia took Natalie by the arm, guiding her down the steep stairs and through a side door into the main cabin. She considered taking her to one of the newly furbished dining room heads but decided the stateroom might be better for the sake of the other guests.

"Come on, Nat," she urged, "you can make it."

Several people glanced up as Tia rushed Natalie past. Thankfully, they made it to the stateroom in time, and like déjà vu, Natalie collapsed to the floor, heaving into the toilet. Tia stooped over to hold back Natalie's shiny blonde hair, wishing there was a way to protect the shell pink dress as well. It looked like it was silk, and probably ruined. Just like this evening would be for Natalie. Tia reached for one of her hair elastics and used it to make a messy ponytail for Natalie.

"I *hate* this," Natalie gasped when she finally came up for breath. "Tell Leo he's got to turn back."

"Turn back?"

"I can't do it," Natalie said in a hoarse voice. *"I hate this boat."*

"But we're on a schedule," Tia explained. "We want to

get photos of the sunset and the bridge. We'll be there in a few minutes. If we go back, we'll miss those—"

"I *have* to go back!" Natalie demanded. "I can't stand another minute of this. Tell Leo to turn around at once." Suddenly she was heaving again.

"Okay . . ." Tia backed slowly from the room, closing the door behind her. She was tempted to ignore Natalie altogether, to just leave her there until they'd secured the photos they'd come for. But she knew that was wrong and selfish. Besides, she thought as she hurried back to the bridge, this was the captain's decision.

"*What?*" Leo demanded after Tia relayed Natalie's frantic message.

"She wants you to turn the boat around."

"What about Melinda's photos? The sunset behind the bridge?"

"I know," Tia told him. "But Natalie is sick."

"Is she *seriously* sick?" he asked her.

"She's throwing up."

"I know that." He wrinkled his nose as he pointed to the splattered wastebasket.

Holding her breath, Tia gingerly picked it up and set it outside. She'd have to bring some disinfectant spray and paper towels up here later.

"I don't want to be insensitive." He kept his eyes on the water ahead of him, moving to give way to another yacht as he tried to allow sufficient room for a sailboat. "But how sick is she? Does she need medical treatment?"

"Not really." Tia shook her head. "She's seasick."

"Then let her ride it out," he said.

"But she said—"

"Look, I'm sorry she's sick. But if it's just plain old sea-sickness, it'll pass. We need to finish what we started here tonight. It's not fair for Natalie to spoil it. Right?"

She gave him an uncertain smile. "Yeah . . . I guess."

"Tell her I'm sorry. Maybe you can get her to drink some Sprite or something. Get her outside into the fresh air maybe."

"Aye-aye, Captain."

He grinned. "Thanks, Tia."

Feeling encouraged and hopeful, Tia hurried back down to the stateroom. But when Natalie heard Leo's response, she grew angry.

"Did you tell him I'm dying down here?" Natalie demanded.

"Well, you're not exactly dying."

"I *feel* like I'm dying." Natalie looked up with red-rimmed eyes and tear-streaked cheeks. "Doesn't it look like I'm dying?"

"Come outside and get some fresh air," Tia urged.

"I can't have the others seeing me like this." Natalie clung to the toilet. "It's too humiliating."

"I'll get you some Sprite and—"

"I don't *want* any Sprite!" she screamed. "I want Leo to turn this stupid boat around. Tell him if he doesn't turn back I'll—I'll jump overboard." She hunched over the toilet again, her shoulders jerking from dry heaves.

Tia waited for her to stop. "You wouldn't really do that," Tia said quietly.

"Oh, wouldn't I?" Natalie's eyes flashed. "If Leo doesn't take me back, I'll jump overboard and the Coast Guard can come pick me up."

"Natalie!"

"*Please*, Tia. I can't stand this. Please tell him to turn around."

"I'll tell him, but I can't promise anything." Tia backed out again. "I need to help Melinda with the photos. Will you be okay for a few—"

"I am *not* okay!" Natalie screeched. "Tell Leo what I said. And get my purse while you're up there. It has my phone in it. If Leo doesn't turn around, I'll call 911 and ask the Coast Guard to rescue me from dying."

Tia just nodded, closing the door and hurrying away.

"You gotta be kidding," Leo said to Tia. "She really said *that*?"

"I'm not making it up." Tia pointed to the pretty beaded bag. "Should I take her phone to her?"

"Not if she's calling the Coast Guard. Does she realize she could be charged with a crime and fined for that?"

"I'm not sure she cares."

Leo looked at Tia with troubled eyes. "What should I do?"

"Turn back," she said quietly. "We'll lose some photos, but really, it's just not worth it."

"Fine." He looked both ways, then started to slowly turn the helm. "Turning back."

"I'll explain to Melinda."

"But you tell Natalie that when she gets off, she gets off alone. She can't expect me to go with her. Understand?"

"Okay."

"Tell her it'll be about half an hour before we get there."

By the time Tia made it to the dining room, several people were asking why the boat was turning around. "Natalie is seasick," she said simply. "Leo needs to get her back on dry land."

She quickly relayed the news to Natalie, and before Natalie

could complain again, Tia went back out into the dining room, quietly explaining the situation to Melinda.

"Seriously?" Melinda scowled as she checked a shot on her camera. "Natalie is forcing us to miss the sunset?"

"Not much we can do about it."

"Is she really sick or just faking for attention?"

"She's really sick. I guess her secret is out now."

"Her secret?"

Tia nodded.

"That she gets seasick?"

"*Extremely* seasick," Tia clarified. "Just being on Leo's houseboat makes her sick. It's a real thing, Melinda."

"Wow, that's pretty weird. I mean, considering who Leo is . . . his love of boats and water. Don't you think?"

Tia shrugged. "Get as many shots as you can for now. Leo will take us back out once Nat's off. We might still get some sunset time. And there's still the fireworks."

The fireworks came sooner than expected for the *Pacific Pearl*. After Leo got the boat docked, he and Natalie exchanged some words—Natalie standing on the dock and Leo standing on deck, with everyone else watching.

"You aren't coming with me?" Natalie yelled at him. "You're not taking me home? Don't you care about me?"

"Are you still sick?"

"Well, no, but"—Natalie held out the skirt of her soiled dress with a crumbling expression—"I'm a mess and I—"

"I'm the captain, Nat. I have to take the boat out to—"

"Of course! You would choose your stupid boat over me!"

"I'm not choosing, Nat. It's just my responsibility to—"

She shook a fist at him. "I can't believe you refused to turn the boat around!"

"I *did* turn the boat around."

"Not at first, you didn't. You only turned it around when I threatened to jump overboard."

"Natalie, you're being—"

"*What?* I'm being *sick*, Leo? Do you even get it? You think this is my fault? Like I can help being sick?"

"No. But we need to go, Nat. I'm sorry you're—"

"Forget it, Leo." She held up her left hand with fingers splayed. "I just wish you'd given me a ring so I could take it off and throw it at you right now. I would!"

"Natalie, don't get so—"

"Don't tell me what to do, Leo. *I'm done.* The engagement is over. The wedding is off. I'm through with you! And I'm through with stupid boats!" She went storming off down the dock.

"Leo," Tia said to him. "If you need to go to her, it's okay. We can do this another time. Everyone will understand. It's not like they're paying guests."

"Forget it," he snapped. "It's over. You heard her. We're done." He stormed across the foredeck. "Get ready, everyone. We're outta here."

His makeshift crew and first mate scrambled to get ready, but it was their expressions that got Tia's attention. Leo's friends looked relieved, as if they felt this was a good change of events. As quickly as the *Pacific Pearl* had docked, she was taking off again. Heading back out into the sunset. But the mood on the boat had changed. The party vibe seemed somewhat subdued now. Although she tried to conceal it, Tia's heart was no longer into it.

24

While Leo was at the helm, attempting to get the boat back out near the Golden Gate Bridge while there was still some good sunset color left in the sky, Tia quietly cleaned and disinfected the corner of the bridge where Natalie had "lost it." As Tia slipped behind him to open the side windows wider to allow more air flow, she was relieved that Leo was so focused on navigating through the heavy nautical traffic that he didn't seem to notice her. She didn't know what she would say to him if he did. Judging by his troubled expression, it was more than just the busy bay that was bothering him. She felt truly sorry for both of them.

Although Natalie's dramatic meltdown had placed a temporary damper on some of the guests, it didn't take long for most of them to return to their previous merrymaking, which hopefully made for some good photos. While the sunset was still glowing, Jake helped Melinda into Leo's rowboat, which they'd been towing. He rowed the boat to various locations as she took some fast photos of the ship from different angles.

"I got shots of the boat with the bridge behind it," Melinda told Tia as she came back onboard. "I also got it with the cityscape and even some remnants of the sunset. Lucky for us, it was a nice long sunset. If these shots aren't light enough, I can probably get Leo to take me out again later in the week."

As the sky was growing dusky, Tia started up the fire pit and laid out the makings for hot dogs and s'mores. With the *Pacific Pearl* slowly cutting through the bay, the real party began. Ties and heels were cast aside, and some got out musical instruments while others started roasting hot dogs. It wasn't long until they were enjoying the fireworks shooting up high from various locations, reflecting across the dark, glossy water with the loud booms of explosives echoing off the nearby hills.

Tia had just finished roasting a bratwurst when she noticed the soft blue light glowing from the captain's bridge. Seeing Leo's face illuminated by the instrument panel, she felt a fresh wave of compassion for him. Poor guy. Talk about a bad night. Ever since his public clash with Natalie, he'd been at the helm, alone and unhappy, and probably embarrassed. As far as she knew, he hadn't even had dinner. Fixing him a generous plate of food, she turned to Melinda. "I'm taking this up to Leo. Want to come along?"

"Not right now. I'm trying to get a good shot of the musicians around the fire with the fireworks shooting off behind them," Melinda said. "Maybe later."

Tia went up by herself. "Thought you might be hungry." She set the plate and an unopened can of soda on the countertop.

"Thanks." He kept his eyes forward.

She moved back toward the door, sensing he wasn't interested in socializing. "I'm sorry about what happened," she said quietly. "I mean, with Natalie."

"Nothing for *you* to be sorry about."

"I know. I just mean I feel badly for you. And for Nat too."

He reached for the soda, popping it open. "By the way, thanks for cleaning up that stinking mess for me."

"No problem." She opened the door. "Anyway, I was thinking that you shouldn't give up, Leo. I mean, maybe you guys will patch things up and—"

"*Nope.*"

"But lots of couples fight." She noticed Melinda coming up the stairs, still carrying her camera.

"That's right," Melinda declared as she entered the bridge. "Lots of couples fight."

"I know that, Melinda." He turned to glare at her. "This was different, okay? It was more than just a little lovers' quarrel."

Melinda sat on the stool next to Leo, sneaking a quick candid shot of the captain at the helm. "Did Tia tell you what Natalie was up to?"

Tia shot her a warning look as she opened the door, preparing for a fast getaway.

"Hold on there, Tia," Leo said sharply. "What's Melinda talking about?"

"*Nothing.*" Tia narrowed her eyes at Melinda.

"What difference does it make now?" Melinda asked her. "They're broken up."

"It was a private conversation," Tia said tersely. "I told you that I didn't want you to—"

"But it was *about* Leo." Melinda grabbed Tia by the hand, pulling her closer to the helm. "Spill the beans."

"Melinda." Tia frowned. "You promised—"

"This is my brother." Melinda placed a hand on Leo's shoulder. "Why would I *not* tell him?"

"Tell him *what*?" Leo snapped. "What're you two yammering about?"

"Just that Natalie planned for you to enroll in Stanford Law School this fall," Melinda supplied.

"*What?*" Leo turned to scowl at both of them. "How is that even possible?"

"Tell him, Tia." Melinda nodded to her.

"I'd rather not."

"Come on." Leo's tone softened. "What did you hear, Tia?"

"It wasn't my intention to eavesdrop." She quickly explained her post by the dining room that night. "I couldn't help but overhear something."

"Out with it," Leo commanded.

Tia repeated the disturbing conversation. "I know Natalie meant it as a good thing," she finally said. "It was supposed to be a wedding gift. A surprise."

"Yeah, right." Leo whacked the wheel with the heel of his hand.

"I need to go back down," Tia said suddenly.

Melinda grabbed her by the elbow. "Tell him about the seasickness secret first," she urged.

"The *seasickness secret*?" Leo scowled.

"Come on," Melinda told Tia. "Leo deserves to know the whole truth and nothing but the truth."

"Fine." Tia looked at Leo, knowing she would sound like a tattletale and that she could be making an enemy here. But maybe it didn't matter. "Natalie told me that she's been keeping her seasickness problem a secret from you. It's not just a one-time thing. She gets horribly seasick whenever she sets foot on a boat. That's why she doesn't like being on your houseboat for more than a few minutes. It's what happened in the rowboat the day you guys came here and she said she had food poisoning. It's why she avoids this boat like the plague. Even when she takes Dramamine, like she did tonight, she can still get horribly ill." She turned to Melinda. "There. Are you happy now?"

"He has a right to know."

"Yeah, but I don't know why I have to be the one to tell him." Tia reached for the door, this time without being stopped. "Excuse me." As she went back down, she felt slightly betrayed by Melinda for dragging her into Leo's mess. Oh, she understood why Melinda wanted her brother to know the truth, but why force Tia to be the bearer of such negative news? That didn't seem right. Especially if and when Natalie and Leo got back together. Because despite Leo's claim that it was over, Tia was not convinced.

Tia was grateful for a nonworking weekend. It was a relief not to cross paths with Leo for a couple of days. When she "accidentally" slept in on Sunday instead of riding her bike to church like she'd told Melinda she planned to do, she didn't even feel guilty. Well, not much anyway.

When the workweek began again on Monday, there was plenty to keep her occupied—and distracted. This was the week to get the galley fully assembled, and she planned to be on hand to supervise every step of the way. When she wasn't in the galley, she was in the stateroom, putting the finishing touches on the menus so she could hand them over to Melinda, who would then come up with some designs for

Julie to choose from, plus add them to the website. Not only that, but Tia had waitstaff and kitchen crew applicants to interview and hire. There was a lot to get done and not a lot of time to do it in.

By the end of the week, the *Pacific Pearl* was almost completely transformed. The galley was finished and functional, with cabinets stocked and ready. The dining room was all set, complete with a bar on one end and an upright piano on the other. The windows were sparkling clean, the decks were shiny and bright, the heads were in great condition. All in all, the *Pacific Pearl* was shipshape.

Except for the captain. Tia attributed Leo's taciturn attitude to last weekend's blowout with Natalie. It didn't take a mind reader to know he was not okay with it. The best Tia could do was try to not cross paths with him.

On Saturday morning, Tia was enjoying being alone on the boat. As if playing house, she went around sweeping up the last of the building debris, dusting and polishing, and basically just admiring the amazing transformation of the *Pacific Pearl*. The plan was for Julie and Roland to come see the final results and enjoy a private dinner cruise with several of their closest friends tonight. The crew and galley staff would be minimal, but Tia wanted to ensure that everything was as perfect as possible. After a week of foggy days, it even looked like the weather was cooperating, because the mist seemed to be melting away by midday.

"Hello?"

Tia strained her ears to hear what sounded like a female voice.

"Anybody aboard?"

Tia stuck her head out of the dining room, where she'd

been putting small flower arrangements on the four tables she'd chosen for tonight's dinner—and there was Natalie, standing on the dock with a perplexed expression.

"Oh, hi, Tia." Natalie waved eagerly, smiling. "Is Leo around?"

"Not right now."

Natalie's smile evaporated. "Do you know where he is?"

"No." Tia shook her head.

"Oh."

Tia waited for Natalie to say something . . . like good-bye. But she just stood there looking slightly lost and totally out of place on the scruffy dock in her white linen pantsuit. "Is there anything I can help you with?" Tia asked in a slightly formal tone, almost as if she was waiting on a customer.

"Please, Tia!" Natalie's voice broke as if she were on the verge of tears. "Can you come out here and talk to me?"

Tia's heart softened as she crossed over the gangway to the dock. "What's up?"

"It's Leo. He's avoiding me."

Tia's sympathy faded. "Well . . . you guys broke up, re-member? In fact, you're the one who pulled the plug."

"I know. But I was so upset. I said things I didn't mean and I—"

"Look!" Tia held up her hands to stop her. "I am not going to get in the middle of this—whatever it is. This is *not* my problem."

"No, of course not. It's just that Leo is ignoring my texts and my calls and he's not home and—"

"You're not listening, Natalie. I'm not going to get involved in this. It's not fair for you to ask me."

"But I thought you were my friend."

"I'm Leo's friend too." Tia stepped onto the gangplank. "I'm also Leo's co-worker, and I think that trumps my friendship with you."

"But I don't know who to talk to."

"Maybe Melinda—"

"She's avoiding me too."

"I'm sorry, Natalie. I honestly am. But there's nothing I can do for you. Maybe you should check with Leo's parents. Don't you work with his dad—"

"Yes, and Jim is as flummoxed as I am. I told him the whole story, and he doesn't understand why Leo is being so stubborn and hardhearted."

"Seriously?" Tia went back down the gangplank, holding her forefinger in the air. "Let's talk about stubborn hardheartedness. How about the fact that you kept your seasickness troubles a secret from Leo? Or that you were conspiring to enroll Leo in law school without his knowledge or approval? Or that you never intended to live on the houseboat with him after you got married? Those things all seem pretty stubborn and hardhearted to me."

"To me too!"

Tia spun around to see Leo coming across the deck of the boat toward them. What was he doing there?

"You lied to me, Tia!" Natalie spat out. "You said Leo wasn't here."

"I didn't know he was here," Tia declared.

"I get it!" Natalie yelled. "I see what's going on now. Good grief, how could I have been so naïve. You've been after Leo right from the start, haven't you, Tia? No wonder it all went sideways on me. It's because of you, isn't it?" She pointed at her with fury in her eyes. "Tell me the truth, Tia!"

Feeling like she was being cross-examined on the witness stand, Tia speechlessly backed away from her, moving toward the boat.

"That's enough, Natalie." Leo came over to stand behind Tia, blocking the gangway and her access to the boat. "You can't turn Tia into your whipping boy. All she's done is try to be a good friend—"

"To you maybe. But she's stabbed me in the back, hasn't she?"

"That's ridiculous. But if you insist on hashing this all out right now, tell me the truth. Wasn't everything Tia just said about you true? You hid your seasickness from me. You never planned to live on the houseboat. You were secretly enrolling me into Stanford. You were doing everything—from pushing for the engagement and then a quick wedding—all just to have your way. My feelings never even mattered to you, did they, Natalie? It's always just been about you."

"I can't help that I get seasick," she said in a pitiful tone. "It's not fair to hold that against me, Leo."

"Except that you kept it from me."

"I was going to tell you."

"When?" he demanded. "On our honeymoon? Right after you told me your plans for me to give up boats and head off to law school? Or after you informed me that I had to give up the houseboat to live in the city? When?"

"Excuse me." Tia pushed past Leo and ran into the dining room. Still stinging from Natalie's accusations, words that were closer to the truth than anyone realized, she just wanted to get away from this—all of it! She didn't think she could stand one more harsh word from them arguing like that. She went to the stateroom, and with a heart that was pounding hard, she closed and locked the door, bursting into tears. It was just like this ten years ago when her parents were fighting and bickering, trying to put her in the middle of their battles. She had hated it then, and she hated it even more now.

25

Tia jumped when she heard someone knocking on her door. "Who is it?" she demanded as she grabbed a tissue to wipe her tears.

"It's me," Leo said. "Can I talk to you?"

She let out a long sigh, then barely cracked open the door. "What?" she asked in a flat tone.

"What's wrong?" He peered at her with a furrowed brow. "Why have you been crying?"

"I—I just couldn't stand it, not for one more minute," she told him. "You guys fighting like that, with me in the middle of everything. It reminded me of my parents, back before they got divorced. I just couldn't take it." Her tears returned.

Leo pushed open the door and took her into his arms. "I'm sorry, Tia. It was wrong for us to do that to you. You shouldn't have been forced to hear all that stupid nonsense— or to be caught in the middle of it. I don't even know how that keeps happening with you, but I know you're right. You have been in the middle . . . a lot. And I'm sorry about that. And sorry you got hurt."

"It's just that it felt like a trigger," she confessed as he held her. "Like it detonated something inside of me, something I probably never dealt with properly before." She took in a jagged breath and stepped away from him. "Maybe it's a good thing. Maybe it's something I need to face up to."

"I hate that I'm the one who forced it on you, though. You've been nothing but good to me, Tia. I really value you and our friendship."

She sniffed. "Yeah. Me too."

"Forgive me for that mess with Natalie. Those things she said about you being responsible for breaking us up were ludicrous. I know you would never do that."

She sighed and shook her head. *Not on purpose, anyway.*

"I think Natalie understands that it's over between us. The engagement is off."

She looked into his eyes. "Are you sure, Leo? I mean, that it's what you want? Even if Natalie—"

"There's nothing Natalie can do that will change how I feel, Tia." He gave a crooked smile. "To be honest, I feel like I dodged a bullet."

"You don't love Natalie?"

"Not like that. Not enough to marry her." He took Tia's hand, pulling her out into the dining room. "I feel awkward having this conversation in there," he said as he released her hand. "But I want you to know the truth about me and Natalie. Do you think you can handle it, or will this make you feel like I'm putting you in the middle again?"

She considered this. "I'd actually like to know—I mean, the truth about you and Natalie."

He pulled out a dining room chair. "Care to sit?"

"Thanks."

"Natalie and I have been friends for our entire lives. You know how she went through her awkward era, the teen years. You saw how insecure she was during sailboat camp. Anyway, I was her friend throughout all of that. Then she went to college, and when she came back a year ago, well, she looked, uh . . ."

"Gorgeous."

"Right. Of course, our families started pushing us together. Natalie started working at the firm, and my dad thinks she's the greatest thing since sliced bread. So Nat and I started dating around Christmas. Not really seriously—at least I didn't think so. But it got to be fairly steady—kind of expected. To be honest, I wasn't quite sure where it was going, or if I really wanted it to go anywhere. But my dad was so pleased about it, and everyone in our families seemed to think we made a perfect match. I guess I allowed myself to get sucked in." He peered curiously at her. "You really don't mind me dumping all this on you?"

"I actually appreciate it, Leo. It's helping me to understand some things that I didn't really get."

"Anyway, like I said, I did love Natalie—although in hindsight I know it was more like the way I love my sister. But the truth is, I'm a guy and I'm human, and I gotta admit that Natalie's new and improved appearance kind of turned my head at first. I honestly wasn't ready for an engagement, though. If she hadn't pressed me that day—that same day that you arrived—I never would've gone there." He locked eyes with her. "Especially after getting reacquainted with you, Tia. I never would've proposed to Natalie."

Tia felt a rush of emotions. "What do you mean?"

"I mean, in a way, Natalie was right about one thing today. You're a big part of the reason my relationship with Natalie went sideways. But it wasn't your fault, Tia. You never did anything to come between Nat and me. Not intentionally anyway. It was simply who you are, the way you are . . . that drove a huge wedge between Nat and me."

"Oh?"

"I tried several times to have a serious conversation with Natalie. I kept hinting to her that I wanted to slow things down, but the more I put on the brakes, the faster she seemed to want it to go. I felt like I was on a runaway train. And I had no idea about the things she was keeping from me. I wish I'd found out sooner, I would've broken up weeks ago. As it was, I was just trying to find the right moment, the right way. I wanted to let her down gently. Didn't want to break her heart. As crazy as it felt at the time, I was actually relieved when she blew me off on the Fourth of July."

"Wow . . . I didn't really know that. I mean, sometimes I'd think you were getting trapped into something. But then I'd spend time with Natalie, and aside from the stuff she was keeping from you, she seemed so sweet and nice and everything."

"She is . . . for the most part. But she's a little spoiled too."

"Melinda told me some things," Tia confessed. "She was concerned."

"Yeah, Melinda had been trying to warn me I was making a mistake."

"You're really glad it's over with?" Tia asked.

His face broke into a wide smile—a smile that reminded her of the boy she'd met on the sailboat ten years ago. "I don't even know how to explain it. I feel like I just got released from a life sentence."

Tia laughed.

"I didn't really want to overwhelm you. Especially after hearing how stressed out you were from getting caught in the middle of my mess with Natalie. But I really do care about you, Tia. I want you to understand what was going on."

"Thanks." She smiled. "I do have one question."

"What?"

"How did you sneak onto the boat without me knowing it?"

"The rowboat."

She nodded. "Oh, yeah. Of course."

"I'm glad I took you girls by surprise. It was good to hear you standing up to Natalie like that, Tia."

"How was she? I mean, when she left? Was she still furious?"

"The good news is, she knows that I meant what I said. That it's over. I'm sure she's upset to find out she isn't getting her way with this. But she'll get over it in time. From what I've heard, there's a guy at the firm who's been pursuing her. Conrad Gibson."

"Conrad!" Tia exclaimed. "That's the guy at the engagement party, the one who was a Stanford alumni that she wanted to write an endorsement letter for you to get into law school."

Leo laughed. "Well, hopefully Nat and her alumni friend will become a couple. That would be excellent."

Tia didn't know what to say now.

"Have I overwhelmed you?"

"To be honest, a little."

Leo slowly stood. "Well, I'm going to give you your space. I know that emotions have been running high around here today. I'm sure we all need a break."

"Thanks." Tia's emotions were still running high, but she agreed with Leo. She did need a break. There was a lot to sort out. Especially if she was understanding him correctly. "There's a lot to do today." She stood, facing him. "Lots to get ready for tonight's mini dinner cruise. I still have prep work to do."

"I need to take the boat for refueling and to fill the water tank and empty the holding tanks." He looked at his watch. "Adam should be here soon."

"Adam?" She was staring into his eyes now, being reminded of how much like the ocean they looked.

"My first mate."

"Oh, yeah. That's right." For a moment they both just stood there gazing at each other, and Tia almost wondered if he was going to kiss her. To her relief he just tipped his head and went on his way. The truth was, she was not ready for kissing just yet. She still needed to process his explanation regarding Natalie. Perhaps to even savor the idea that Leo really cared about her. Did that mean he loved her? Or would this turn out how it had with his last fiancée? Only time would tell. She didn't plan to rush things. She didn't want to fall into the Natalie trap and push him. No, she would just bide her time . . . wait and see . . . take what comes.

As she worked in the kitchen, she hummed happily to herself. When she felt the engines starting, she got such a sense of peace and satisfaction that it nearly brought tears of happiness to her eyes. She felt like her life was truly on track, like she was exactly where she was meant to be. No matter what lay ahead, it seemed clear that the tide was changing. She felt exceedingly hopeful.

As she sliced a red onion, she suddenly remembered how her hopes had risen before, only to be dashed later on. How many times had she been deluded and disappointed when it came to Leo? Hopefully that wasn't going to happen again. Just the same, she was determined to go carefully. No running ahead.

"I'm here," called a female voice from up in the dining room.

"Haley," Tia called back eagerly. "I'm down in the galley." She'd hired this young woman as her sous chef a few days ago. Tonight would be their first time to work together. "You're early," she said as Haley came into the galley.

"Yeah. I was so excited to see everything all put together, I decided to come early. The dining room looks fabulous." Haley looked around. "So does the galley. Wow. This is great."

"I only set two of the tables upstairs," Tia said. "But we'll be seating four tables tonight, so maybe you can get the other two. Like I said on the phone, we're not having wait-staff tonight. It's just you and me. But it's only sixteen guests, so I think we'll be fine."

"You're serving everyone the same thing?"

"Yes. Just like a regular dinner party—all friends of Julie and Roland, the owners of the boat." Tia smiled. "No paying guests means no tips tonight."

"No problem."

Julie and Roland arrived at 6:00, taking time to look around and admire the completed renovations. "Everything looks beautiful," Julie told Tia. "Amazingly beautiful."

"I can hardly believe this is the same boat my parents had," Roland admitted. "What a transformation."

"I cleaned up the stateroom," Tia told him. "If you get tired, feel free to take a break in there."

"I'm actually feeling pretty strong," Roland said. "But thanks."

"There's our captain," Julie said happily. "How are you, Leo?"

"Doing really well, thanks." He smiled at both of them.

"I heard your news . . . the broken engagement," Roland said quietly. "I'm not sure what to say. Condolences?"

"More like congratulations," Leo told him.

Roland blinked. "You're serious?"

"Totally. I feel like I dodged a bullet."

"Oh, well, marriage isn't *that bad*." Roland slipped his arm around Julie.

"Not when it's with the right woman." Leo grinned at Tia, making her cheeks grow warm.

"That's for sure and for certain." Roland beamed at him. "Makes all the difference in the world."

Tia turned to Julie. "Do you and Roland still want to play host and handle the drinks? My sous chef Haley is here, and she's experienced as a bartender too."

"We'll handle it. You girls just focus on dinner," Julie said.

"What are we having for dinner?" Roland asked.

"Crab-crusted salmon, risotto, roasted veggies, and a few other surprises."

Roland's eyes lit up. "I'm salivating."

"I'll send Haley up with some hors d'oeuvres for you guys to enjoy on the foredeck," Tia told him. "And I chilled a pinot grigio for you."

"Lovely."

She turned to Julie. "We'll bring the rest of the hors

d'oeuvres up before 7:00, shortly before the guests arrive. Those can be served on the foredeck too, as long as it's warm enough out there."

"Perfect." Julie sighed. "This is a day I've been waiting for."

"We'll sail at 7:30," Leo told her.

"This is so exciting." Julie grabbed Roland's hand. "Isn't it?"

He rubbed his beard with twinkling eyes. "It really is."

Tia felt indescribably happy as she returned to the galley. After all their hard work, all the ups and downs of the last month, it seemed that they were finally able to enjoy the fruit of their labors. As she put the finishing touches on the hors d'oeuvre plate, she said a silent prayer for Julie and Roland, asking for a special blessing for them and their friends this evening.

Before long the boat was moving through the bay, and Tia was loading a tray full of gorgeous salad plates into the dumbwaiter for Haley to serve to the guests. The plan was to text each other by phone, something Tia had devised, to save trips up and down the stairs between the galley and dining room. So far, it was working.

By 8:30, the guests were still enjoying their entrées, with Haley in attendance. During this lull, Tia decided to take a dinner up to Leo. Adam had already made a visit to the galley for his own food.

"Wow, that looks fabulous." Leo stared down at the salad and dinner plates in her hands. "But where's yours?"

"I already ate." She smiled as she set it on the counter, extracting silverware and napkin from a pocket of her chef's jacket. "I thought you might like this."

Leo reached over, she thought for the food—but instead

he wrapped an arm around her waist, pulling her to him. "I'd rather have this," he teased.

She laughed, enjoying the closeness of him.

"I like your chef's outfit." He grinned down at her.

"Not very feminine, though."

"I wouldn't say that." He touched her cheek. "Everything you do is feminine, Tia."

"Oh . . ." She turned and looked out the window into the bay. It wasn't nearly as crowded as it had been on the Fourth of July. "Looks fairly calm and quiet out there."

He nodded. "Yeah. It's a nice evening for a cruise." He turned her back toward him. "Remember that other time we were looking out over the San Francisco Bay . . . ten years ago?"

"Yeah." She felt a rush of excitement. Just like ten years ago, he pulled her toward him and kissed her—only this kiss was more. So much more.

"Oh my." She caught her breath as she stepped away. "I guess I shouldn't distract you. Wouldn't want to cause some nautical disaster."

He laughed. "That wouldn't be good."

"It's so beautiful out there," she said as he started to eat. "I can understand why this is a job you wouldn't get tired of." She looked at him. "Or would you?"

"I don't know." He turned the wheel a bit. "Sometimes I think it would be fun to captain a boat to more exotic places. Maybe even around the world."

"That would be fun."

He looked at her. "You'd like that?"

"Absolutely." She nodded. "I mean, I wouldn't want to leave Julie and Roland too soon. But I'd love to cook on a boat that was traveling farther. That would be amazing."

He pointed to the crab-crusted salmon he'd just forked into. "Now *that* is amazing." He shook his head as he chewed. "So are you."

"Thanks." She smiled shyly. "I should get back down to serve dessert."

"And what might that be?"

"Just cream tarts topped with fresh berries."

"Sounds good to me."

"I'll bring you one later."

"Thanks." He reached over to gently touch her cheek. "For everything."

Despite her kitchen clogs, her feet felt as light as fairy wings as she went down the stairs to the galley. She couldn't remember a time when she'd ever felt this happy. Although it was hard to imagine that life could go on like this for longer than just a few perfectly idyllic moments, she felt hopeful. Maybe it could.

26

The next two weeks were busy and blissful. Leo and Tia and their crew fell into a harmonious rhythm after several slightly stressful dinner cruises. Fortunately, they were "special offer" cruises that Julie had booked for a reduced fare, and the guests had been gracious and understanding, promising to come back again after they got all the kinks worked out.

By the end of the fourth dinner cruise, Tia felt like the kinks were mostly out. By the fifth cruise, she felt the kitchen staff and wait-staff were working together like a well-oiled machine. Or nearly. Although it was hard and intense work, it was rewarding to see the happy guests at the end of a cruise. The tips were good, which in turn brought out the best performances from her staff. They were on their way!

Tia chatted on the phone with her dad once a week, usually on Saturday mornings. She eventually hinted to him that she might've found romance. She was hesitant to say too much, worried she might put a jinx on it. But she could tell Dad was happy to hear this news. She suspected it might even encourage him to get his wedding date with Deanna nailed down. At least she hoped so. Sometimes it seemed the only thing holding him back was his concern for her, as if he was unwilling to be happily committed unless she was.

In their time off during the non-cruise days of Monday and Tuesday, Leo remained attentive and interested. So much so that Tia felt mixed emotions. On one hand, she loved it, but on the other hand, she was slightly concerned over what other people might think. After all, he'd barely broken things off with Natalie. She didn't want to be perceived as "the other woman." For that reason she was trying to keep their activities limited to chores around the boat or just hanging around the waterfront—including a lot of fishing from Leo's little rowboat, which was surprisingly fun.

"Let's spend the day in the city today," Leo said on Monday morning as they sat together on the deck, having coffee and the sticky cinnamon rolls that Leo had supplied.

"The city?" Immediately Tia imagined crossing paths with Natalie or someone else from the law firm, and despite the unlikelihood of this, it made her uneasy.

"I know you wanted to continue your tour of Golden Gate Park, and it's supposed to be a gorgeous day today," he said enticingly. "What about the Embarcadero? You said you wanted to see the new restaurants there."

"I do. That sounds wonderful," she confessed.

"Then let's do it."

"I don't know." She took a slow sip of coffee.

"Why not?"

"It probably sounds silly, but it's been such a short time since the breakup with you and Natalie," she admitted, "that it just makes me uncomfortable."

"It's been more than three weeks," Leo pointed out.

"I know . . . but according to Melinda, your father is still getting over it. How would it look to him if he knew you were already, uh, kind of involved with someone else?"

Leo shrugged. "I'm not sure I care."

"Well, I do."

"Just so you know, my mom is already aware that I'm 'involved with someone else.'" He grinned. "And she's all for it. Apparently you made a super impression on her that day you borrowed her kitchen."

"You mom is a delight."

"When do I get to take you home for dinner? I mean a dinner you don't cook."

Tia sighed as she twisted her claddagh ring. She still had the heart pointing away from her and suddenly realized that its meaning no longer applied to her. Her heart, as far as she was concerned, was taken. She slipped off the ring, turned it around, and was just putting it on when he stopped her.

"What're you doing?"

"Just turning it around."

"Why?"

"Just because." She grinned at him.

"Because it was upside down?" He held out his hand. "Can I see it for a minute?"

"Sure." She handed the ring over, letting him examine it and even slip it onto his pinky finger, although he could only get it halfway down.

"Pretty." He handed it back to her, watching as she slipped it on with the heart's tip pointing toward her now.

"Anyway, call me prudent, but I just think maybe we should

290

give our relationship another week or so before we go public," she told him. "A month sounds appropriate."

"Since Nat and I were only engaged about that long, a month should be sufficient, eh?"

She nodded. "I think so."

"When the month is up, where would you like to go?"

She thought about this. "I'd really like to wander around Fisherman's Wharf."

"It's a date." He grinned. "In the meantime, I can't complain about this." He waved out to the bay. "Want to go fishing again today?"

"Absolutely." She laughed. "You've got me hooked."

"What a girl!"

"Well, that fish we caught last week was pretty fabulous," she reminded him. "In fact, it gave me an idea. We should talk to Julie about offering fishing dinner cruises. The guests could reel in their suppers."

"Brilliant!" He stood and stretched. "Guess I'll go get the gear ready."

She picked up their coffee cups. "I'll go get myself ready."

On Saturday morning, as Tia was receiving a food order for that evening's cruise, she spotted a figure in the distance, striding down the dock toward the boat. Tia peered curiously at the woman in the light blue dress and suddenly realized it was Natalie. Tempted to duck back into the dining room as if she hadn't seen her, Tia froze in place. *Why was she here?* As badly as she wanted to make herself scarce, she knew that hiding was childish. She made a meek wave. What did Natalie want? Probably Leo. Fortunately, he hadn't arrived yet.

The last time Tia had seen Natalie, she'd been enraged at Leo, and she'd pretty much accused Tia of stealing her fiancé. Really, Natalie hadn't been too far from the truth, although Tia would insist no stealing had been involved.

"Hey Tia," Natalie called out. "Got a minute?"

"Uh . . . yeah." Tia asked the delivery guy to put the boxes in the galley as she went down the gangplank to stand in front of Natalie. "What's up?"

"I've been wanting to talk to you," Natalie said a bit sullenly.

"Well, here I am." Tia braced herself, almost wishing she'd stayed on the boat.

"I've been rethinking some things I said to you a few weeks ago. It's no secret that I was extremely agitated that night—you know, after getting so seasick and everything. Anyway, I'm afraid I insinuated that you were the reason Leo and I broke up." She made a weak smile. "I realize that was wrong, Tia. I'd like to apologize."

Tia blinked in surprise. "Really?"

"Yes. That was very inappropriate and immature on my part. I'm truly sorry."

"You were distraught and upset," Tia said gently. "I can understand."

"Maybe so, but it didn't give me the right to lash out at you like that."

Tia felt torn now. On one hand, she wanted to just forgive Natalie, forget it, and move on . . . but on the other hand, what would Natalie think when she discovered that Tia and Leo actually were starting a relationship? It wasn't as if they could keep this news from her. Especially considering that Leo's mom and sister were already in the loop.

"I hope you'll accept my apology."

"Of course." Tia bit her lip, nodding.

"Thank you." Natalie looked around the boat, almost as if she hoped to spy Leo.

"He's not here yet," Tia said. "At least I don't think so. I haven't seen him."

"Oh, well, I sort of wanted to apologize to him too."

"Uh . . . right." Tia took in a deep breath. "Actually, I'm glad you're here, Natalie. I, uh, I have something to tell you too."

"What?" Natalie's brow creased as she pushed her sunglasses on top of her head, studying Tia with unblinking blue eyes.

Tia wished she'd had some time to prepare her words. This wasn't easy to say—and was something that could be easily taken wrong. "Well, it has to do with Leo," she began. "And me."

Natalie stiffened a bit.

"You need to know that I never did anything wrong. Nothing I regret. Not while you and Leo were together. But the truth is, I was interested in him—"

"*What?*"

"Just hear me out, please, Natalie. I'm not sure if you remember this or not, but I was at the sailing camp with you and Leo ten years ago."

"Yeah. I didn't recall you at first, but Leo told me about that."

"I doubt he mentioned that he kissed me."

"Leo kissed you?" Natalie looked shocked.

"On the sailing trip. I was only sixteen at the time. It was my first kiss—it kind of rocked my world—and I always remembered it. So when Leo picked me up at the airport last month, well, I was totally stunned. I had no idea that he was my aunt's boat captain or that she even knew him. I couldn't believe our paths had crossed again. I mean, it was ten years later, so I was pretty ecstatic." Tia sighed. "Then I found out he was engaged, and I was devastated. When I met you at dinner and I saw you were so beautiful, so perfect, I realized it was hopeless. Leo was taken."

"But if we hadn't been—"

"Listen to me, Natalie. Even though I was brokenhearted, I swear to you, I *never* did anything to steal Leo from you. Not intentionally, anyway. I tried to distance myself the whole time. But both you guys kept drawing me in, trying to make me a friend when all I wanted was to set some boundaries. Let me tell you, it wasn't easy being around you guys all that time either. I was pretty miserable."

"Seriously?" Natalie just stared at her.

"I didn't really want to tell you," Tia confessed. "But I think you have the right to know. And I hope you won't hold it against me."

"Wow." Natalie slowly shook her head. "I had no idea."

Tia made an uneasy smile. "I hope we can still be friends."

"Friends? You still want to be my friend?" Natalie stared curiously at Tia.

Tia had actually given this a lot of thought. Because Leo's and Natalie's families were such close friends, she'd hoped that somehow she'd be able to restore her friendship with Natalie. "I know it might take some time, but I still hope we can be friends."

"I do too," Leo called as he came down the gangplank to join them. Tia hadn't realized he was already here. He must've come on the rowboat today.

"Leo." Natalie scowled at him. "Were you listening to *everything?*"

"I only heard part of it, Nat. But I agree with Tia. I'd like to preserve our friendship too."

Natalie shrugged. "Yes, that would be the grown-up thing to do. I am trying to take the high road . . . to be an adult."

"Natalie came here to apologize to me," Tia explained to Leo.

"As long as you're here, I might as well apologize to you too, Leo," Natalie said in a slightly stilted way. "I'm sorry for the way I deceived you. That was wrong. And I'm sorry for getting so angry at you that night . . . for making you look like a jerk just because I was seasick and you needed to stay with the boat. I realize that wasn't fair. Please forgive me."

"I do forgive you," he said eagerly. "I hope you'll forgive me too."

"For what?" she asked curiously.

"For getting engaged when I obviously wasn't ready."

"Oh . . ." She nodded with a knowing expression.

"That was a stupid move on my part, Natalie. I don't even have a good excuse. Except that I just wasn't thinking clearly."

"Well, don't forget how I pressured you." She made a sheepish smile.

"Anyway, I'm really sorry for hurting you. I hope we can still be friends again someday."

She sighed. "Yeah . . . so do I."

They all just stood there for a long minute, then Tia stretched her arms out toward both of them. "Group hug?" she said hopefully. There on the dock, the three of them actually hugged. Who'da thought?

When Natalie stepped back, she tilted her head to one

side, pointing an accusatory finger at the two of them. "Tell the truth—are you guys a couple now?"

"Not exactly," Tia said. "I mean, I wanted to wait until—"

"Yes, we're a couple," Leo declared as he slipped an arm around Tia's waist. "No point in beating around the bush about it."

"I just didn't want to rush things," Tia explained to Natalie. "For your sake, you know?"

"It's okay." Natalie held up her hands. "It's probably time for everyone to move on." She glanced at her watch. "Including me." She gave a big bright smile as she smoothed a windblown strand of blonde hair away from her eyes. "Later, kids." Just like that, she turned and strode back up the dock, looking just as poised and graceful as if she were walking down a red carpet or fashion runway. The delivery guy who was just coming down the gangplank let out a low, appreciative whistle as he watched her.

"She really is beautiful," Tia said quietly as the delivery guy got into his truck.

"Not as beautiful as you," Leo whispered in Tia's ear.

"What?" Tia asked doubtfully.

"I mean it." He leaned over to kiss her. "You have no idea how gorgeous you are, do you?" He gently tugged her ponytail. "Just one more thing I totally love about you."

She smiled. "Thanks."

27

After the air was cleared with Natalie, Tia was much more open to real dating. As promised, their first official date was an afternoon on Fisherman's Wharf the following Tuesday. They started with a walking crab cocktail, followed by a late lunch at Alioto's. It wasn't as much about the food as it was about the location and history. Tia was just letting it all soak in. Even more than the location, it was about being with Leo.

"Now what?" Leo asked as they exited the restaurant.

"I just want to be like a tourist," Tia told Leo as they strolled down Pier 39.

"Then we should go to K-Dock to look at the sea lions," he told her.

The fog was just coming in as they watched the sea lions lounging around on the dock below them. "I hope this doesn't spoil your lunch," Leo said. "I mean, the smells and sounds aren't exactly appetizing."

"I think this is great. I love it." She laughed as she pointed out a large sea lion squeezing in between a couple of slumbering sea lions, causing one of them to roll off the dock and into the water. "Now that is a rude awakening."

Because the air was getting chilly, Tia asked if they could stop in a tourist shop. "I want a San Francisco sweatshirt," she explained. After trying on several, they bought matching ones, wearing them out of the store.

"Now we really look like tourists," Leo said as they walked.

"Good." Tia chuckled to imagine what someone as fashionable as Natalie would say to see the two of them like this. Not that she cared.

"You know what I'd like to do?" Leo said suddenly.

"What?"

"Go to the Wax Museum," he said eagerly. "I haven't been there since I was a kid."

"Yes!" she exclaimed. "Perfect."

They spent the next hour holding hands as they perused the exhibits in the Wax Museum. By the time they left, Tia felt very much like a twelve-year-old again.

For the next few weeks, they spent some of their days off exploring different parts of San Francisco and some of their time just hanging together or fishing. It all seemed idyllic, and sometimes Tia felt she was living out a dream. The more she got to know Leo, the more she believed they were truly suited for each other. Oh, it wasn't that they liked all the same things. For instance, she loved Chinese food, but he wasn't a fan. Even so, he didn't mind going to Chinatown with her. In return, she didn't complain when he ordered from the American side of the menu.

They also spent some time with Julie and Roland, as well as with Leo's family. Julie and Roland were completely supportive of this "new" relationship, but Leo's dad was still being a little standoffish. At least that was how Tia felt, although Melinda assured her it was just his way. Fortunately, Leo's mother made up for him. Joy went out of her way to welcome Tia with open arms whenever Leo brought her home.

All in all, Tia felt that as a couple they were not only having a lot of fun but making real progress in getting acquainted. There were moments when she half expected Leo to pop the question—although she still felt it was too soon. No way did she want him to rush into anything. Not like he'd done with Natalie. She would never say or do anything to push or pressure him, but she knew their relationship was about as good and solid as it could be. And it was wonderful!

A few days after Labor Day, Julie called a business meeting with Leo and Tia. They met in the dining room with coffee and blueberry muffins, and Julie announced that due to a lack of reservations going into the fall, they would only be offering two dinner cruises a week, on Fridays and Saturdays. "Only one dinner per night," she told them. "No more early bird dinners and sunset dinners."

"I sort of figured that was coming," Tia admitted.

"I suppose I didn't fully consider this last spring. I mean, the seasonal nature of the dinner cruises and how that might impact employees. I was so focused on getting the business started—and then Roland got sick."

"Well, we all knew this was going to be learning by trial and error," Tia reminded her.

"And we haven't done too badly," Leo added.

"Well, I'm sorry I didn't think it through better," Julie said. "I realize that probably means some of your staff and crew will have to look for more permanent employment, or maybe get second jobs. I do want to keep both of you on your regular salary for the off-season if I can. I still need to go over the books a bit more."

"I was asked about captaining for an Alcatraz cruise line," Leo told her. "It's just day work and wouldn't interfere with the dinner cruises. Would you mind if I looked into it?"

"No, of course not," Julie told him.

"I can always quit that if I need to," he said. "I mean, when the season picks up again. Or next summer."

"That's good to know." Julie turned to Tia. "Will two dinners a week feel like enough work for you?"

Tia shrugged. "It's been so busy this summer that it sounds sort of good, right now anyway."

"Well, I'll understand if you need to look for something else too." Julie frowned. "But I won't be happy to think I've complicated your lives like that. So that you both need two jobs to get by, I mean."

Tia smiled. "Say, we might be able to focus on booking some more special events—anniversaries, weddings, birthdays, bar mitzvahs, and whatnot. That could help fill the calendar in a bit."

"That's true." Julie brightened. "The more established we get, the more I expect we'll have bookings. Don't you think?"

"Absolutely." Tia nodded. "Our guests seemed to have enjoyed themselves. Hopefully they'll spread the word."

"I'll give you both a copy of the off-season budget. You can do as you feel best with your staff and crew," Julie said. "But by mid-October, I expect we'll be working our off-season schedule."

After Julie left, Leo turned to Tia. "I have something to show you," he said mysteriously. "Come with me."

"Okay."

He led her outside and across the foredeck, taking her out to the bow. "Remember the first time we stood together in the bowsprit of the sailboat?"

She laughed. "Of course."

He leaned over to kiss her. "Good."

"How could I forget?"

He nodded with a hard to read expression.

She peered curiously at him. Something about this felt unsettling. Almost as if he was about to say something important—like *good-bye*. "You said you had something to show me." She peered out over the water, which was gray-blue and enveloped in fog. "What is it?"

Leo reached out to take her hands in his and then got down on one knee. "Tia D'Amico," he said in a serious tone, "I love you with my whole heart and I want to spend the rest of my life with you."

"Wh—what?"

"Tia, I'm asking you, will you please marry me?"

Tia was dumbstruck. And happy. And speechless.

"I know this is sudden." He was still on one knee. "But I've given it lots of thought. And when you know it's right, you *know* it's right. Believe me, Tia, I know this is right. Will you marry me? Will you come live on my houseboat with me?"

With tear-filled eyes, Tia bent down to hug him. "Yes!" she exclaimed. "I will marry you, Leo. You name the time and the place and I will become your wife."

He stood, wrapping his arms around her and pulling her close for a nice long kiss that made her feel like her knees were melting. "To seal the deal." Leo reached into his shorts pocket, extracting a small hand-carved wooden box. "This is for you."

She opened the lid and there, nestled in dark blue velvet, was the most magnificent ring she had ever laid eyes upon. Two stones—one pale blue and one darker—entwined in wavelike bands of platinum. It was perfect.

"How did you do this?" she asked as happy tears trickled down her cheeks. "This is it. The ring I dreamt about as a girl."

"I know."

"But it's really it. It looks just like I imagined it would. How did you—"

"Remember that time you told me you'd have to marry a guy who was born in December?"

She stared at him. "December?"

He grinned as he pointed to his chest. "December eleventh. My stone is blue topaz. Yours is aquamarine. They look great together, don't you think?"

"Beautiful." She shook her head in wonder. "But where did you find this ring?"

"I had it made." He lifted it from the box. "Let's see if it fits."

Tia was dumbfounded as Leo slid the new ring onto her left hand ring finger. "It fits. How did you know what size I wore?"

He pointed to the claddagh ring on her right hand. "Remember when I tried that on my pinky? I just told the jewelry artist and he had me try on ring blanks until it felt right on my pinky. He assured me he could adjust the ring if you need it."

She stared down at it, shaking her head. "No, it fits perfectly."

"You really like it?"

"I love it." She looked up at him. "But not nearly as much as I love you."

"I love you too." He kissed her again.

Going Ten Knots, They Tied the Knot

Tia D'Amico and Leo Parker, surrounded by close friends and family, met to exchange wedding vows on the foredeck of the *Pacific Pearl* on October 25. As the boat cruised beneath the Golden Gate Bridge, the bride and groom said "I do."

Jake Harrison stood up as the groom's best man and Melinda Parker as the bride's maid of honor. The bride wore flowers in her hair and a tea-length dress of gauzy white cotton trimmed in antique lace. The groom wore khaki pants and a collarless white shirt. No tie. None of the wedding party wore shoes.

The boat's railing was trimmed with garlands of ivy and white peonies, and although there was a slight breeze, the sky was mostly clear for the ceremony. The fog rolled in afterward, but not enough to dampen the spirits of the wedding party as they gathered around the fire pit where informal music was shared by guests. As the sky grew dusky, the many strings of white lights glowed cheerfully, adding to the general feeling of festivity and celebration.

The wedding dinner was a simple affair of surf and turf prepared by the sous chef and galley crew and enjoyed by all in the ship's dining room. Afterward, toasts were made and members of the wedding party danced the night away as the boat sailed around the San Francisco Bay.

The happy couple left for a short honeymoon aboard a chartered fifty-foot sailboat, where they plan to enjoy a five-day cruise down the California coastline. The groom is employed as captain of the *Pacific Pearl*, a dinner cruise boat, and the bride works as the head chef. Upon return, they will reside in the groom's recently restored houseboat in Sausalito—where we expect they will both live happily ever after.

Keep Reading for a
Sneak Peek of the Next Book
in the

FOLLOW
YOUR HEART

Series

 COMING SUMMER 2017

1

Nicole Sherman had no idea why her mother had slipped into the back of her art classroom this afternoon, but since this seventh-period class she was teaching was half over, Nicole pretended not to notice. It wasn't easy to ignore that platinum blonde hair styled within an inch of its life. Her sixty-five-year-old mom wore a slightly catty expression as she slid into a vacant chair. Sitting up straight, she pristinely clutched her faux Coach purse in her lap and, unlike the real students, looked attentive.

Nicole cleared her throat, continuing her lecture on the Renaissance period and trying not to be distracted by her mom, although her pale blue DKNY pantsuit looked comically out of place amidst the high school students. Slouching in their "uniforms" of shredded denim, faded tees, grubby flip-flops, and strange hairdos, these teens were bored and antsy and probably too warm since the temperature in the art room was pushing 80 degrees.

Nicole clicked to the next image projected on the screen overhead. She always reserved the Renaissance for the last week of her art history class. Not because she was saving the best for last but because it would be irresponsible to leave it out completely.

"Raphael is considered one of the premiere painters of the High Renaissance." Nicole stared at the somber self-portrait up on the screen. Even Raphael looked restless and discontent. "Born Raffaello Sanzio in Urbino, Italy, this artist is best know for his religious works, and in many ways, his style was more lifelike than that of his predecessors." Feeling herself surrender to the heat-induced stupor, she wondered why the art department was the only building with no air conditioning. She clicked to the next image.

"Raphael did numerous Madonna and child paintings in various settings. Perhaps he simply wanted to get it just right." She tried to inject interest into her voice. "Most would agree that he did." She clicked to *Portrait of a Young Man*. "It's interesting how Raphael captured the young man with that sideways glance—as if he's got mischief on his mind."

Really, she wondered as she clicked to the next image, *is this how you're planning to spend your life?* Boring these disinterested high school students with information they probably wouldn't retain past their final exam on Friday—if they kept it that long. What was the point? She glanced at the class as she clicked to the next image. To her surprise, a hand raised. Was someone really going to ask a question? But then she realized it was only her mother—waving eagerly like a first-grader. Some of the students were looking at her with a smidgeon of curiosity.

Nicole bit her lower lip. To allow her mother to speak up

was dicey at best. Caroline Sherman was unpredictable—she tended to speak first and think later. It might amuse these teens, but Nicole wasn't ready to witness her class degenerate into adolescent chaos. It was the last week of school, and as Principal Myers liked to say, the natives were restless. Why encourage them?

"Miss Sherman?" her mother called out urgently. "I have a question."

"Class," Nicole said in a flat tone, "our unexpected visitor happens to be my mother." She forced a smile, hoping to appear more mannerly than she felt. "I'd like you to meet Mrs. Sherman." She looked directly at her mother. "You have a question?"

"Yes, Miss Sherman, *I do*." Her mother's blue eyes twinkled as she stood up. "I'm curious. Have you ever seen any original works of this particular artist, Raphael? And if you have, will you please tell us about it?"

Nicole considered the question. Of course, her mother already knew the answer, but for some reason she wanted Nicole to share with the class. Nicole took in a deep breath, noticing that her students actually looked somewhat attentive now. Perhaps this was a teachable moment.

"As a matter of fact, I have seen a few pieces of Raphael's original art." She told them about how she'd spent a year touring Europe after graduating from college. "It was a really sweet gift from my parents and turned out to be an amazing trip for me. Seeing the actual works of the people I'd studied made the art come to life for me. And when I walked past the pond where Monet had painted the lily pad painting, I could almost feel his presence." She told them about visiting the Louvre and some of the Renaissance works there. To her pleasant surprise, most of her students perked up, and some of them were actually listening with genuine interest.

She continued to tell them about Florence, Italy, pointing out that Raphael and some of his contemporaries had lived there. "You can imagine how it would inspire them to be living around other artists, exchanging ideas and—" She was cut off by the bell, signaling that her last class and the school day had ended. "That's all for today," she called out as the students gathered their backpacks and things and made a mass exodus.

A girl named Alyssa paused by the door. "That's pretty cool, Miss Sherman. I wish I could go to Europe like you did."

"Yeah, me too," the boy behind her said wistfully.

"Maybe you will," Nicole said hopefully.

After the students had exited, Nicole smiled at her mother. "Thanks for asking that question, Mom. It was just what we needed."

Caroline Sherman laughed as she walked to the front of the classroom. "Seemed like you were losing them, honey. I figured a little maternal prodding couldn't hurt."

"Well, I've never been particularly fond of the Renaissance Period." Nicole shut down the program on her computer and turned off the projection screen. "I appreciate what it did for the art world and all that, but it's just not my cup of tea. You know?"

Her mom gave her a little hug. "I understand completely."

Nicole closed her laptop. "Why are you here?"

"Because I knew you were stuck."

"Huh?" Nicole frowned. "How could you possibly—"

"I meant stuck in general, Nikki."

"What do you mean? Stuck how?" She studied her mom's

carefully made up face. For sixty-five, this woman looked pretty good.

"Oh, you know . . . the things you were telling me last weekend at Michael's birthday party—about how you felt sort of lost after breaking up with Peter and you felt stuck in your job."

"I said that?" Nicole tried to remember how much she'd divulged at her nephew's birthday party.

"You sounded like you were looking for a change."

Nicole sighed, remembering how she'd been feeling a little envious of her older sister's picture-perfect life last weekend. Oh, she knew Katy had her own challenges. But maintaining her career and raising three boys with a man she loved— sometimes it looked pretty good. "I was obviously kind of down that day, Mom. I didn't mean to dump on you about—"

"No, no, that's not it. It's just that I have something exciting to tell you, Nikki. And since you're all done with classes today, why don't you let me take you out for a cup of coffee." She waved her hand like a fan. "Or maybe something icy. Good grief, it's like a sauna in here. How can you stand it?"

"With all these windows, it gets pretty stuffy in here. Especially this time of year. This building doesn't have air conditioning." Nicole wondered why she was so defensive about her "sauna."

"It's been unseasonably warm this week," her mom offered.

"Anyway, I'd be happy to escape for a while." Nicole went over to the door that she'd propped open with a heavy clay pot and let it close. "Hopefully it'll cool down some after the sun goes behind those trees. But I need to come back here when we're done. I have to fire up the kiln." She pointed to the pottery lined up on the counter. "I need to get those fired before the end of the week. I've been trying to run it at night because of the heat."

"My poor girl," Caroline said with sympathy. "They've got you working in an honest-to-goodness sweatshop here."

Nicole laughed as she went for her bag. "A lot of people would love to have my job," she called from her office. "One more year until tenure." Even as she said this, she wasn't certain she cared. Was tenure about job security or getting stuck in a job she didn't really love? What was the point? She locked her office and hurried back out, curious as to what her mother had to tell her.

"My old friend Vivian Graham called me today, and we had a very interesting conversation." Caroline's brows arched mysteriously.

"That is somehow related to me?" Nicole couldn't quite imagine this as she held the door to Starbucks open for her mom.

"Well, as it turns out, it just might. You see," Caroline continued as they stepped into the short line, "Vivian and Bruce are celebrating their fortieth anniversary this summer by taking a world cruise. Can you imagine *three months* of being pampered on a luxurious ship that goes all around the world?" She sighed. "But then, they're rich."

As they picked up their iced mochas, Caroline continued to rattle on about how "fortunate" Vivian and Bruce were, but after they were seated, Nicole held up her hand like a stop sign. "Okay, Mom, can you please get to the part about why this involves me? I've had a long day and an even longer school year, and my brain is starting to get a little fuzzy."

Caroline made a sly-looking smile. "Well . . . do you recall that Vivian owns a gallery in Savannah?"

Nicole tipped her head to one side. "That kind of rings a bell. Didn't we look at a vacant building when we were in Savannah that last time? Vivian was talking about getting it for an investment?"

"Yes. That's right. Vivian bought the building. A few years later she opened an art gallery—I guess it was about a dozen years ago. The Graham Gallery, she said it's called. It took a while for it to catch hold, and then there was the recession. But apparently it's fairly well established now. I guess it's been kind of like her baby—even more so after her boys were grown and all. It actually sounds rather nice."

"Uh-huh." Nicole tried to imagine this as she sipped her iced mocha.

"While Viv was telling me all about her gallery and these art exhibits she has lined up for the upcoming summer, complaining about how hard it would be to leave it all behind to go off on her *fabulous world cruise*"—Caroline rolled her eyes, then laughed—"well, anyway, I got this brilliant idea."

"Yes?" Despite her weariness, Nicole felt her curiosity piquing.

"It was slightly miraculous how this idea occurred to me—almost like a divine inspiration."

"Seriously?" Nicole made a doubtful frown.

Caroline nodded firmly. "Don't be such a skeptic, Nikki. It's entirely possible that God gave me this idea. Anyway, I suddenly realized that you, my dear, were exactly what Vivian needs."

"What she needs?"

"To manage her gallery."

Melody Carlson is the award-winning author of over two hundred books, including *The Christmas Joy Ride* and *Once Upon a Summertime*. Melody has received a *Romantic Times* Career Achievement Award in the inspirational market for her books. She and her husband live in central Oregon. For more information about Melody, visit her website at www.melodycarlson.com.

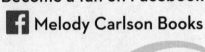

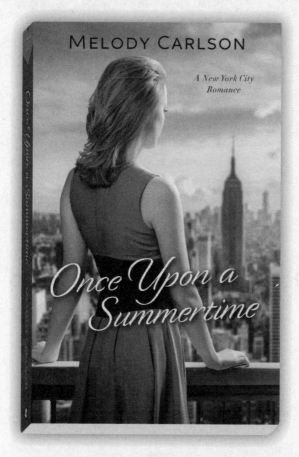